THE WITCH MAKER

*Sally Spencer titles available from
Severn House Large Print*

Blackstone and the Tiger
The Dark Lady
Dead on Cue
Death of an innocent
A Death Left Hanging
The Enemy Within
The Golden Mile to Murder
The Red Herring

THE WITCH MAKER

A Chief Inspector Woodend Mystery

Sally Spencer

Severn House Large Print
London & New York

This first large print edition published in Great Britain 2005 by
SEVERN HOUSE LARGE PRINT BOOKS LTD of
9-15 High Street, Sutton, Surrey, SM1 1DF.
First world regular print edition published 2004 by
Severn House Publishers, London and New York.
This first large print edition published in the USA 2005 by
SEVERN HOUSE PUBLISHERS INC., of
595 Madison Avenue, New York, NY 10022.

British Library Cataloguing in Publication Data

Spencer, Sally
    The witch maker. - Large print ed. - (A Chief Inspector Woodend mystery)
    1.   Woodend, Charlie (Fictitious character) - Fiction
    2.   Police - England - Fiction
    3.   Rites and ceremonies - England - Fiction
    4.   Detective and mystery stories
    5.   Large type books
    I.   Title
    823.9'14 [F]

    ISBN 0-7278-7430-6

Printed and bound in Great Britain by
MPG Books Ltd, Bodmin, Cornwall.

Prologue

The Vale of Hallerton, Central Lancashire, March 1604

For three days and three nights the wind howled like a soul stretched beyond the point of endurance on the executioner's rack. It loosened slates and rattled doors. It snapped tender young saplings, and brought down mighty oaks which had stood unchallenged for generations.

Nor was the wind left to do its work alone. Like the Devil himself, it brought its minions with it. There was a thunder which could have been the roar of a wounded beast. There was a lightning which lit up the night sky as if it were hellish day. Rain flailed down on men, animals and buildings, with a ferocity that had never been known before. It seemed to the terrified villagers that it would never end.

And then, as suddenly as it had appeared, it was gone.

★ ★ ★

5

She could see them assembled on the village green, waving their hands in extravagant gestures and pointing towards her cottage. They were drunk. She knew that from the way they were swaying as they spoke. But it did not bother her. Men taken in drink often thought they had found courage, but it was usually no more than the courage to *talk* bravely. And though they might hate her – and many, if not all of them, undoubtedly *did* – it would lead to naught.

'And *why* will it lead to naught, Graymalkin?' she asked the black cat crouching in a dark corner of the room. 'Dost you know? Does thy small, clever brain hold the answer?'

The cat considered her words for a moment, then emitted a cry which was neither a purr nor a growl, but instead more closely resembled the wail of a distressed infant.

Meg Ramsden laughed delightedly. 'Aye, thou art right, that *is* how they sound,' she said. 'Like children. Like babes in arms. Because whether in the bed or in the book, I have control over them. And they know it.'

Several new men appeared on the scene. Four of them were carrying a heavy stone pillar on their shoulders, two others had spades in their hands.

'Let them play their games, Graymalkin,' Meg Ramsden said. 'Let them try to inflict on me the fear which clings to *them* like the morning mist. They will not succeed.'

She reached up to the shelf on the wall, pulled down a heavy, leather-bound ledger, and opened it out on the table. Though she'd had lessons from the parish priest while he shared her bed, she had never truly learned to read. But that mattered not a jot. All the *important* words were in her head, and the words on the page, which she now ran her slim fingers over, were no more to her than a magical symbol of her power. Still, she knew enough to recognize some of the spidery writing for what it would represent to others.

'This be Edward Thwaites,' she said, pointing to two of the magic words. 'And what be that next to his name? Why, it be figures, Graymalkin – figures which be burned on his soul like the devil's brand.'

A noise came from the distance. At first it sounded as if the thunder – much weakened by its previous rage – was about to return. Then Meg began to distinguish the individual parts of the noise, and realized that it was no more than the angry mutterings of the men.

'So brave. So very brave!' she crooned softly. 'But how far will such bravery take them? Will it stay with them as they cross the Green? Or will it, like water in a leaky pail, drain a little more away with every step they take, so that by the time they reach my door, they will be nothing be empty vessels? We know the answer, do we not, Graymalkin?'

There was a hammering on the door.

As if they thought that she was so afraid of them that she would bolt it to keep them out!

As if they thought they were the ones with the power!

'Hast thee lost so much of thy spirit that thee needs to knock on thy own door, Harold Dimdyke?' Meg called out contemptuously.

There was a pause, then the latch was lifted and the door swung open. And suddenly the tiny kitchen was full of desperate worried men – men who, even now, were marvelling at their own resolution.

One man stepped clear of the pack. Harold Dimdyke. So nervous that he was twisting the rim of his hat – which he had instinctively removed – in his hands.

'This was a storm the like of which we have never seen before,' he said, almost stumbling over his words.

'It was longer than most,' Meg replied indifferently.

'It was a sign,' muttered one of the other men – Jack Peters, the blacksmith.

'A sign of what?' Meg asked.

'A sign that evil is afoot.'

Meg threw back her head, and laughed. 'Evil!' she repeated. 'If it is a sign of anything, it is a sign that the men of this village are so frightened that they will jump at their own shadows.'

'Milk has turned sour,' said a third man.

'Milk has always turned sour during a thunderstorm,' Meg countered.

'A calf, born at the very height of the storm, had two heads,' claimed a fourth man.

And then a torrent of words – of accusations – was unleashed.

'Maddy Brookes has a fever!'

'Jethro Sykes has lost the sight in one eye!'

'A wild dog the size of the lion that was killed by Samson in the Bible has been seen stalking the village!'

'But even that is not the worst,' Harold Dimdyke said gravely.

'Then tell me what is,' Meg responded – still calm, still amused.

'The porch of the church was destroyed by the storm. The house of God has fallen to the forces of darkness.'

So that was where the stone pillar she had seen the men carrying earlier had come from, Meg thought. She might have known. It had lain there – felled by the storm – and they had simply taken it, like the scavengers they were.

'So many signs!' Meg said. 'So many portents!' She swept her hand through the air, as if to brush away all the ignorance and superstition which had flooded into the room. 'You bring me no more than tales to frighten children with! Is that not so, my little Graymalkin?'

But, looking down, she saw that the cat, without her even noticing it, had somehow disappeared.

'We must take our fate in our own hands,' Harold Dimdyke said, his voice steadier now.

'And how wilt thee do that?' Meg wondered.

'We must burn the witch!' said a voice at the back of the small mob.

And everyone else agreed – 'Yes! Yes! We must burn the witch! Burn her! Burn her!'

And now, for the first time, Meg began to feel a little of her confidence ebb away. 'I am no witch,' she said.

'Then why dost thou have thy books, full of spells and incantations?' asked the blacksmith.

'Thou knowest it is no book of spells, Jack Peters,' Meg said sharply. 'Thou knowest exactly what it contains. For thou art in it!'

'*How* can I know?' Peters countered. 'For I am a poor man – a simple, honest man – and I cannot read.'

'Then ask Roger Tollance,' Meg suggested. 'For is it not he who made the marks? Is he not he who kept the records?'

She had expected them all to be answered

by that. She had never expected – never would even have dreamed – that the mob would part, and Roger Tollance would advance to the centre of the room.

He stopped, not more than a foot from her, and her nostrils were filled with the stink of cheap ale and his bodily functions. She looked him up and down with the same contempt she had always shown him. He was a man who might have achieved much – a scholar by local standards – but now she owned his talents, buying them as cheaply as she could have bought the services of the lowest swineherd.

'Tell them of my books, Roger Tollance,' she said. 'Tell them what my books contain.'

He would not look her in the eye. Instead he turned to face the men from whose ranks he had so recently been drawn. 'They are the words of the Devil,' he said in a frightened voice. 'The Devil's own words, writ in his own hand.'

'Then thou art the Devil himself, for it was thy hands which wrote it,' Meg told him.

Roger Tollance swallowed hard, and shook his head violently. 'Not I,' he said.

'How can thee say that when they have all seen thee do it?' Meg asked scornfully. 'When they have all stood in this same room and watched thee scratch with thy quill?'

'If my hand did make the marks, it was through no choice of my own,' Roger

11

Tollance protested. 'It was the Devil's will which was guiding me. But I am free of him now.'

'Thee liest!' Meg protested.

But then Harold Dimdyke lifted his hand to silence her. 'We have heard enough,' he said solemnly.

One

The hammering on the front door of the police house seemed like nothing more than a bad dream at first, and Constable Michael Thwaites – who had soon convinced himself that a bad dream was exactly what it was – turned over in his bed and hoped it would soon go away.

But it did *not* go away. Rather it grew ever louder and more demanding, until even a portly middle-aged police constable who valued his beauty sleep could no longer ignore it.

Thwaites rolled carefully out of bed. As his feet made contact with the cold lino-leum, he promised himself – for perhaps the hundredth time – that sometime next week he'd get around to laying that roll of carpet which, for well over a year, had been propped up reprovingly in the corner of the bedroom.

The knocking continued – almost demented both in its force and rapidity by now.

Thwaites reached for his tartan dressing

13

gown, which was hanging on a hook next to the bed. Now if he could only find his slippers...

The man at the door seemed intent on waking up the whole village. Thwaites abandoned the search for his footwear with a deep sigh, and made his way carefully down the stairs.

He knew his visitor. Indeed, in a village the size of Hallerton, it would have been a miracle if he hadn't.

'Now what's all this about, young Kenneth?' Thwaites asked sternly.

Kenneth Dugdale, who was the local milkman and couldn't have been called 'young' for at least a couple of decades, gestured wildly with his hands.

'Murder!' he gasped. 'Out on the Green!'

'Murder!' Thwaites repeated, wondering if this were all no more than a dream after all.

'Tied to the Witching Post!' Dugdale said. He placed his hands loosely around his own neck and stuck out his tongue for a moment. 'Strangled!'

Thwaites was suddenly more than aware of his own inadequacy. He was a local bobby, he told himself. He handled petty theft – not that there was much – and the failure to buy dog licences. He wasn't equipped to deal with this.

But there was someone who *was* equipped, he thought, as a sudden wave of relief

14

washed over him!

'Have you told the Witch Maker?' he asked the milkman.

Dugdale opened his mouth to answer, but nothing came out. He tried again, with the same result.

'Have you told the Witch Maker?' Thwaites repeated.

Dugdale shook his head.

'No?' Thwaites said angrily. 'Why not?'

'Because it *is* the Witch Maker,' Dugdale said, forcing the words out with almost superhuman effort.

The remnants of the morning mist were still swirling around the blackened stone Witching Post as Thwaites approached the Green. But even with the mist – and even from a distance – it was clear that the milkman had been right. A man was hanging limply from the post, and that man was none other than the Witch Maker.

'What are you goin' to do?' asked Dugdale, who, much against his will, had been dragged back to the scene of the crime.

What *was* he going to do? the constable wondered.

He knew what most rural bobbies would do. They'd seize on this murder as an opportunity to get themselves noticed by the brass in Whitebridge. But he didn't *want* to be noticed. Like everybody else in the village,

15

all he wanted was for the outside world to leave him alone.

'Should I ... should I go an' ask his brother, Tom, to come an' deal with it?' Dugdale asked desperately.

Constable Thwaites was tempted – very tempted – to say yes, they should let Tom take charge.

Because though the man had no official position of any kind, some of the Witch Maker's authority had rubbed off on him – as the Witch Maker's authority *always* rubbed off on members of his immediate family.

But that wouldn't work!

It simply wouldn't work!

He was sure of that, because once before the village had tried to keep a violent death to itself – and had paid a heavy price for it!

'You watch the body for a few minutes, will you?' the constable asked the milkman.

'An' what will you be doin' while I'm standin' here?' Dugdale wondered worriedly. Then he saw that Thwaites was looking across the Green at the bright-red phone box, and his worry became a complete panic. 'You're never goin' to...' he gasped. 'You're surely not thinkin' of...?'

'I don't like it any more than you do, but I don't have a lot of bloody choice, do I?' Thwaites snapped.

Before his resolution could fail him, the constable turned and strode rapidly towards the phone box.

Did it still work? he fretted as he closed the gap between himself and his salvation.

Say it had broken down – at some point in the ten years since it had been installed – would anybody have noticed? No one he knew had ever used it. Why should they, when all the people they could ever wish to talk to were no more than a short walk away?

He pushed the door, but the box wouldn't open. He tried again – and then a third time – before he realized that what he should have been doing was pulling, not pushing.

Once inside, he reached for the receiver with a hand which had visibly begun to shake, and lifted the instrument to his ear.

There was a dialling tone! Thank God!

With the index finger of his other hand, he began to dial. The number could not have been simpler – nine-nine-nine – yet twice his finger skidded and he had to dial again.

Finally, he was through. 'Emergency,' the operator said, in a cool, reassuring voice. 'Which service do you require, please?'

'I ... there's been a ... the Witch Maker's gone an' got himself...' Thwaites said help-lessly.

'Take a deep breath and start again,' the operator advised him. 'Which service do you require. Police, fire or ambulance?'

'Police!' Thwaites gasped. 'For God's sake, get me the police!'

Two

Chief Inspector Charlie Woodend had a much pleasanter awakening than Constable Thwaites that June morning. The sun – playing softly on his cheek – began the process of bringing him round, and the sweet singing of the moorland birds outside his window completed the task.

He was aware of how light on his feet he felt as he made a cup of tea to take up to his still-sleeping wife, Joan, and of how caressing the air was as he walked out to his car. It might have fallen to his lot to have to deal with the nastier side of human nature, he reflected as he turned the ignition key – and to be supervised in that work by a couple of prats who couldn't tell their arses from their elbows – but whatever burdens were placed on him, there were some mornings when it seemed really good to be alive.

The feeling of well-being stayed with him all the way to police headquarters. True, he was held up for quite some time by road works – somebody had told him there were four thousand holes in Whitebridge, Lancashire, and, watching the council workmen fill in one of them with asphalt, he could well believe it. True, too, he would have rather the Chief Constable's car had *not* been parked in its allotted spot – would have preferred it, in fact, if Marlowe had been attending one of those conferences on senior-level policing which were always held conveniently close to a good golf course. But these were but minor irritations, and on such a fine day he was quite prepared to live and let live.

He smiled at the constable on duty outside the main entrance, and at various colleagues who were entering the building at the same time he was. He smiled at the desk sergeant.

Then the sergeant said, 'Mr Marlowe would like to see you immediately, sir.'

And the smile melted away.

'A bit late in this morning, aren't you, Charlie?' asked the Chief Constable, moving documents around on his desk in that irritating way that he had.

'Road works,' Woodend explained.

Marlowe frowned. 'Perhaps you should have taken that into account when you decided what time to set off from home. But I suppose that's neither here nor there at the moment.' He picked up one of the pieces of paper he had been shuffling. 'Have you ever heard of something called the Hallerton

Witch Burning?'

'Aye,' Woodend said. 'Takes place once every twenty years. Quite a spectacle, in its way.'

'So you've seen it yourself?'

'Not the last one. Couldn't make it. I was up to my neck in muck an' bullets at the time.'

'I beg your pardon?'

'The last one was in 1944, sir. There was a war goin' on, in case you've forgotten.'

Marlowe's frown deepened. He had spent his entire war in a cushy billet in Chippenham, and knew that Woodend was well aware of the fact.

'We were all a little inconvenienced during the period of hostilities,' he said frostily. 'So, it was an earlier Witch Burning you saw, was it?'

'That's right, sir. The one that happened in 1924, when I was no more than a nipper.'

'Even so, you probably have more idea of what it's all about than I do.' Marlowe glanced down at the paper again. 'Apparently, the chap in charge of it, who, for some reason, is called the Witch Maker—'

'He's the one who makes the Witch,' Woodend supplied helpfully.

'—this Witch Maker, was found murdered this morning. On the very spot, so it would seem, where this Witch Burning is to take place. There's already a uniformed team on the scene, led by a sergeant from Lancaster, but since time is pressing, I'd still like you to get up there as soon as possible.'

'What do you mean?' Woodend asked. 'Time is pressin'?'

'The Witch Burning, which, as you've already pointed out, only happens rarely, is due to take place on Sunday, which is only three days away.'

'Well, unless we can crack this case in record time, they'll just have to call it off, won't they?' Woodend said.

'No, Chief Inspector, they will not,' Marlowe said firmly.

'I'm sorry, sir?'

'The Witch Burning will go ahead as planned.'

'But it can't!' Woodend protested. 'The place is crowded for a Witch Burnin'. The handloom-weavin' folk-art freaks travel from all over the country to see it. There's busloads of tourists who come an' rubber-neck. I can't have them tramplin' all over the crime scene.'

'The Witch Burning is a major cultural event,' Marlowe said. 'It reflects both the richness and the diversity of this county's history.'

'You sound like you're quotin' straight out of some kind of pamphlet,' Woodend said.

'I may be,' the Chief Constable replied. 'But that does not alter the facts. I've had people – *important* people – ringing non-stop since the news broke. They all want the burning to go ahead – and so it will.'

'Even if that means the murderer gets away with it?'

'Hallerton's a small village, and it's obviously a local crime,' Marlowe said airily. 'I doubt there can be more than a handful of possible suspects. It's surely not too much to ask that you pin the killing on one of them by Sunday, is it?'

'An' what if I don't?' Woodend asked.

Marlowe smiled. It was not a pleasant sight. 'Then I shall be forced to form a very unfavourable opinion of the way in which you have conducted the investigation,' he said.

Three

The moorland road was not built for speed. It weaved and twisted its way around ancient property lines which had long since ceased to be of interest to anyone. It climbed, then dipped, then climbed again. At some points it was wide enough for two cars to pass each other comfortably, while at others it had barely the breadth to accommodate a single vehicle. Woodend seemed to have noticed none of this. He took the corners on two wheels and slammed his foot down hard on the accelerator whenever there was more than a few yards of open road ahead of him.

Sitting in the passenger seat of the Wolseley, Monika Paniatowski took it all calmly. She was, if truth be told, a bit of a mad bugger behind the wheel herself. Besides, she had learned from experience that when her boss was furious – as he undoubtedly was now – a few close encounters with dry-stone walls were just what he needed to calm him down again.

'He wants me to have it wrapped up by

Sunday,' the Chief Inspector said. 'Wants it *pinned* on somebody – his words, not mine – by the time the Witch Burnin' gets under way.'

'What exactly *is* the Witch Burning?' Paniatowski asked. 'Does it have anything to do with the Pendle witch trials?'

They had begun to climb a fairly sharp slope, and the engine of the Wolseley groaned its displeasure at its driver's choice of gear. Woodend ignored the complaint.

'No, it hasn't a lot to do with the Pendle trials,' he answered his sergeant. 'In Pendle it might have been barbaric, but at least it was legal. It was the authorities from Lancaster who actually arrested the witches, an' the official executioner who hanged them. In Hallerton, on the other hand, it was more a case of do-it-yourself justice. The villagers themselves arrested Meg Ramsden, conducted the trial and carried out the execution – all within an hour.'

'And they got away with it?' Paniatowski asked incredulously.

'Some of them did. The authorities could not try the whole village for the murder, naturally. But the crime couldn't go unpunished either, so the high sheriff had the ones who'd played the biggest role arrested.'

'And who might they have been?'

'The fellers who actually tied the poor bloody woman to the post an' burned her.

Who else?'

'What happened to them?'

'They were hanged in Lancaster Gaol. An' on the day of their execution – at the very moment when the trapdoor was due to be opened – the village burnt Meg Ramsden in effigy.'

'Why?'

'There you've got me, lass. Maybe as an act of defiance. Anyway, whatever their reasonin', twenty years to the day after the men were hung, the people of Hallerton burned a second effigy. An' they've kept on doin' it – every twenty years without fail – ever since.'

They had almost reached the crown of the last hill before Hallerton. Woodend slowed, and then pulled over – perhaps because the drive had calmed him down, perhaps because he was starting to regret his mechanical cruelty to his faithful car engine.

'Come on, Sergeant, it's time to spy out the land,' he said.

Paniatowski joined him on the edge of the slope, and together they looked down at the village.

Not that there was a great deal to see. The hamlet was made up of perhaps a hundred and fifty dwellings. Most of them were clustered around the main street, though there were a few outlying farms. The village green stood out as a bright patch in the midst of all the mounds of grey stone, and the cars –

almost like models at this distance – were distinctive enough to be clearly identified as police vehicles.

'Welcome to the seventeenth century,' Woodend said dourly.

If Paniatowski heard him, she gave no sign of it.

'Somethin' on your mind, lass?' Woodend asked.

'This was the sort of place that Bob used to bring me to,' Paniatowski said wistfully – and almost to herself.

'An' it is *used* to, isn't it?' Woodend asked.

There was an edge to his voice, because he remembered – even if she didn't – that the affair between Detective Inspector Rutter and Detective Sergeant Paniatowski had almost been enough to ruin both their careers.

'Yes, it's *used* to,' Paniatowski replied. 'We only see each other now when we have to.'

Was that strictly true? Woodend wondered.

Had the passion which had burned between them completely died down? Or did they perhaps still contrive official reasons – reasons that probably fooled even *themselves* – to spend time together?

It was none of his business really, he told himself. They were both grown-ups and had the right to slash their own paths to hell if they wanted to. But Bob Rutter had been his protégé, the son he'd never had. And as for what he felt about Monika ... well, that didn't really bear examining too closely at all.

'Look at that!' Paniatowski said.

'Look at what?'

'That! Just beyond the village.'

Woodend turned his gaze in the direction his sergeant was pointing. In a field close to the main road – a road, which, either by design, or accident, completely bypassed the centre of the village – there were signs of considerable activity. At one end of the field, a number of battered-looking caravans were parked almost in a circle – like a wagon train in the western films. At the other end, a couple of dozen men were busily involved in erecting temporary structures, most of them roughly round in shape, all of them painted in garish colours.

Woodend groaned. A funfair. A bloody funfair. He should have expected this. Should have *remembered* it. There was *always* a funfair at the Witch Burnings. But it was the last thing he *needed* there to be.

'When do you think it arrived?' he asked his sergeant.

Paniatowski considered the question. 'Judging by how far they've got already, I'd say they got here yesterday afternoon at the latest,' she pronounced, 'which, of course, was several hours before the murder.'

'Wonderful!' Woodend said.

Paniatowski looked down at the village again. On the surface, there was nothing abnormal about it, she thought. There were dozens of other villages which were almost identical. Yet even from a distance, it was starting to make her flesh creep.

She lit up a cigarette. 'It doesn't really mean anything though, does it?' she asked lightly, in an attempt to dispel her growing unease.

'*What* doesn't really mean anything?' Woodend asked.

'The Witch Burning. I mean, it's just a harmless tradition, isn't it? Like dancing round the maypole, or hanging up a stocking for Santa?'

'I wouldn't be so sure of that,' Woodend said, walking back to the car.

It was not the answer Paniatowski had been hoping for. 'You wouldn't?' she said. 'Why not?'

'Them two men who were hanged for the murder of Meg Ramsden – they were brothers.'

'So what?'

Woodend opened the driver's door of the Wolseley. 'An' their name was Dimdyke,' he told her.

Paniatowski almost choked on her cigarette.

'Dimdyke?' she repeated, after she'd finished coughing. 'But that's the name of the

28

current Witch Maker! The man who was murdered this morning!'

Woodend slid into the driver's seat. 'Aye, it is,' he agreed. 'Makes you think, doesn't it?'

Four

All the villages she'd ever visited had been almost inordinately proud of their fêtes, Paniatowski thought. And that pride showed even before you got to the village itself – in the advertisements the fête committees had erected all along the country lanes leading to the place. She remembered some of the ones she'd seen in the past – huge, brightly coloured hand-painted signs offering countless delights from sack races to donkey derbies; elaborate papier-mâché models of warm and cuddly woodland creatures; streamers and balloons – all manner of inventive and endearingly amateur inducements. At the boundary of Hallerton, all she saw was the standard county-council-issue sign – a metal plaque with black raised letters on a white background which announced only the name of the village.

'I thought you said the festival was a pretty big thing,' she said to Woodend, as they drove past it.

'An' so it is,' the Chief Inspector replied. 'People come from all over to gawp at it. The one I saw attracted busload on busload of tourists, includin' a fair number of Yanks.'

'Well, you'd never guess any of that from what we've seen so far,' Paniatowski commented.

'I said it got a lot of visitors,' Woodend told her. 'What I didn't say was that the visitors were made to feel particularly welcome. In fact, from what I remember, the locals gave the outsiders a bit of a cold shoulder.'

'Strange,' Paniatowski said.

'Aye, it is,' Woodend agreed. 'But there's nowt as queer as folk – an' from what I've heard there's no folk as queer as them that come from Hallerton.'

They had entered the village proper. The main street was cobbled, and barely wide enough for two cars. On either side of it stood stone cottages, their small windows seeming to gaze disapprovingly at what passed before them. The feeling of disquiet that Paniatowski had felt on the hill only intensified now that she was in the village itself. It was almost, she thought fancifully, as if they had driven into the mouth of a snake and were now making their way through its dark and dangerous body.

The village came to an end as abruptly as it had begun, and ahead of them was the village green.

But it wasn't like other village greens she'd seen, Paniatowski thought. In this, as in so

31

many other things, Hallerton managed to be different.

True, she added in fairness, the police cars and the crowd which had gathered must have somewhat distorted its normal appearance. Yet even allowing for that, it was still not the restful place that most greens were.

It was impossible to imagine cricket matches being played there on lazy summer days, for example. And it was inconceivable that courting couples would stroll round it as they discussed their future together.

It was, despite its lush grass, a *dark* place.

Woodend parked his Wolseley next to an unmarked Land Rover, then glanced across at the Green. Standing next to the Witching Post was the Land Rover's driver – a small dark figure in a heavy sheepskin jacket and light, colourful sari.

'I see Doc Shastri's already here,' he said to his sergeant. 'You have to admit one thing about yon lass – she's as keen as mustard.'

Paniatowski felt a stab of jealousy. She knew it was unworthy of her, but she still couldn't help it. Until the arrival of Dr Shastri, she'd been the only female in Central Lancashire closely involved in the investigation of violent crime, and whilst – on the one hand – she welcomed the addition of another woman to the job, she could not quite avoid – on the other – mourning slightly the fact that she had lost her own uniqueness.

A policeman in his early thirties, with sergeant's stripes on his arm, marched briskly over to them and saluted.

'Sergeant Gough, sir,' he said. 'From Lancaster headquarters. We've secured the area.'

'Good,' Woodend replied, not quite managing to hide his grimace.

The sergeant noticed the expression. 'Is there something wrong, sir?' he asked.

Woodend sighed. 'Just your choice of words. "Secured the area" – for God's sake! It only used to be the senior officers, with their arses firmly anchored to their office chairs, who talked in that kind of jargon. Now it seems as if even ordinary decent bobbies have got in on the act. Whatever happened to good old Lancashire English, an' callin' a spade a bloody shovel?'

Gough looked flustered. 'I'm sorry, sir, I didn't mean to—'

'Nay, lad, don't apologize,' Woodend said. 'You've just done right. You'll need to use all that fancy talk if you're to get on in the modern police force. Is there a local bobby around?'

'Yes, sir. Constable Thwaites. I've sent him home.'

Woodend raised an eyebrow. 'An' why was that?'

'He ... er ... he was surplus to requirements, sir. My team knew what to do, and it

33

seemed to me we could get on with it more efficiently if we didn't have to stop to explain everything to him.'

'*That* bad, was he?' Woodend asked.

'I beg your pardon, sir?'

'You're a good lad,' Woodend told him, 'an' it's only right you stick up for other officers – even if they're not your own mates. But I do need a clear picture of what's really goin' on. Understand what I'm sayin'?'

Gough swallowed. 'Constable Thwaites seemed a little overwhelmed by the whole thing, sir,' he said. 'I thought it might do him good to have a bit of a break back at the police house.'

Woodend nodded. 'You're probably right about that,' he agreed. 'But I *will* need to speak to him, so make sure he's here when I get back from examinin' the body, will you?'

He turned and walked towards the crowd. It was densely packed, but without Woodend saying a word it somehow managed to part in order to let him pass.

Crowds always *did* part for him, Paniatowski thought, following in his wake. It wasn't because he was a big man – though he undoubtedly was. Nor was it that he looked as if he'd turn nasty if he didn't get his own way – because for all his size, no one would ever have taken him for a bully. There was just something about Cloggin'-it Charlie – some presence, which, if it could have been bottled, would have made his fortune.

Dr Shastri, an exotic bird of paradise in the sea of grey which surrounded her, smiled broadly when she saw Woodend and Paniatowski approaching.

'Well, if it isn't my two favourite law-enforcers,' she said in her singalong voice. 'Both I, and my friend at the post, are delighted to see you. He's not very talkative, to be honest, but I get the distinct impression he is tired of hanging around, and would appreciate being taken down soon.'

Woodend grinned. 'Bein' a bit ghoulish is all very well in its place, but I'm really gettin' seriously worried about the state of your mental health, Doc,' he said, not meaning it.

The dead man was in his early forties. His face was bloated. His eyes bulged. That he was still upright was due only to the fact that his arms and legs were tethered firmly to a heavy stone post which had been turned jet black by generations of witch burnings.

A second piece of rope, shorter and thinner than the one attaching him to the post, was wrapped around the victim's neck. A loop had been made in this shorter rope, and before it had been tightened, an iron bar had been inserted.

'He's been garrotted,' Dr Shastri said. 'As a method of execution, it has much to recommend it. It's very simple, very effective – and very traditional.'

'How do you mean? Very traditional?' Woodend asked.

The doctor shook her head in mock despair. 'You English!' she said. 'You live in this damp, drizzly country all your lives, and you do not even know your own history.'

'Educate us, then,' Woodend suggested.

'It is popularly believed that when people were burned at the stake, they were alive for much of the time the fire was consuming them,' the doctor said. 'In fact, that was very rarely the case. The burning was a cleansing process, you see, rather than a method of execution. Before the fire had properly caught, it was common for the executioner to show mercy by strangling the condemned person – just as has happened here.'

'So *we* might be ignorant buggers, but we're lookin' for a murderer who *does* have a sense of his own history,' Woodend said pensively.

'Which probably includes just about everybody who lives in this village,' Paniatowski pointed out.

'True,' Woodend agreed. He turned back to Dr Shastri. 'How long's he been dead?'

The doctor shrugged her shoulders. 'I would guess at somewhere between five and eight hours. I might be able to be a little more specific when I've had the opportunity to stick my little thermometer up his backside.'

36

Woodend nodded. 'Anything else you can tell me?'

'There is a bump on the back of his head the size of a duck egg. It's my belief that when he was brought here, he was unconscious.'

'So he never knew what was happening to him?'

Dr Shastri shook her head. 'I did not say that, my dear sir. I did not say it at all. If we go around to the other side of the post, I think you will find his hands most interesting.'

Woodend followed the doctor and squatted down so that his eyes were on a level with the dead man's hands. Several of the nails were broken, and there was some evidence of bleeding.

'He struggled,' the Chief Inspector said.

'Indeed he did,' the doctor agreed. 'Not that there was much point in it. His bonds were quite secure, and the post is as solid as a rock.' She laughed at her own joke. 'I have no doubt that when I carry out my full examination I will find traces of stone dust under his fingernails.'

'So he was unconscious when he was brought here, but he came around as he was being killed?' Paniatowski said.

'That's one possibility,' Woodend agreed grimly. 'But there is another one which is equally likely.'

'And what's that, sir?'

'That he didn't just *happen* to regain consciousness while he was bein' throttled. That his killer *waited* for him to come round before he started the garrottin'.'

Five

Constable Thwaites supposed that most policemen who had stumbled across a murder would have gone out of their way to set themselves apart from the general public, but he wasn't most constables, and this was no ordinary general public.

He had no desire to isolate himself from the rest of the villagers. In fact, what he wanted to do – *desperately* wanted to do – was to join them.

To immerse himself in the collective consciousness.

To almost drown in it.

So it was that, when he emerged from the comparative safety of his police house and arrived on the Green, it was towards the people confined behind the barrier that his legs automatically took him.

He was nearly there when he saw the look in the eyes of the people he had known all his life – and lost his nerve.

'Betrayer!' the eyes said.

'Judas!' they called him.

And he couldn't ignore what the eyes were

39

saying – couldn't even plead his own case with the people to whom the eyes belonged – because there was at least a part of him which knew that they were right.

He froze for a moment, then turned on his heel and skulked away. The legs now urged him to keep on walking – to tramp the moors until, through sheer exhaustion, they gave way under him. But his brain and – more importantly – his heart, had now taken over. And they told him that he couldn't leave the village however hard he tried – because he was part of it, and it was part of him.

He came to a halt in front of the Black Bull. His heart was thumping; his breaths were coming in short gasps.

Got to get a grip on myself! he thought desperately. Got to be able to find the strength – from *somewhere* – to deal with that bugger from Whitebridge.

He tried to remember whether he had actually *chosen* to become a policeman or whether it had been chosen for him. But this was the village, and such thoughts – such choices – had no meaning. Yet of one thing he was very sure: from the moment he had donned the blue serge uniform, he had behaved in the way the village expected of him.

'Until now!' he moaned softly.

Until this morning, when he had taken it upon himself to bring the outside world into a place where the outside world did not belong.

But what other option had he had? What else was he *supposed* to have done? Was he to allow the fate of the village to be guided by someone who still only shaved every other day?

Thwaites turned his attention – and that decreasing portion of his mind he still had control over – to the Witching Post.

The big man in the hairy sports coat must be Woodend, he thought. They had never met, but he had heard enough about the chief inspector's unorthodox approach to police work to be convinced that – from the village's point of view – headquarters could not have sent a worse officer to investigate the case.

The woman who was with the chief inspector – the attractive blonde with the stunning figure and the nose which was perhaps just a little too large for Lancashire tastes – was a stranger to him. But from the way she stayed so close to Woodend, there could be no doubt that she was his bagman – and that made her a danger, too!

Woodend turned his back on the Witching Post, and walked over to where the sergeant from Lancaster was standing. They conferred for a few moments, then Thwaites saw the uniformed sergeant point in his direction. The constable had been expecting that, of course – but it still sent fresh waves of dread coursing through his body.

Monika Paniatowski saw the portly local constable standing in front of the pub, shifting his weight first on to one foot and then on to the other. He was nervous, she thought, but that was only to be expected from a rural bobby preparing to meet the Big Cheese from Police Headquarters. What he didn't know – but was about to find out – was that this wasn't a normal Big Cheese at all. It was Charlie Woodend – 'Common-Touch' Charlie – and within a couple of minutes, the constable would be wondering why he'd ever felt any concern.

As Woodend and Paniatowski drew level with him, Constable Thwaites gave the Chief Inspector a rusty salute. Woodend acknowledged it with a brief nod, which managed to convey the impression that he didn't set much store by that kind of formality.

'I don't suppose you get many smart-arses from Headquarters up in this neck of the woods,' Woodend said.

The remark seemed to knock the constable completely off balance.

Monika Paniatowski smiled to herself.

This was classic Woodend, she thought. Bluff, open and unconventional – and all the more effective because, while it was true it was something of an act he was putting on,

42

it was also – in essence – the *real* Charlie Woodend speaking.

The constable was still searching for a response to Woodend's unexpected remark.

'I ... er...' he began.

Then he seemed to quite lose the will to continue.

'You're a bit intimidated by it all,' Woodend suggested. 'Well, don't worry about that, Constable Thwaites. If I was in your position, I'd feel exactly the same way.'

'Yes, sir,' Thwaites replied dully, as if he didn't know what was going on, but still felt he had to say *something*.

'The difference is, Thwaites, that unlike some of the other smart-arses they *might* have sent, I know when I'm out of my depth – an' without your help, I'll drown in this bloody village,' Woodend concluded.

It was at this point in Woodend's act that the local constable usually started to realize that he wasn't dealing with just another boss from Whitebridge, Paniatowski thought – this point at which his chest would start to swell slightly as he understood that there was a possibility that he, a mere hayseed, could actually be of real value to the investigation.

But that wasn't happening here! Rather than Woodend's rough charm plumping up the constable's self-esteem, it seemed to be throwing Thwaites into an even deeper panic.

'Local lad, are you?' Woodend asked.

'Yes, I am.'

'Good. So you should know all there is to know about Hallerton.'

'I suppose I do, sir.'

'Then tell me about the Witch Makers. Are they always picked from the Dimdyke family?'

'Picked?' Thwaites said. 'What do you mean, sir, "picked"?'

Woodend sighed. 'Is the Witch Maker always a Dimdyke?'

'Well, yes,' Thwaites said, as if it were the most obvious thing in the world.

'So they're a bit like a royal family, are they? The Witch Maker's son automatically inherits the position, regardless of his ability?'

'The Witch Maker doesn't have sons,' Thwaites said. 'Nor daughters, neither.'

Woodend grinned. 'How's that managed?' he wondered. 'Do they cut his balls off when he takes on the job?'

'No!' Thwaites said, clearly scandalized that Woodend could suggest such a thing even in jest. 'It's just that he never marries.'

'Never?'

'Never.'

'Not in the entire history of the Witch Burnin'?'

'No, sir.'

'An' why's that, pray tell?'

44

'He has no time for a family.'

'Oh, come on,' Woodend scoffed. 'I'm a chief inspector. Do you think I'm not busy? When I'm on a case I can work round the clock for weeks on end, but even I've found time for a family.'

But had he really? he asked himself as he felt a sudden shudder pass through him. Certainly he had a wife and a daughter, but, given the pressures of his work, how much of a husband and father had he actually been?

'The Assistant Witch Maker starts learnin' his craft when he's ten years old,' Thwaites said, his expression clearly indicating amazement that it was necessary to explain *any* of this.

'Go on,' Woodend encouraged.

'He completes his apprenticeship at the time of the next Witch Burnin', which is another ten years. Then the old Witch Maker retires, an' he takes over. Ahead of him, he's got ten years on his own – refinin' his skills – and ten years teachin' all he knows to *his* apprentice. By the time he steps down, he's forty years old. You can't really expect a man to think about startin' a family then, now can you?'

'Some men do,' Woodend pointed out.

'Not our Witch Makers,' Thwaites said. 'It's a heavy burden they carry for the rest of us, an' it takes its toll. There's not many ex-Witch Makers who live to see another

Witch burned.'

'If they want to learn what it's like to work under pressure, they should try bein' Mid Lancs detectives,' Woodend said unsympathetically. 'So, because of his position, Harry Dimdyke was a single man. But I take it he has relatives in the village.'

Thwaites frowned. 'We *all* have relatives in the village, sir. We all *are* relatives in the village.'

'But some relatives are closer than others,' Woodend pointed out.

'I see what you mean, sir,' Thwaites admitted, relieved. 'Harry's *closest* relative was his brother, Tom.'

Woodend surveyed the crowd, which had hardly moved an inch since he'd arrived on the scene. 'Point him out to me, will you, Constable,' he said.

Thwaites glanced around. 'He's not here,' he said.

'An' why's that? Is he off travellin' somewhere?'

'No, sir. We don't do much travellin' from Hallerton.'

'You must have done durin' the war.'

'A few of us were called up then,' Thwaites admitted, 'but we never got posted far away from home. An' I suppose that since the end of the hostilities a few other folk might have been as far as Whitebridge or Lancaster. But that's the extent of it.'

'So if the dead man's brother's not travellin', where the bloody hell is he?' Woodend demanded. 'Hasn't he heard what's happened? He surely must have done, in a village this size.'

'Oh, he's heard, all right. As a matter of fact, he was here earlier.'

'Then why isn't he *still* here?'

Thwaites looked perplexed. 'Well, I suppose the main reason for that is that he had to go.'

Woodend suppressed a sigh. '*Why* did he have to go?' he asked patiently. 'Was he overcome by emotion or somethin'? Did he find the strain of watchin' it all just *too* much to bear?'

'No, sir. At least, I don't think so.'

'Then what is the reason, in your opinion?'

'I imagine he'll have left because he'll have work to be gettin' on with.'

'Work? What kind of work?'

'The Witch.'

'The Witch?'

'It's only three days to the Burnin'. There's still a lot to do.'

'Let me see if I've got this straight,' Woodend said. 'His brother's just died – in one of the most horrible ways it's possible to imagine – an' he's gone straight back to workin' on the Witch.'

'That's right,' Thwaites agreed. 'What else would you expect him to do?'

47

Six

It was a strange procession they made through the village – the portly constable leading, the big man and the pretty blonde following. Curtains twitched as they passed, doors creaked open once they had gone. This was a village in the heart of Lancashire, but it felt to the Chief Inspector and his sergeant as if they were entering a dark and unknown kingdom.

Woodend found himself thinking about the villages he'd known as a lad. They really *had* been a world unto themselves back then. Though never more than ten miles away from the nearest town, they might as well have been a hundred from it for all the contact they had with it.

Then more people had found themselves able to afford motor cars, and everything had changed. Executive housing estates had sprung up – as if by magic – on the edges of villages which had remained undisturbed for hundreds of years. And following in the wake of the office workers, came the men from the factory floor. True, they might have to content themselves with sitting behind the wheels of less flash vehicles than those driven by the pioneers, but they still saw no reason why they and their families should not share the country life with their bosses.

Hallerton, however, had obviously been untouched by this revolution the internal combustion had brought about. The stone cottages still looked just as their builders had intended them to – squat, hunkering structures, groaning under the weight of oppressive stone roofs. There were no picture windows recently added here. No electric doorbells replacing the blunt metal knockers. The Venetian blind had not secured so much as a foothold in this village where mock-lace curtains still reigned supreme.

The Witch Maker's barn stood perhaps a hundred yards from the edge of the village proper. Like the rest of the buildings in Hallerton, it had been built from stone quarried not three miles from the spot on which it stood. Yet though it was no taller than any of the cottages, it somehow managed to seem more imposing and formidable. In front of the barn stood a sheep pen which looked as if it had been thrown together from any material which came readily to hand, and was clearly intended to be only a temporary enclosure. Inside the pen, half a dozen sheep were nibbling at a pile of freshly cut grass.

'What's this place used for when they're not makin' the Witch?' Woodend wondered aloud.

This question, like so many of the previous ones he'd asked, seemed to confuse Constable Thwaites. 'I'm not sure I know what you mean, sir,' he said. 'They're *always* makin' the Witch.'

The constable pushed on the heavy oak door, and it swung open just wide enough for the three of them to enter.

The barn was a dark, dank place, full of shadowy corners. There were a few largish gaps in the wall, through which sunlight had managed to struggle into the building, but as if exhausted by the effort, the rays fell only weakly on the compacted earth floor.

Most of the effective illumination was provided by half a dozen oil lamps, which filled the air with the stink of paraffin. Smoke rose from these lamps – grey snakes of it – and slithered through the air before wrapping itself around the blackened rafters of 400-year-old dead oak. It was, Woodend thought, the perfect location in which to make a Hammer Horror film.

There were three people in the barn – an older man, a younger man and a girl. The men were bent over a large workbench. The girl was sitting somewhat apart from them, on an upturned orange crate. All three glanced up to look at the new arrivals, but the two males, at least, showed very little interest when they saw who those new arrivals were.

The older man was thick-set and middle-aged, and even in the gloomy light of the barn it was possible to see that he bore a remarkable resemblance to the corpse that had only recently been cut down from the Witching Post. The younger man had not yet fully developed the shape he would assume as a mature adult, but was broad and well muscled. On the evidence of his stub nose, broad forehead and rough jaw line, there was little doubt that he was the older man's son.

The girl was something else! She had long golden hair. And deep blue eyes, which were blank now – but could probably express a world of meaning when she wanted them to. Unlike the men's noses, hers was long, slim and delicate. Her mouth was wide, and her lips were inviting – or perhaps pleading. Woodend had long since stopped being attracted to young girls, yet he was forced to admit to himself that she was one of the most beautiful creatures he had ever seen.

The older man spoke. 'Somethin' the matter here, Constable Thwaites?'

Somethin' the matter? Woodend repeated silently. Your brother's just been murdered – that's what's the matter!

'This is Mr Woodend, Tom,' Constable

Thwaites said. *'Chief Inspector* Woodend.'

'Oh aye,' Tom Dimdyke replied, clearly unimpressed by both the man and the title.

'Mr Woodend would like to ask a few questions,' Thwaites continued uncertainly.

'There's nothin' of importance I can tell him, an' I've no time for idle chit-chat,' Dimdyke replied.

'Don't you care who killed your brother?' Woodend asked.

'Of course I care,' Dimdyke said angrily. 'But findin' our Harry's murderer can wait.'

'It can *wait!*'

'Yes, it can. But Meg Ramsden can't. She's due for a burnin' three days from now.'

Woodend remembered the Witch Burning he'd attended as a boy, forty years earlier. The figure tied to the stake had been very realistic, he recalled – almost frighteningly human-like. Even now, he could still picture the long blonde wig she had been wearing – and the eyes which seemed to gaze helplessly into the jeering crowd. Yet even allowing for that, he could not see the task taking so long that a brother's murder had to be put to one side until it was completed.

'Why don't you come an' see for yourself?' Tom Dimdyke said, reading his mind.

Woodend took a step forward, and Dimdyke and his son moved to one side so he could get a better look at what they had been working on.

Despite himself, the Chief Inspector let out a gasp of amazement. He had been expecting a crude dummy packed with bunched-up newspaper and other stuffing. What he was being presented with instead was a perfect representation of a human skeleton, which, had it not been made of wood, he would have been prepared to swear was the real thing.

'Somethin' wrong?' Tom Dimdyke asked, with a half smile forming on his lips.

'I ... I don't remember it as a skeleton,' Woodend said.

'Oh, it won't be a skeleton when it's tied to the Witching Post,' Dimdyke told him. 'We'll have fleshed it out by then.'

'Fleshed it out,' Woodend repeated, feeling stupid.

'There's a skin that goes over the frame. It's made out of cow hide. An' between the skin an' the skeleton, there's the fat of half a dozen sheep that have been freshly butchered.'

'The sheep that are grazin' outside now?'

'That's right. The ones that are grazin' outside.' Dimdyke laughed. 'Waitin' to be led like lambs to the slaughter.'

'But what I don't see—' Woodend said.

'What you don't see is why, when the skeleton's covered with sheep fat an' hide, it has to be so accurate,' Tom Dimdyke said, completing his sentence for him.

53

'That's right.'

'Because it has to be as much like Meg as it's humanly possible to make it,' Tom Dimdyke said. 'What do you notice about the fourth rib on the left side of her chest, Mr Policeman?'

Woodend bent down to take a closer look. A jagged line ran across it, as if it had been half sawn through. 'It's cracked,' he said.

'Aye, it is,' Tom Dimdyke agreed. 'Meg Ramsden fell when she were bein' taken down from the cart. She broke her rib so badly that them that was holdin' her could feel it pokin' out.' He shook his head regretfully. 'It was an accident. Nobody wanted to hurt her.'

'Nobody wanted to hurt her! She was about to be burned at the stake, wasn't she?'

'That was necessity, not punishment. Anyway, as I were sayin', she fell an' broke her rib. That's why *this* rib's been prepared like it has – so it'll break like Meg's did just before she died.'

'What's the point of that?'

'It's the way it has to be.'

And it made sense, Woodend thought to his own amazement. In a way that he couldn't even begin to explain to himself, he fully accepted that it was essential the effigy had just the same broken rib – and broken in *exactly* the same place – as Meg Ramsden did when she was tied to the stake.

'Now that *you're* the Witch Maker—' he said.

'Me!' Tom Dimdyke interrupted. 'You think *I'm* the Witch Maker?'

'Yes.'

'An' what *made* you think that?'

'Well, I assumed that since you said you had a lot of work still to do on the Witch...'

'I do – more than you could even begin to imagine. But only under the supervision of my lad, who would have been Witch Maker four days from now anyway, even if Harry hadn't been killed.'

Woodend looked from Dimdyke to his son and back again – and saw the obvious pride that the older man had in the younger.

'Me! Take over from Harry?' Tom Dimdyke scoffed. 'You know nothin' about it. Bein' Witch Maker calls for *dedication*. We all have to make sacrifices for the Witch Burnin' in this village, but the Witch Maker an' his assistant make the greatest of the lot. The assistant builds his first Witch when he's ten.'

'I've already told Mr Woodend that, Tom,' Constable Thwaites said, in an obvious attempt to ingratiate himself.

'Then he builds another ... an' another ... an' another...' Dimdyke continued, as if Thwaites had never spoken. 'Until finally he builds one that's fit to take Meg's place at the stake. Do you think that's easy?'

55

'No,' Woodend admitted. 'I don't imagine it is.'

'There's no childhood for the lad born to be Witch Maker. There isn't the time. But like I said, it's a sacrifice that has to be made.'

Woodend wondered how any man could willingly condemn his small son to such an undertaking.

'Have you actually made a sacrifice *yourself*, Mr Dimdyke?' he asked caustically.

Tom Dimdyke nodded gravely. 'Oh aye. Twenty year ago now. It was hard – but it was necessary.'

'An' what form, exactly, did *your* sacrifice take?'

Dimdyke's eyes hardened. 'That's none of your bloody business!' he said.

And Woodend realized that it *was* none of his bloody business – though not in the way that Dimdyke meant.

His business, he reminded himself, was tracking down murderers who existed very firmly in the second half of the twentieth century. And with that realization came another. That something strange had happened to him in the previous few minutes. That almost without knowing it, he had been sucked into the mysteries of the Witch Making – into a world which had only vague points of contact with the reality he had known out in the sunlight.

'What can you tell me about your brother's movements last night?' he demanded, re-asserting the solid sense of self which he had carried around with him for most of his life.

'I've told you once, I've got too much on my hands to waste time talkin' to you,' Tom Dimdyke said.

'Maybe you've been so busy you haven't noticed that I represent the law,' Woodend said, aware that he sounded like nothing so much as a small child challenging an adult – and not giving a damn. 'I'm not *askin'* for your co-operation, Mr Dimdyke. I'm *tellin'* you I want it. An' if you get in my way, I'll have this place sealed off until the investigation's over. Which will mean you won't be allowed in here at all, and there'll be no bloody witch to burn!'

Dimdyke gave him a gaze which would have turned a lesser man to stone, and made even Woodend start to wobble.

'If I was you, I'd think twice before I started threatenin' somethin' like the Witch Burnin',' he said.

'H ... help him, Dad!' the girl said, speaking for the first time. 'All he w ... wants to do is find out who killed Uncle Harry. H ... help him!'

Dimdyke looked thoughtfully at his daughter for a moment, then turned to Woodend and said, 'All right, what do you want to know?'

'I've already told you. I want to know about your brother's movements last night.'

Dimdyke shrugged. 'He would have been here. The Witch Maker never leaves the Witch alone in the week before the Burnin'.'

'What about you?' Woodend asked Wilf Dimdyke. 'Were you here as well?'

The young man nodded. 'Yes.'

'All night?'

'No. I stayed until about half past eleven, then I went to the Black Bull for a couple of pints.'

'You're not lyin' to me, are you?'

'My lad doesn't lie!' Tom Dimdyke said angrily.

'But the pub would have been closed by then,' Woodend pointed out.

'No it wouldn't,' Tom Dimdyke said. 'It's thirsty work bein' the Assistant Witch Maker – an' the pub doesn't close until he's slaked it.'

'An' bugger the licensin' laws?' Woodend asked, interestedly.

'There's laws an' laws,' Tom Dimdyke said. 'In this village we know which ones matter – and which ones don't.'

'It doesn't work that way,' Woodend explained. 'Nobody gets to choose the laws they'll follow an' the ones they'll ignore.'

'Yes, they do – at least in Hallerton,' Dimdyke said with certainty. 'What do you think the Witch Burnin' is all about, if it's

58

not to show that some things are above the law?'

'Well, your ancestors certainly seem to have had that attitude,' Woodend agreed. 'They disregarded the law – but they also paid the price!'

'An' not just th ... them,' said the girl, with a sudden fierceness. 'We're s ... still payin' for what they did, even now. An' we always *w* ... *will*.'

Even without the stutter, it would have been hard to say for certain whether her voice was full of anger or full of pride, Woodend thought. Perhaps it was a little of both.

'So the last time you saw your uncle was at about half past eleven?' the Chief Inspector said, returning his attention to Wilf Dimdyke.

'That's right.'

'An' you didn't notice anybody suspicious hangin' about when you left?'

'No.'

'He wouldn't!' Tom Dimdyke said. 'They are far too sneaky to be seen if they don't want to be.'

'Who's too sneaky?'

'The fairground folk.'

'You think one of them's the killer?'

'Who else could it have been?' Tom Dimdyke asked, sounding genuinely surprised.

Seven

The Green was a great deal quieter than it had been earlier in the day. The body had been removed in an ambulance, and then, no doubt as a result, the crowd had drifted away. Looking at the barriers fencing off a large section of the area – and at the two uniformed constables who were patrolling them – a newly arrived visitor might well have been forgiven for wondering what all the fuss was about.

Woodend surveyed the scene himself, then turned and fixed his gaze on the Black Bull.

'I think we've all earned a drink,' he told Sergeant Paniatowski and Constable Thwaites.

'I'm in uniform, sir,' the constable pointed out.

The Chief Inspector ran his eyes quickly up and down the other man's blue serge uniform, and grinned.

'So you are,' he said, as if he'd only just noticed the fact. 'Still, thirst can do strange things to a man. In my case, it's makin' me think I see you wearin' a brown suit.'

'I don't understand, sir.'

'Don't be thick, Constable. I'm sayin' it won't bother anybody – least of all me – if you come an' have a pint.'

'I'd rather not, if you don't mind, sir,' Thwaites said, shaking his head. 'I'd be much happier gettin' myself off home.'

'An' I'd much rather you had a drink, so I can pick your brains,' Woodend told him. 'So you'd better follow me.'

Then he pushed open the pub door and stepped inside.

Some changes had obviously been made to the Black Bull since it had evolved from being a simple village ale shop – but not a great many. Its exposed beams were low enough for the unwary to bang their heads on. Its flag floor was uncarpeted, and the bottle-glass windows gave only a hazy, distorted view of the world outside. It was, in other words, the sort of pub that Woodend couldn't normally praise too highly. So why, he wondered, did this particular boozer make him feel so ill at ease?

He walked over to the bar. 'You take a seat while I get them in,' he told the sergeant and the constable. 'Bitter, is it, Thwaites?'

'I don't want anythin', sir,' the constable said firmly.

'Please yourself,' Woodend told him.

He turned his attention to the landlord, a stocky middle-aged man with a publican's

61

typically red face. He smiled, and was rewarded with an unwelcoming glare in return.

'Pint of best bitter an' a double vodka, please,' he said.

'The bitter, I can manage,' the landlord said, with some show of reluctance. 'But there's no call for that other stuff round here.'

'No, I don't suppose there is,' Woodend agreed. 'Make it a gin and tonic instead, then.'

The landlord reached for a pint glass, slipped it under the tap, and pulled back the pump as if it were the hardest thing he'd ever done in his life.

'Wilf Dimdyke says he was in here last night,' Woodend said conversationally.

'An' so he was,' the landlord agreed.

'Thing is, he says he didn't get here until half past eleven.'

'That's right.'

'Which is an hour after you should have been closed.'

The landlord shrugged, as if it really didn't matter. 'So summons me,' he suggested.

Woodend paid for the drinks and took them over to the table where Paniatowski and Thwaites were sitting.

The Chief Inspector handed his sergeant her drink, then turned to the constable and said, 'Yon Tom Dimdyke seems to think the killer came from outside the village. What's your opinion on the matter, Constable?'

'He's right,' Thwaites said firmly.

'So Harry Dimdyke was killed by one of the folk from the fairground, was he?'

'He'd have to have been.'

'Why?'

'Why what?'

'Why would any of the fairground people have wanted to kill him?' Woodend said, speaking slowly and carefully, as if he were explaining matters to a particularly slow child. 'We can rule out robbery, both on the grounds that there was absolutely nothin' worth stealin' in the barn—'

'We don't know that for sure,' Thwaites interrupted. 'Harry could have had somethin' valuable on him.'

'...an' because I've never heard of a case of robbery yet in which the robber took his victim somewhere well away from the scene of the crime an' then garrotted him.'

'Maybe it wasn't robbery, then,' Thwaites suggested. 'Maybe one of the fairground people had a grudge against Harry.'

'In that case, he'd have to be a *world champion* grudge-holder.'

'I beg your pardon, sir?'

Woodend sighed. 'Even if it's the same fair – an' we haven't established that it is yet – it's one hell of a long time since it last came to Hallerton. Now as far as I know, most

63

fairground workers don't have the same approach to life as office clerks do. They don't put in their forty years on the same job for the sake of the gold watch they'll collect at the end.'

'They could have—'

'Most of the fellers who were with the fair twenty years ago will either have left it, retired or died by now. An' even if we stretch belief to breakin' point, an' allow that one or two blokes who are here now might have been workin' for the fair the last time round, how likely is it that one of them would have waited nearly a quarter of a century to get his revenge for somethin' Harry did to him back then?'

'Maybe it was a *family* grudge,' Thwaites said. 'You know how clannish these carnival folk can be.'

'A bit like the people of this village?'

'It's not the same, sir. It's not the same at all.'

'Let's assume for a minute that one of the fairground people *wasn't* the killer,' Woodend said. 'Who is there in the village who might not be too unhappy to see Harry Dimdyke dead?'

'Nobody. He was the Witch Maker.'

'Is that the answer to every question in this village?' Woodend asked, exasperatedly. 'That he was the bloody Witch Maker?'

Thwaites face creased, as if he really *did*

want to explain – really *did* want Woodend to understand – but, despite that, he was still having trouble finding the words.

'The village is nothin' without the Witch Burnin',' he said finally.

'Oh come on,' Woodend said, doing his best to sound reasonable – and just missing the mark. 'I know the Witch Burnin' brings a lot of visitors' money into the village, but that's only once in a generation, isn't it? There has to be more to this place than that.'

'It's not a question of money, sir,' Thwaites said petulantly.

'Still, there must be plenty of it comin' in durin' the Witch Burnin'.'

Almost as if it had been done on cue, a loud voice behind them said, 'I've told you before, I don't want your custom. Not your custom – an' not any your mates' custom, either.'

Woodend turned. The speaker was the landlord, and he was addressing a young man with long greasy hair, a kerchief round his neck, and a gold ring in his ear, who standing at the other side of the bar.

'I don't have to drink it here,' the young man said reasonably. 'If you don't want me in your pub, I'll take it back to my caravan.'

'There's sellin'-out shops in Lancaster that'll give you what you want,' the landlord told him.

'But that's fifteen miles away!'

65

'Fifteen miles or a thousand, I don't give a bugger. You'll still get nothin' from me.'

'I don't see why you won't—'

'I've a right under the law to refuse to serve anybody I don't want to serve. An' before you say any more, there's a police constable sittin' at that table. Do you see him?'

'I see him,' the young man said, in a surly manner.

'Then bugger off before I set him on you.'

The young man slunk out of the pub, and a smile which seemed both proud and complacent came to Constable Thwaites' face.

'You see?' he asked.

'No, I don't,' Woodend admitted.

'Zeb won't serve the fairground people, an' neither will the shops. We don't want their money – an' we don't want them.'

'So why are they here?'

'The Witch Burnin's a public event, an' as such, it has to be licensed. The county council wouldn't grant that licence unless we agreed to allow it to be open to everybody – an' that includes the fair.'

'But you'd rather nobody came?'

'That's right. It's like I told you – there's no point to a bridge unless it runs over a river, an' there's no point to Hallerton without the Witch Burnin'.'

'You're jokin', aren't you?' Woodend asked incredulously. 'You have to be!'

'It might seem like a joke to you, sir,'

66

Thwaites told him reprovingly, 'but that's how we see it.'

'So everythin' that goes on around here has no purpose if it doesn't support the Witch Burnin'?' Woodend asked, trying to understand.

'That's right, sir.'

'Why?'

'Because that's the way it's always been.'

'This is the 1960s,' Woodend said. 'There's a television in nearly every home in the land these days. There's planes that can fly you all the way to Australia in little more than a day. Bloody hell, the Yanks'll be puttin' a man on the moon in a few years.'

'But what's that got to do with us, sir?'

Woodend sighed again. 'Let me see if I can get this straight,' he said. 'You claim that nobody in the village would want to kill Harry Dimdyke because he was the Witch Maker?'

'That's right, sir.'

'Which, as far as you're concerned, means that he could never have got up anybody's nose? Which, in turn, means that nobody could ever hold a grudge against him, or want him dead?'

'Yes, sir.'

'You told me two things earlier. The first was that the Witch Maker never marries, an' the second was that the burden of his office makes him an old man before his time.'

'That's quite correct, sir.'

67

'But even dead, Harry Dimdyke looked far from clapped out. In fact, I'd go so far as to say he seemed to be a very vigorous man who'd never have been happy with a life of celibacy.'

'I'm afraid you've lost me there, sir.'

'Most murders have either money or sex lurkin' somewhere in their background. We ruled out one, so that must leave the other. Harry Dimdyke wasn't gettin' his oats at home, so where was he gettin' them?'

Thwaites glanced down at the table. 'I wouldn't know about that, sir,' he mumbled.

But he would, Woodend thought. He'd bloody *have to*!

'Was he havin' an affair with somebody's wife?' the Chief Inspector pressed. 'Is that the big secret you've been tryin' to keep from me?'

Thwaites said nothing.

'Well? *Was* he dippin' his wick in somebody else's candle holder?'

'I'm afraid I couldn't say, sir,' Thwaites replied stonily.

'This is a village!' Woodend exploded, unable to keep his temper under control any longer. 'You can't fart in a place like this without everybody knowin' about it. An' you're tryin' to tell me you don't know whether or not Harry Dimdyke was gettin' a bit on the side?'

'Yes, sir.'

68

'If I think you're holdin' back on me, I can make things difficult for you,' Woodend threatened. 'In fact, with a little bit of effort, I can make them bloody impossible. So, for your own good, can I suggest you start pullin' with the rest of the team?'

'I know nothin' about Harry Dimdyke's private life which would assist your investigation,' Thwaites said stiffly.

'How many more years have you got to serve before you're eligible for a pension?'

'Four an' a half.'

'You could lose that pension, you know. If you were kicked off the Force for misconduct, your pension rights could go right down the drain. Is that what you *want* to happen?'

Thwaites took a deep breath. 'I *want* to live out my time in this village, sir. I'd rather do it with a pension than without one, but if it comes to a choice between one an' the other, I'll choose the village.'

'An' what about justice?' Woodend demanded. 'Am I the only one who wants to see Harry Dimdyke's killer arrested?'

'We *all* want to see him arrested,' Thwaites said levelly. 'But we know that whoever killed him, he wasn't one of us. Can I go now, sir?'

'Aye,' Woodend said wearily. 'Bugger off back to your cosy little police house, an' give a bit of thought to what it'd be like to lose it.'

Eight

Woodend looked across the pub table at the chair in which – until a couple of minutes earlier – Constable Thwaites had been sitting so uncomfortably. It was strange, he thought, but the constable seemed to make more of an impression with his absence than he had ever managed to do with his presence.

'I didn't handle our friend, the local bobby, very well, did I?' he asked his sergeant.

'It's hard to imagine how you could have handled him worse,' Paniatowski replied.

Plain-speaking had always played a larger part in their working relationship than social niceties, Woodend thought, and all Paniatowski was doing now was speaking plainly. So he had no right to feel offended. None at all.

Yet he did. Worse, although he knew there was absolutely no justification for it, he felt a sudden urge to strike out.

'How long have you been an expert on human relations, Sergeant?' he demanded, unreasonably.

'Sorry?'

'I should have thought that after the complete bloody mess you made of things over that affair with Bob Rutter, you'd have been a little tolerant of other people's failin's.'

Paniatowski said nothing. There was nothing she *could* have said. Because she recognized the underlying truth of her boss's statement – acknowledged that she and Detective Inspector Bob Rutter had indeed made a complete bloody mess of things.

It was Woodend who finally broke the silence which had fallen between them. 'I'm goin' to make a phone call,' he said. 'If you want another drink, order it – an' I'll pay for it when I get back.'

Bob Rutter had been a stickler for tidiness even before his wife's blindness had made it imperative that everything should always be in the right place – and his desk was a fair reflection of his overall attitude. His in-tray and out-tray were both placed precisely in parallel with the edges of the desk, and the correspondence resting in them was neatly squared-off. His pencils were all well-sharpened, his blotting paper changed every couple of days. Order reigned supreme.

There was only one personal item in evidence. It was a photograph, in a silver frame, placed in such a position that Rutter would see it every time he reached for his phone. The woman in the photograph was smiling optimistically in the direction of a camera she was unable to see. She had dark hair and olive skin. She was unquestionably beautiful, but he would have loved her just as much even if she hadn't been.

There was a photograph at the other end of the desk to balance the one of Maria, Rutter thought, looking at the empty space. But this second one was invisible to everyone but him. The woman in it was blonde. Sometimes he saw her as smiling, sometimes as angry. She was not blind except – on occasion – to the consequences of her actions. Nor was she exactly beautiful. But he loved *her* too.

The phone rang, cutting through his introspection, and he reached for it gratefully.

'You busy?' asked the voice on the other end of the line.

'I've not got anything on that I can't shelve for a while, sir,' Rutter said. 'Why? What do you want? Something to do with this new murder you're investigating?'

'Aye, that's right. I'd like you to spend a bit of time in that dusty basement that our beloved Chief Constable has the nerve to call the "Criminal Records Resources Centre".'

'And what should I be looking for in the CRRC?'

'I'm not entirely sure,' Woodend admitted. 'Anythin' relatin' to criminal activity in the village of Hallerton, I suppose.'

'That's a bit vague.'

'I know it is, but I don't really *have* anythin' more specific to give you. I'm tryin' to build up a picture of the place, you see, an' the locals are bein' rather less than helpful.'

'Monika's with you in Hallerton, is she?' Rutter asked, before he could stop himself.

'Yes, she is. Why wouldn't she be?'

'No reason,' Rutter said, then added hastily, 'How far back would you like me to go with my search?'

'Ideally, to 1604.'

'What?!'

'That's just a bit of gallows humour,' Woodend explained, 'but I suppose you have to be here in this village to really appreciate it.'

'Probably,' Rutter agreed, having no real idea of what his boss was talking about. 'So how far would you *really* like me to go back?'

'Fifty or sixty years. An' I want you to give me *everythin'* you turn up – however trivial or inconsequential it might seem to you.'

'Understood,' Rutter said.

He replaced the receiver and glanced at the picture of his wife. It was only by an effort of will that he didn't turn in the other direction and look at the picture which wasn't really there.

Woodend returned to the table. Paniatowski hadn't ordered another drink. In fact, she seemed to feel no great urge to finish the one she still had in front of her.

'We'll be needin' somewhere to stay for the night, an' this seems as good a place as any,' the Chief Inspector said, thinking, even as he spoke, that the words sounded strained – that it was as if, in order to reach Monika, they'd have to climb over a huge barrier first.

'Shall I have a word with the landlord when he gets back?' Paniatowski asked, her voice neutral, almost machine-like.

'Gets back?'

'Well, he's not here now.'

Woodend glanced across at the bar, and saw that his sergeant was right. There was absolutely no sign of Zeb, the under-friendly mine host of the Black Bull. He had probably slipped into his own quarters for a few minutes.

And why shouldn't he have? Though the pub had been quite full when the two detectives arrived, they were now the only customers.

'Not exactly popular, are we?' he asked his sergeant.

'Not exactly,' Paniatowski agreed, in the same dull tone she had employed earlier.

Something was going to have to be done, Woodend thought.

'I'm sorry about what I said earlier, lass,' he told Paniatowski.

'It's all right,' the sergeant replied, but without much conviction.

'It's not all right – an' we both know that. If I've learned one thing in my years on the Force, it's that it's very easy to pass judgement on other people, but unless you've walked around in their shoes for a while, you probably don't know what you're talkin' about.' He took a slug of what remained of his pint. It tasted like urine. 'The only excuse I've got for speakin' like I did – an' it's not a very good one – is that this bloody place has unsettled me.'

'This *place* – or this *case*?' Paniatowski asked.

'Seems to me they're one an' the same thing,' Woodend told her.

Nine

The church and the primary school in Hallerton were located at the edge of the village, just as they were in so many other moorland communities. They looked across at each other, but were separated by the almost-straight road which ran all the way to a different world called Lancaster.

Woodend glanced down the road. Then, closing his eyes, he tried to picture it as it must have looked three hundred and fifty years earlier, in the days after Meg Ramsden had been burned at the stake. It was unlikely to have been paved back then – and even after only a few days without rain, any horses travelling along it would have thrown up a cloud of dust which could be seen for miles.

How dry had the road been when the High Sheriff's men came? Had the villagers stood on this very spot and watched the dust cloud grow ever larger? Had they listened to the sound of the hoofs – no more than a distant rumble at first, but gradually getting louder, until it filled their ears?

Yes, they probably had. And though they

must have known what the Sheriff's men's mission was, they'd made no attempt to run away.

Perhaps they'd gone to pray for guidance, Woodend speculated, turning towards the church. But given what he'd already learned about the people of this village, that didn't seem likely. And even if they had gone into the church, it wouldn't have been *this* church, because it was a hundred years old at most.

He took a closer look at the building. It didn't seem quite *right*. True it had all the features typical of its time. There was a steeple, covered with the blue slates which would have to have been imported all the way from North Wales. There was a lych-gate, with a bench on which the bearers could rest the coffin during its final journey to the grave. So what was missing?

Woodend took a step back, and suddenly saw what was wrong. This church was smaller – much smaller – than any of the others in the area. It was almost as if the builders had been inspired less by faith and hope and more by a foreknowledge of the size of congregation the structure would eventually have to cater for.

He switched his attention to the school. It, too, resembled many others he had come across on the moors. It was constructed of the same blocks of dressed stone as the church, and roofed with the same blue-grey slates. The windows were high, in order to let in light while denying the children the opportunity of being distracted by views of the outside world. The playground was as austere and forbidding as any prison exercise yard.

The school had probably been built a few years later than the church, Woodend guessed, perhaps in the late Victorian era. At that time education had been regarded with grim seriousness, and even though boys and girls of the same family were often compelled by economic circumstances to share the same bed, the sexes entered the school by separate doors.

The church clock struck a quarter to four, the doors of the school opened, and the children streamed out. Woodend watched them with interest. They were obviously pleased to be free of their educational confinement, yet there was something orderly about the way they left the school – almost as if they were an army in retreat.

Woodend lit a cigarette and watched them until they had disappeared into the village. Then – on impulse – he strolled over to the school. Faced with the choice of entering through the boys' door or the girls' door, he was amused to find that his legs automatically inclined him towards the one used by the boys.

He passed through the cloakroom and into the hallway. Several classroom doors faced him, but only one of them was open. He knocked lightly on it, and stepped into the room.

A woman – a member of staff, presumably – was sitting on the teacher's desk. She was around forty, he estimated. She had long greying hair which was a tangled mess, and a large ladder in one of her nylon stockings which looked far from recent. She had just lit up a cigarette, and was sucking on it with a greed which surprised even a champion chain-smoker like him.

The woman looked up. 'Yes?'

'I was just passin', an' I thought I'd drop in,' Woodend said. 'I hope you don't mind.'

'Mind?' the woman replied. 'Why should I mind?'

'I'm a policeman,' Woodend told her. 'I'm investigatin' the murder in the village.'

'Oh yes?' the woman said, without displaying any real interest.

It was then Woodend saw the bottle – a quarter pint of cheap brandy – which was lying on the desk next to a set of dog-eared exercise books. The woman noted that he had seen it, but made no effort to cover it up.

'It struck me that you an' the other teachers might be able to give me an insight into the life of the village,' the Chief Inspector pressed on.

The woman seemed to find the remark hysterically funny.

'The other teachers?' she said. '*What* other teachers?'

'You're the only one?'

'Looks like it, doesn't it?'

'But I must have seen fifty kids come out of this place.'

'Fifty-seven! What's your point?'

'You surely don't handle them all on your own, do you?' Woodend asked, astonished.

'There's very little choice – considering that no one else will come and work in Hallerton. Besides, it's not as arduous as it seems. It's not as if they actually want to learn anything, beyond the very basic reading and writing skills. And why should they? Most kids in this country don't know what they'll be doing *tomorrow*, but these little buggers know what they'll be doing *forty years* from now – and nothing I offer them is going to make very much difference to that.'

'Even so, just keepin' them in order must be a bit of a problem. Fifty-seven kids crammed together in one room! It's not a job I'd like to take on.'

The woman sneered. 'It's a piece of cake,' she said.

'You're jokin'.'

'I don't make jokes. This place has drained away any sense of humour I might once have had.' The woman took another drag on her cigarette and coughed violently several times. When the fit subsided, she said, 'You've seen the little swine at their liveliest today. They're excited, you see.'

'Yes, murders do, unfortunately, seem to thrill small children,' Woodend said.

'Oh, it's not the murder that's got them going,' the teacher said scornfully. 'It might have done a few weeks ago – especially since it was the almighty Witch Maker himself who was killed – but not now.'

'Not now?'

'Not so close to the big event itself. They've been waiting for the Witch Burning all their short dull lives.'

'You don't seem to have much rapport with the children you teach,' Woodend said.

'Rapport!' the teacher repeated. 'How can you have rapport with a pudding. And that's what they are! Puddings! They just sit there. I tried – once upon a time – to awaken a curiosity in them for the world outside Hallerton. They weren't interested. I told them fairy tales to stimulate their imaginations. What a waste of time that was! The only story they care about is the story of Meg Ramsden – and they already know more about that than I'd ever care to learn.'

'I take it from what you've said that you're not a local woman yourself.'

'No, thank God! But if I *had* been a local woman – if I'd known what the people in the

81

other villages round here know – I'd never have taken the job in the first place. It's soul-destroying, working here.'

'So why do you?' Woodend wondered.

The woman glanced across at the brandy bottle. 'I've no choice,' she said, without any hint of shame. 'I need a job – and this is the only place which will have me.'

'Drink problem?' Woodend guessed.

'It's no problem at all – as long as I can get my hands on one.'

Woodend shook his head, but said nothing.

'I've always had a slight inclination towards the drink,' the woman continued. 'It runs in the family. But it's only since I've been working here I've realized what a real friend it can be. You couldn't do this job sober. Believe me, I've tried it a couple of times.'

'Have you checked the toilets since the children left, Miss Simpkins,' said a stern but rich baritone voice from the doorway.

Woodend looked up. The speaker was a man in his early thirties. He was wearing a tweed jacket – somewhat less hairy and more stylish than his own – and a clerical collar.

'What?' the woman asked, as if she still didn't quite comprehend what was happening.

'The toilets,' the vicar repeated, contemptuously. 'You are to check the toilets once the children have gone, in order to make sure they haven't left anything there. We agreed on that at our last meeting.'

For all that she was a lush, Woodend thought, the man could have been a bit pleasanter in the way he spoke to her – especially considering his calling.

'You *do* remember, don't you, Miss Simpkins?' the vicar said.

'I suppose so,' the teacher answered, sliding rather awkwardly off her desk, then walking with exaggerated care to the door.

Once he was sure she had gone, the vicar ran his eyes over Woodend's clothes, and clearly found the Chief Inspector's appearance did not come up to scratch.

'This is a school,' he said.

'Aye, I've noticed,' Woodend agreed.

'And are you a parent of one of the children who attend this school? Or are you, perhaps, a member of Her Majesty's School Inspectorate?'

'Neither.'

'In that case, and since this institution is not open to the general public, I wonder if you would tell me who you might be?'

'I *might* be the bishop's special representative, come to see if any of the clergy are skivin' off,' Woodend said.

'I beg your pardon!' the vicar said, outraged.

'Granted,' Woodend replied, with a slight smile. 'But as a matter of fact, I'm nothin' to do with the diocese. What I am, is the chief inspector of police from Whitebridge who's come to investigate the murder.'

'Ah, I see!'

The look of supercilious suspicion vanished from the vicar's face and was replaced by an expression which said that, despite Woodend's obvious failure to dress the part, he was now prepared to accept the policeman almost as an equal.

'You must excuse our Miss Simpkins,' the man of the cloth continued. 'You seem to have caught her on a bad day.'

'Is that right?' Woodend asked. 'To tell you the truth, I was beginnin' to wonder if she ever had any good ones. Still, she's not workin' under ideal conditions, is she – not with fifty-odd kids in her class an' a boss who looks at her as if she's somethin' he's found on the heel of his shoe?'

The vicar coughed awkwardly, while he decided what to do next. 'Would you like to see the church?' he asked finally.

'Aye,' Woodend agreed. 'Might as well, now I'm here.'

Ten

Wilf Dimdyke gave Meg Ramsden's carved left foot a last going-over with the sandpaper, then stepped back to look at the results.

It was still not right, he told himself. He still hadn't quite captured the way the foot should look – the way the foot *had* looked on every effigy which had been produced since the first one.

'Bugger it!' he said.

'What's the matter?' his father asked, alarmed.

'The foot.'

'What's wrong with it? It looks fine to me.'

It would do, Wilf thought. It would look fine to *anybody* who was not seeing it through the eyes of a Witch Maker.

'There's no point in fiddlin' with it any more,' he said. 'I'll just have to carve a new one.'

'There's not time for that!' Tom said, his concern now teetering on the edge of panic.

'There'll be time,' Wilf told him. 'There always is.'

'But what if there *isn't*? What if, when it comes round to Sunday mornin''—'

'Dad!'

Tom Dimdyke looked down at the ground. 'I'm sorry,' he mumbled. 'I shouldn't have said anythin'. It's not my place.'

'It's all right, Dad.'

Tom shook his head. 'No, it's not. You're the Witch Maker now, an' what you say goes.'

'Maybe you were right about the foot,' Wilf said. 'Maybe I can improve this one enough so that I don't have to carve a new one.'

But he didn't believe it – and now neither did his father.

Wilf picked up a chisel with one hand and a mallet with the other, and considered the foot. But while part of his mind was struggling with the technical problems he faced, another was considering the change in the nature of his relationship with his father.

He should have expected the change, he thought. He *had* expected it! It was natural. It was part of a pattern which had repeated itself eighteen times since the village had taken the momentous decision which changed its destiny.

Yet it was still hard to come to terms with – because whatever else might have happened, Tom was still his *dad*.

His sister, Mary, was too young to remember anything about their mother. But he wasn't! He'd been just old enough to sit by her bed – holding her hand and watching her cough up blood – as she slowly died of consumption.

Her death had devastated his father – even a small boy like him could tell that. But Tom was a man – a *real* man – and he'd put his own grief aside and got on with the business of bringing up his children. There'd been offers of help, but he would have none of them. The kids were his responsibility, and if that involved doing women's work, then so be it. He'd painstakingly learned how to cook, and how to wash and change his daughter's nappies. The house was a credit to him, the neighbours said. And so it was.

Other memories came back to Wilf as he worked on the effigy's foot. He remembered sitting on the older man's knee and giggling furiously while Tom tickled him under the chin. He remembered them going down to the river together at a time when his fishing rod was taller than he was himself, and how Tom – with almost infinite patience – had taught him how to use it.

Tom's word had been law. If he gave you a clip on the ear, you didn't ask why. You *knew* why! It was because you had earned it; because – even if you didn't fully understand your crime – you accepted that you'd done wrong. Not that there *were* many clips around the ear to speak of. Tom had ruled the house through love, not through fear.

And now this!

Now, on becoming Witch Maker, he was experiencing a great sense of loss. It was almost as if...

It was almost as if the man he had known since his earliest childhood had suddenly become a stranger to him.

'You do what you have to do with Meg,' Tom said encouragingly. 'An' whatever you decide, I'm sure your Uncle Harry would have been more than happy with the way you've taken care of his Witch.'

He meant well, Wilf thought – but he didn't understand. None of them understood.

They all believed that the Witch Maker's greatest moment came as he stood on the Green and watched the Witch burn, just minutes before he stepped down from his position to make way for his successor.

How could it not be so? they asked themselves.

He had served his term – had endured all the sacrifices that being the Witch Maker entailed – and now, the heavy burden of responsibility almost lifted from him, he could look on with pride as his Witch went up in smoke and flames.

But it *wasn't* his Witch.

His Witch – the one he had truly put his heart and soul into, the one he had made the *most* sacrifices for – had been built while he was an apprentice, and consumed by a fire twenty years earlier.

The Witch Maker reached the height of his skill during his apprenticeship. After that, he became no more than a teacher – training his successor to build *his* masterpiece.

Wilf knew all this as only a Witch Maker could. Knew that while the Witch Maker had the *authority* in the village, it was the Assistant Witch Maker who had the *power* – because true power came only through the act of creation, and once he became Witch Maker, a man's creative days were over.

'Pass me another piece of sandpaper,' he said to his father.

He realized, even as he spoke, that it sounded more like a command than a request, but before he had time to soften his words his father had place the sandpaper in his hand without comment.

He was above being corrected now, he thought. He was above being questioned. He was the Witch Maker.

Eleven

'At first glance, the church seems to have very little architectural merit,' the vicar said in a tone of voice which suggested that he was about to embark on an oft-repeated lecture. 'Nonetheless, there are certain features of it which I am sure that even you, as a layman with little specialized knowledge, should find interesting.'

Woodend scowled. His Nonconformist background had made him naturally suspicious of vicars with a High Church leaning, but this feller would have got right up his nose whatever line of work he'd been in.

'Look, for example, at the steeple,' the vicar continued. 'You'll notice that the weather vane—'

'Why don't we just cut the crap?' Woodend suggested, mildly.

The vicar looked as if he'd just been struck by an errant thunderbolt. 'What did you say, Chief Inspector?' he asked icily.

'You didn't bring me here to see the church,' Woodend pointed out. 'You wanted to get me away from the school – and especially, you wanted to get me away from Miss Simpkins.'

The vicar seemed unsure of how to react to the comment. For a moment, it looked as if he would choose outrage again, then his expression shifted to one of haughty Anglican disdain. Finally, however, he decided to opt for at least *temporary* honesty.

'You're quite right, of course,' he agreed. 'The poor woman has a lot of troubles in her life, and as both the vicar and the chairman of the board of school governors, I try to shield her from the consequences of her own weaknesses as much as I possibly can.'

Especially since, if she left the school, you'd find it almost impossible to replace her, Woodend thought.

But aloud, all he said was, 'What do the other governors of the school think about her?'

'There aren't any,' the vicar admitted.

Then there wasn't much to be chairman of, either, Woodend reflected.

'Only one teacher, an' only one governor,' he said. 'Seems like a rum kind of school to me.'

'It's a "rum kind" of village – as you're no doubt already coming to appreciate,' the vicar said. 'In most villages, seats on the governing body of the school are very much sought after. As are seats on the parish council. A title gives *ordinary* people some

91

kind of status, you see. But in this village there is no parish council, and no one – seemingly – is willing to serve on the board of the school.'

'Couldn't you recruit them from the pulpit?' Woodend suggested, with only a *touch* of malice. 'That's what most vicars I know do when they want to press some poor bugger into reluctant service.'

The vicar laughed bitterly. 'If they came to church, that might work,' he said. 'But they don't.'

'Which means that you can take Sunday off, does it?' Woodend said whimsically.

The vicar glared at him. 'I have two parishes in my care. This one and Throckston. I hold my services in Throckston.'

'There's more of a congregation there, is there?'

'My church in Throckston is reasonably full, given the times we live in,' the vicar said. 'Certainly it is fuller than the churches officiated over by some of my colleagues.'

'But the only business you can drum up in Hallerton is for births, marriages and deaths, is it?'

The vicar shot him another look of dislike, thought of twisting the truth slightly, then opted for honesty again.

'Here it's just *deaths*,' he said. 'If they want someone to be buried in my churchyard, they *have* to come to me. But I think if they could do it without permission, I wouldn't even see them then.' He paused for a moment. 'You obviously have no interest at all in my church, but perhaps you'd care to have a look around my churchyard.'

The invitation was delivered casually, but Woodend was not fooled. He had made the vicar feel inadequate, and now the vicar was planning to get his revenge by making the smart-mouthed bobby feel the same. How he hoped to achieve his aim in the church-yard was anybody's guess, but it might be interesting to find out.

'Yes, I'd be delighted to take a look,' he said.

They walked through the lych-gate. The closer they got to the church, the more Woodend could see how neglected it was. The churchyard, on the other hand, was as neat and tidy as a formal garden.

He stopped to examine one of the tomb-stones.

OSWALD WARBURTON 1896–1912
Only child of Walter and Catherine.
Sadly missed.

The youth had been dead for over fifty years, and the parents, too, must have passed on long ago. Yet this grave – like all the others around it – had been kept in immaculate condition.

'You shouldn't be surprised,' the vicar said, reading his mind. 'In Hallerton, the past is all that matters. In Hallerton, the dead are more important than the living – far more important.'

Was this what the vicar had brought him to see? Woodend wondered. Was this the surprise that the man had been aiming at? If it was, then it was a pretty watered-down revenge by anybody's standards.

'Yes, they really do care about their dead,' the vicar said. 'Which makes it all the more surprising that the one thing you find in every other village churchyard is missing here.'

So that was it, Woodend thought. Something he should have spotted already – and hadn't.

'What have I missed?' he asked.

The vicar chuckled with very unpriestly glee. 'You're supposed to be the detective,' he said. '*You* work it out.'

Woodend looked around and saw graves, yew trees, and the pump at which mourners could fill their flower vases with water. Everything which should be there *seemed* to be there.

'I don't know what's missin',' he confessed.

The vicar chuckled again. 'Then perhaps you should consider going into another line of work entirely,' he suggested. 'Still not got it?'

'No.'

'Would you like me to give you a big clue?'

For a second Woodend was tempted to tell him to stuff his clue, then curiosity overcame him.

'Aye, go on,' he said.

The vicar's smile was now so wide it looked as if it might crack his face in half.

'Were you ever in the Army?' he asked.

'Yes.'

'In peacetime? Or during the war?'

'Durin' the war.'

'Then even if you're a very dim detective indeed, you shouldn't need a better clue than that.'

Of course he bloody shouldn't, Woodend agreed silently, as enlightenment dawned.

His war had been bad enough, but the one which had preceded it had been even worse. One million young British men had died fighting in the Great War – the so-called 'war to end all wars'. The soldiers had been slaughtered like cattle, and there was no village in the country – not even the tiniest hamlet – which had not lost some of its sons.

And there was no village – not even the tiniest hamlet – which did not have its own war memorial.

Some of the memorials were large and imposing. Some were very unprepossessing monuments indeed. The richer parishes had used marble, the poorer an altogether more modest stone.

But they all had one!

Except Hallerton!

'What happened to the cenotaph?' Woodend asked. 'Was it taken away at some point?'

'As far as I know, there's never been one *to* take away. Certainly, there's no mention of one in any of the church records.'

'That's incredible,' Woodend said. 'I wouldn't have thought it possible.'

The vicar smirked. 'There are more things on heaven and earth than are ever dreamed of in a dull policeman's philosophy,' he said.

Twelve

Hettie Todd sat on the steps of the caravan she shared with her mother, idly watching the fairground workers putting up the rides. She loved the life which went with belonging to the funfair. She loved the aroma of out-door cooking, and the strong smell of hot diesel from the generators. She loved the bright flashing lights, and the loud tinny music. It didn't bother her to be always on the move, because it was the people you shared the space with – not the particular space you happened to be occupying that night – which really mattered.

The men had been hard at it all day, she thought. They didn't care that there had been a brutal murder only a few hundred yards from where they toiled. They wouldn't have reacted any differently if the whole village had been massacred. They had a job to do, and what went on beyond the bound-aries of the fair was no concern of theirs.

Their job – their whole function in life – was to create a fantasy world in which to envelop all those who came to visit it. Create it – and then destroy it. Because only a few days after it had gone up, it would come down again, and the funfair would move on, leaving behind it only the echoes of laughter to prove that it had ever been there.

Hettie smiled, self-mockingly.

Create a fantasy world! Echoes of laughter!

She might see it like that, but the men certainly didn't. To them, the machinery of the fairground – the exotic world which they built and then demolished – was nothing more than bolts to be slid in place and nuts to be tightened. Fairground folk might have the power to *create* an escape from reality, but within themselves they were the most practical, down-to-earth people in the whole world. And there was good reason for that – for while outsiders might view them as nothing but idle gypsies and slackers, they knew just how hard their lives could be.

It sometimes puzzled Hettie that she should muse and contemplate in this way. Where did these strange thoughts which seemed to fill her mind come from? Why did she alone – of all those involved with the fair – seem to think them?

She searched her own past – not for the first time – for some clue as to her singularity.

She had been born on the road. But that, in itself, was not unusual. Half the folk working on the fairground had come into the

98

world that way, for though nature imposed its own timetable on pregnant women, the carnival season put in place an even more demanding one.

Then there was the fact that she was illegitimate. She'd once heard one of the men refer to her as 'Zelda Todd's bastard', but she hadn't really taken offence. 'Bastard', within the world of the carnival, was no more than a descriptive term. There were, as everyone was well aware, plenty of other bastards working on the fair.

Nor had her upbringing been radically different to anyone else's. During the season, she and all the other kids had worked all the hours that the god of carnivals had sent. Out of season, they'd all camped on whatever piece of land some local council had grudgingly set aside for them, and attended whichever of the local schools could come up with the least plausible excuse for refusing to admit them.

Had it been this schooling which had made her different? Again, she didn't think so. She had quite enjoyed her snippets of education – certainly more than most of the carnival children, who had no desire to be thought of as 'scholars' – but she had felt no more of a sense of loss than the others did when the time came to get on the road again.

So what *was* the reason she was so odd? She wished she knew. She really wished she knew!

It was as these thoughts ran through her mind she saw – with a sinking heart – that her mother was standing by the Caterpillar, and was in deep conversation with Pat Calhoun.

She had no doubt what the conversation was about. Her mother wanted her married. Or at least – since carnival folk did not set much store by bits of paper – Zelda wanted her *attached*.

'You're gettin' old,' her mother never tired of telling her.

'I'm not old at all, Mam!'

'When I was your age—'

'I was already on the way. I know that! But it doesn't make any difference. I'm not ready!'

But would she *ever* be ready?

True, Pat Calhoun was her *mother's* choice, but she had to admit that he wasn't a *bad* choice.

He was tall.

He was well built.

He could be called handsome, in a sandy-Irish sort of way.

Though he could get violent when he'd had a few drinks, which of the carnival men couldn't? And unlike a few of the other men, he had never turned his violence on a woman.

So all in all, her mother had not made a

bad choice for her. And yet ... and yet ... somehow it didn't feel right.

She had been expecting her mother and Pat to turn and look towards the caravan, as they usually did when they were talking about her. But they didn't. Instead they were gazing intently in the other direction – towards the village. And now she considered it more carefully, they didn't have their normal time-to-discuss-the-Hettie-problem-again faces on, either.

There was none of Zelda's usual persuasive cajoling in her expression – *'Hettie knows, deep down, that it's you she really wants, Pat. All you have to do is let her know that you're serious.'*

Nor was there any of Pat's diffidence in his – *'Hettie's a free spirit, Zelda. You should know that. All I can do is wait. If she makes her mind up that she wants me, she knows where I am.'*

No, there was none of that at all. Neither looked exasperated with the other, as they usually did. What they *did* look was worried!

Zelda pointed in the direction of the village green. Pat shook his head. Zelda pointed again, jabbing her finger violently through the air this time. Pat looked at the ground, scuffed his feet, and said nothing.

Now what the bloody-buggering hell was that all about? Hettie wondered.

Thirteen

It was well past six o'clock when Woodend noticed the old handloom weaver's cottage which stood in splendid isolation on the other side of the Green to the pub. It was the fact that it looked well cared for – but not lived in – that intrigued him, but it was not until he got closer to it that the mystery of what it was – and why it was there – was solved.

The answer came in the form of a small sign – skilfully hand-painted but still obviously amateur – which was mounted on the wall next to the door.

'The Meg Ramsden Museum,' Woodend read aloud.

There were no opening times listed, nothing about the cost of admission. If it was being run for a profit, then whoever was behind it was keeping very quiet about the fact.

The door was ajar, if not exactly open. Woodend pushed it, and it swung further, to reveal a long room which must once have been a handloom-weaving gallery. That it *was* a museum was obvious from the exhibits, which were displayed in free-standing cabinets or else mounted on the walls. Woodend looked around for the inevitable box which would invite voluntary contributions, and could find none.

'They don't want your money,' said a voice.

Woodend glanced in the direction it had come from. Standing at the other end of the gallery, partly hidden by one of the displays, was a tall, bald man in his fifties, dressed in a heavy wool jacket with leather elbow patches.

'What was that you said?' the Chief Inspector asked.

'I was merely remarking they don't want your money. They don't really want *you*, if truth be told. The only reason they open the museum to the public at all is because, if they didn't, it would be like admitting that they'd got something to be ashamed of. And they'd never do that.'

Woodend took a few steps further into the room. The other man was wearing a white-and-green checked shirt and knitted brown tie beneath his jacket, and there were a number of tiny holes in the shirt which indicated that he was a pipe smoker. He was, Woodend guessed, either a schoolteacher or university lecturer with a keen interest in local history.

'Are you from the police?' the man asked.

'That's right,' Woodend agreed.

'Thought you must be.'

'An' why's that?'

'Because you're certainly not a local. Nor do you have the look of a casual sightseer who's wandered in here by accident and is now wondering if it's worth the effort staying for a while.'

'I take it you're not a local either,' Woodend said.

The other man laughed. 'Quite correct. I'm an outsider too. John Tyndale's the name.'

'Charlie Woodend.'

'Yes, I'm an outsider, all right. I was born and raised not ten miles from here, but to the people of Hallerton, that's about as foreign as coming from Outer Mongolia.'

'Aye, I got the impression it was a bit of a tight-knit community,' Woodend said.

'That's not the word for it,' Tyndale told him. 'If you examine the history of most villages in this area, what you'll be tracing is a gradual decline. And then you come across Hallerton!' He paused. 'But I don't want to bore you,' he added, half-apologetically.

'I'm not bored at all,' Woodend assured him. 'I'd be very interested to hear what you've got to say.'

Tyndale smiled with the gratitude of someone well used to seeing others flee when he embarked on his particular obsession.

'The decline began in the eighteenth century,' he said. 'The aristocracy back then suddenly decided that they could make more money out of farming their land as large-scale units than they could from renting out small pieces of it to the local peasants. What followed was what was called the Enclosure Movement. It created a lot of landless labourers – and not only in Lancashire, but all over the country. The condition of the poor had never been very wonderful, but suddenly it had become a great deal worse. Many villages literally died.'

'But not Hallerton?' Woodend said.

'But not Hallerton,' the other man agreed. 'A lot of the people lost their livelihood, but they somehow managed to scrape by and stay where they were. Then we come to the second wave in the depopulation, if I can call it that – the Industrial Revolution which occurred in the nineteenth century. Britain was suddenly the workshop of the world, and Lancashire, with its cotton mills, coal miles and iron works, was the very centre of that workshop. Towns sprang up all over the place, and the inhabitants of those towns – as well as the workers in the factories which were responsible for their growth – were drawn mainly from the countryside.'

'An' that wave managed to miss Hallerton as well?'

'Indeed it did. If you examine the registry in most villages around here, you can probably trace one or two families back three or four hundred years. In Hallerton, you can trace them all back.'

'Do you mean "all"?' Woodend asked, with a smile. 'Or do you just mean "most"?'

'I mean *all*,' Tyndale said emphatically. 'A lot of these rural areas were cut off from the outside world for most of the winter, so it was quite a common practice for your son to marry your neighbour's daughter. But in Hallerton, it was more than common. There are very few examples of Hallertonians marrying outsiders. Almost none, in fact.'

'So Meg Ramsden's descendants still live in the village.'

'Not having any children of her own, there are no *direct* descendants,' Tyndale said, 'but I think it would be fair to say that Meg's bloodline runs through everyone here.'

'No children of her own?' Woodend repeated. 'Wasn't that unusual in those times.'

'Very,' Tyndale agreed. 'And that fact alone may have had a direct bearing on her fate.'

'How do you mean?'

'Well, Point One: if she'd had the distraction of children, she might never have become the woman she *did* become. And Point Two: the villagers would probably never have burned her if she'd been a mother. Of course, if you take Point One to its logical conclusion, Point Two becomes largely irrelevant, because they'd never have considered burning her anyway.'

'You've lost me,' Woodend admitted.

Tyndale laughed, self-deprecatingly. 'I'm sorry,' he said. 'When you know as much about the history of this village as I do, you're bound to make the occasional leap in your mind which leaves your listener behind. What I meant to say was that Meg's childlessness – either as a result of being barren or because she deliberately chose not to have children – was probably a very significant factor in her later decision to devote much of her considerable energy to...'

But Woodend was no longer listening. A shaft of late-afternoon sunlight had suddenly penetrated one of the small windows, illuminating a portrait which had previously been in semi-darkness. And it was this portrait which Woodend was now staring at – wide-eyed and awestruck.

The picture was, as far as Woodend could tell, at least three hundred and fifty years old. It was painted in oils, after the style of the Flemish School. Van Dyck or possibly Rubens. He wasn't sure which.

The background was dark – as was the fashion of the day – and the subject of the portrait was wearing a black dress with white lace at the collar and cuffs. The woman's hands rested demurely on her lap, but there was nothing demure in her expression. Rather there was a sexuality about it which most portraits of the time tended to suppress – a sexuality which seemed to have overpowered the artist and forced him to discard all the rules and conventions.

Woodend let his eyes dwell for a moment on the long blonde hair, then let them travel to the deep blue eyes, the slim nose and the sensuous mouth. Behind him, he heard the other man laugh.

'Most people react like that to Meg's portrait,' Tyndale said, misreading – understandably – what was going on in Woodend's mind. 'I suppose it's natural enough. When they're told they're going to see the picture of a witch, they expect to see a crone with a twisted nose and a face covered by warts. It comes as a real shock to them to realize just how beautiful she was.'

'She *was* beautiful!' Woodend gasped.

'And she knew it. She was so well aware of it, in fact, that she wanted her beauty celebrated. The artist she commissioned came all the way from York to paint her picture – which was several days' journey in those times. And, as you can see, he was a *real* artist. What Meg paid him for his work would have kept a whole family in this village alive for a year. I sometimes wonder if she knew that by having it painted, she was contributing to the resentment which eventually lead to her death. And then I wonder if she would really have cared if she *had* known. Vanity can sometimes blind even the wisest woman, don't you think?'

But Woodend had stopped listening again, and was off in a world of his own. He had never believed in ghosts, and in the picture of Meg Ramsden he saw nothing to change his mind. Yet what he was seeing still came as a shock. The portrait had been painted three hundred and fifty years earlier. The artist who had created it had long since turned to dust. Yet the face was still alive.

And not just on canvas! Woodend had seen it for himself – in the flesh – not more than a couple of hours earlier. It was the face of Mary Dimdyke!

Fourteen

The barn door swung open, and Mary Dimdyke entered, carrying a large mug of tea in each hand.

'By the cringe, but you're a sight for my sore old eyes, Mary, lass,' her father said.

Mary smiled. 'You're n ... not *old*, Dad.'

Tom Dimdyke returned the smile. 'There's days when I feel a hundred an' fifty,' he said. 'I'm not like this young lad here – our Witch Maker. Just gettin' out of bed is enough to bugger me these days.'

There was more banter behind the words than there was truth, Mary thought. Her dad was as vigorous as he'd ever been. And what pride he'd put into those three words – 'our Witch Maker'.

'I've b ... brought you some tea,' she said, holding out one of the mugs to her father.

Tom Dimdyke looked at it longingly, but shook his head. 'Not at the moment, thank you, lass.'

'S ... somethin' the matter with it, Dad?' Mary asked. 'I m ... made it the w ... way you like it – so st ... strong you could st ... stand

110

your spoon up in it.'

'I'm sure it's just right, Mary, love, but I think I'll hold off on it a while,' her father told her, all the while making a frantic sideways gesture with his eyes.

And suddenly Mary understood what he meant, and why he looked so uncomfortable.

'Here's your t ... tea, Wilf,' she said, holding out the other mug to her older brother.

Wilf took the mug with the barest nod of his head, and turned his mind back to the problem of Meg's left foot.

'I think I'll have my mug now,' Tom said, and when Mary gave it to him, he slurped it down greedily.

'Will you be w ... wantin' me to bring you anythin' else?' Mary asked.

Tom looked uncertain. 'I'm not sure,' he said. 'Will we be wantin' anythin' else, Wilf?'

The young man made no reply.

'I was askin' if you thought we'd be wantin' anythin' else,' Tom Dimdyke said, louder this time.

'A few ginger biscuits would be nice,' his son replied, not looking up from his work.

'Aye, a few ginger biscuits would be grand,' Tom agreed gratefully. He ran his eyes quickly up and down his daughter's slim frame. 'You look a proper picture, lass,' he said.

Mary glowed with pleasure. 'Th ... thanks, Dad.'

'Move into the doorway, where I can get a better look at you.'

Mary stepped back. 'Is th ... this all right?'

'Perfect,' Tom said. 'The way the sunlight catches your hair is lovely. It'll look perfect on Sunday.'

The glow disappeared, and Mary rocked on her heels as if she'd been hit by a hammer. 'But I th ... thought...' she gasped.

'You thought what?'

'I th ... thought that after everythin' that's h ... happened...'

'Everythin' that's happened?'

'Uncle H ... Harry...'

'Your Uncle Harry's death was a terrible, terrible thing, but it changes *nothin'*,' Tom told her firmly.

Mary felt hot tears start to trickle down her soft cheeks. 'W ... Wilf!' she sobbed.

Her anguish was so obvious that it managed even to permeate her brother's Witch-absorbed mind.

'What's the matter?' he asked.

'D ... Dad says that even though Uncle H ... Harry's dead, I'll still have to go th ... through with it.'

'There's no point in appealin' to your brother, because he can't do anythin' about it,' Tom said, his voice suddenly harsh and unyielding.

Wilf's body stiffened. 'What was that, Dad?' he asked.

'I said there's no point in your sister appealin' to you.'

'Is there not?'

'No, there bloody isn't.'

For a moment it seemed as if Wilf would accept his father's judgement on the matter. Then Mary sobbed again.

Wilf straightened up. 'She's my sister,' he said.

'An' she's a child of this village,' his father told him. 'She has Meg Ramsden's blood runnin' through her veins.'

'That doesn't mean—'

'Yes, it does. You *know* it does.'

The two men – father and son – faced each other across the effigy. Their fists were bunched, their eyes locked, and their noses almost touching.

A panic swept over Mary, so intense she felt that she could almost drown in it.

She had caused this, she told herself. She alone had set the two men she cared most about in the world at each other's throats. If it came to blows, their father would win, despite the fact that Wilf was younger and stronger – because her brother, for all his rough talk, was gentle and kind, and simply did not have Tom's determination.

'D ... Dad! W ... Wilf!' she pleaded. 'There's n ... no need for this! We d ... don't

113

want any trouble!'

'Stay out of this, Mary,' Wilf said, his gaze still fixed on his father's. 'So you think you can overrule me, do you, Dad?'

'It's not me,' Tom said.

'Isn't it?' Wilf looked around the barn. 'Well, I certainly don't see anybody else here.'

'You're the Witch Maker now,' Tom said. 'I honour you for that. You have my respect, an' – whenever it's necessary – you have my total obedience an' all.'

'So if I say that I don't want our Mary to have to go through the ordeal of havin' her—'

'But even though you are the Witch Maker, there are some things you don't have any choice about,' Tom interrupted.

His father's eyes had begun to moisten over, Wilf noticed with astonishment.

His big, strong dad – the man who carried him for miles on his back when he was a kid – was almost on the point of tears which were every bit as deep and bitter as Mary's. It wrenched at his heart to see his father in such distress. But there was still Mary to consider – still Mary to protect.

'If my position means anythin' at all—' he began.

'Bein' the Witch Maker doesn't give you freedom,' Tom told him. 'I thought you'd have realized that by now.'

'Then what does it do?'

'It's a burden. It's a responsibility. It binds you to what *has* to be done – even more tightly than it binds the rest of us.'

Fifteen

Throckston was only four miles from Hallerton. Yet it would have been impossible to confuse the two, Woodend thought as he parked the Wolseley outside the Wheatsheaf Inn.

It wasn't just that the outward signs of the twentieth century seemed to have reached this village in a way they had never managed to reach its neighbour. It wasn't even that the locals watched the two police officers' arrival with frank curiosity, but without any sign of hostility. Put simply, it was obvious from the moment he and Paniatowski stepped out of the car that even the air in Throckston seemed lighter and easier to breathe – as if, unlike the air in Hallerton, it was not forced to carry on it the heavy weight of three hundred and fifty years of history.

They took their luggage out of the boot of the Wolseley, and walked across the car park to the pub. A man sitting on the wall nodded to them, and they nodded back. The dog sitting at the man's feet looked up and wagged its tail.

'It feels good to have got away from darkest Hallerton,' Woodend said.

'Yes, it does,' Paniatowski agreed heartily. Not that there'd been any choice in the matter. The landlord at the Black Bull had been adamant that he had no rooms available for them – or for anybody else, for that matter.

But every pub in this part of Lancashire let out rooms, Paniatowski had protested.

Maybe all the rest did, the landlord had replied. He wouldn't know about that. But he did know that this one didn't.

How about bed and breakfast places? Paniatowski had asked. Were there any widow ladies in the village who would welcome the chance to supplement their pensions by providing accommodation for a couple of police officers?

If there were any, the landlord told her, he didn't know about them. And neither, it seemed, did Constable Thwaites.

Thus, they had been forced to come to Throckston.

And thank God they had, Woodend thought, as he pushed open the public bar door and heard the happy buzz of conversation which had been wholly absent from the public bar of the Black Bull.

The landlord of the Wheatsheaf was a jolly, red-faced, balding man, wearing a bright check waistcoat which strained against his

117

ample beer paunch.

As he slid the register across the counter for Woodend to sign, he said, 'So you're investigatin' that murder of the Witch Maker, are you?'

'That's right,' the Chief Inspector agreed.

'Well, you'll have your work cut out for you, there's no doubt about that,' the landlord assured him. 'They're funny folk over in Hallerton. Always were, an' always will be.'

'You seem be talkin' from personal experience,' Woodend said.

'*Bitter* experience,' the landlord replied. He chuckled. 'An' I'm not talkin' about the kind of bitter that comes out of my pumps.'

'Tell me about it,' Woodend suggested.

The landlord needed no further urging. 'Well, when I was younger – an' didn't know any better – I tried to get off with a girl from Hallerton myself,' he said. 'A lovely lass, she was, by the name of Bessie Potts.' He sighed, and a faraway look came into his eyes. 'But it never came to anythin'.'

'Why was that?' Woodend asked. 'Didn't she fancy you back?'

'Oh, she fancied me, all right.' The landlord paused and patted his stomach. 'I wasn't born with this, you know. When I was young, I had a belly as flat as a washboard, an' an arse so tight you could have cracked walnuts in it. So as you can imagine, I never had any difficulty pullin' women.'

118

'Except for this Bessie Potts,' Woodend prompted.

'Like I said, she wasn't the problem. She'd have gone for a ramble on the moors with me at the drop of a hat. But she never had the chance, did she? I went to pick her up for what I suppose these days you might call "our first date" – an' she wasn't there.'

'But someone else was?' Woodend guessed.

'You're so smart you should be a detective,' the landlord said, laughing heartily at his own joke. 'Yes, you're right, somebody else was there – half a dozen somebody elses, as a matter of fact.'

'Local lads?'

'That's what you'd have thought, isn't it? But it wasn't *lads* at all. These fellers were all old enough to have been my dad.' He chuckled again. 'Nasty enough to have been that dad of mine, an' all.'

'Did they hurt you?'

'No, though I suppose it would have made a better story if they had've given me a beltin'.'

'So what *did* they do?'

'They made it as plain as the nose on your face that if I didn't take their first "friendly" warnin', there wouldn't be another one. An' we're not talkin' about a few bruises, you know. They as good as said that if I showed my face in the village again, they'd make sure I'd lose the use of my legs. An' I believed them at the time – so I've never been there from that day to this.'

'Probably wise,' Woodend said.

The landlord shrugged. 'Aye. Probably.' He glanced up at the clock. 'Supper should be ready in about half an hour. I know for a fact that the missus is makin' a Lancashire hotpot – but she can soon do you somethin' else if you think that won't suit you.'

'Do *you* think it'll suit me?' Woodend asked.

'Well, though I say so as shouldn't, it's the best hotpot I've ever tasted. An' it always wins first prize at the village fête.'

'Then I'd be a fool to turn down the opportunity to try it for myself,' Woodend said.

He had picked up his bag and was heading for the stairs when the landlord's cough made him turn round again.

'Was there somethin' else?' he said.

'Not really,' the landlord said wistfully. 'I was just thinkin'.'

'About what?'

'There were lots of other pretty girls around at the time I was after Bessie. Some were *almost* as pretty as she was, an' I married one of them.'

Woodend smiled. 'But?'

'But I still can't help wonderin' if my life would have been any different if I'd ignored that "friendly" warnin'.'

Sixteen

It was nice to be back in the normal world, Woodend thought. Nice to be sitting in a bar with Monika Paniatowski by his side, a pint glass in his hand and his stomach well-lined with the landlady's justly famous Lancashire hotpot.

It was only a temporary release, of course. The following morning they would return to dark, brooding Hallerton, and attempt to solve a murder that no one there seemed particularly keen to *have* solved. In fact, he couldn't even put aside thoughts of the village for even that long, because there was a phone call he needed to make.

He took a swig of his pint and stubbed out his Capstan in the already-overflowing ashtray.

'I'd better go an' call Bob on the off chance he's come up with somethin' useful,' he said.

'Yes, that's probably a good idea,' Monika Paniatowski said, her voice giving away nothing of the turmoil that was raging inside her.

Woodend stood up. 'Shouldn't be long,' he

said. 'But if you start feelin' bored, you can always order another round.'

He was at the point of turning towards the door when his sergeant said, 'Could you ask Bob ... could you ask Inspector Rutter...'

'Yes?'

'I ... I miss my little car. Could you ask Inspector Rutter if it would be possible for one his lads to drive it up here in the morning?'

'Aye, I'll do that,' Woodend said, wondered what it was she'd really been going to ask him to ask Rutter. 'I'll tell you somethin', Monika – I've known mother hens that lavished less attention on their chicks that you devote to that car of yours,' he continued, in an attempt to lighten the atmosphere.

Paniatowski smiled weakly. 'You know how it is with the things that are important to you,' she said.

Yes, Woodend thought. Yes, I believe I do.

Bob Rutter had lost track of time – he always did when he immersed himself in reports – so it was not until the insistently ringing phone reminded him there was a world beyond that of cardboard folders that he even realized it had gone dark outside.

He picked up the phone. 'DI Rutter.'

'See if you can find out why there's no war memorial in Hallerton,' said a familiar voice on the other end of the line.

Rutter was not quite sure that he had heard correctly. 'A war memorial?' he repeated.

'There should be one, an' there isn't. I'd like to know why. It might not have any relevance to the case, but at least it'll put me one up on that smug bastard of a vicar.'

'Are you feeling all right, sir?' Rutter asked worriedly.

'No, I'm not. Nobody who knows he has to go back to Hallerton in the mornin' could be feelin' all right. It's not somethin' that I'd wish on my worst enemy.' Woodend paused. 'So have you come up with anythin' that might help me solve the case in a hurry, an' give me the excuse to leave the bloody place behind me?'

'I'm not sure,' Rutter admitted. 'Aside from murder, there doesn't seem to be much crime in Hallerton.'

'Well, that's a comfort,' Woodend said sourly.

'I'm been comparing the crime sheets from Hallerton with those of the other villages round it,' Rutter continued. 'The rest of the villages record a marked increase in petty theft and burglary since the war. Nothing really significant, you understand – bicycles taken, a few pounds stolen – but in Hallerton there isn't even that. I don't know why that should be. Perhaps the local constable keeps a tighter grip on things than the constables in the other villages do.'

'Or *somebody* keeps a tighter grip,' Woodend said.

'I beg your pardon, sir.'

'Nothin'. Just thinkin' aloud. Have you got anythin' else for me?'

'There've been four suicides the last fifty years, two of them in the last ten. Isn't that rather high for a small place like Hallerton?'

'I haven't got the statistics, but it *is* quite common for small farmers to take their shotguns an' blow off their own heads. An' in a way, who can blame them? They work their bollocks off, year an' year out, an' it only takes one particularly bad run of weather to ruin them. The banks won't help – there's no real money in it for them – and the poor bloody farmer's got nobody else to turn to. If the government cared about the land as much as it says it does, it would never allow...' Woodend paused again. 'Sorry, lad, I was off ridin' my hobby horse for a second, wasn't I? Tell me about these farmers.'

'They *weren't* farmers,' Rutter said.

'Weren't they? I'd just assumed they'd—'

'They were all women, and none of them was even a farmer's *wife*.'

Woodend whistled softly. 'Is there any common thread runnin' through these suicides?'

'Well, there's their age,' Rutter said.

124

'Oh aye? How old were they?'

'They were all in their middle-to-late twenties.'

'An' do we have any clue as to their motives?'

'None. According to the reports, they were all healthy and had everything to live for.'

'If you can call spendin' most of your time in Hallerton *livin*',' Woodend said. 'Did they have anythin' in common *apart* from their age? Were they all from the same family, for example?'

'The records seem to suggest that everybody in the village is related – through some obscure link in the past – to everybody else.'

'But no *close* relationship? What about the most recent two? They weren't first cousins or anythin', were they?'

'No. Absolutely not.'

'So what else might have connected them?'

'Nothing comes immediately to mind. One ran the village store with her husband, and the other was the postman's wife.'

'So they were both married,' Woodend said, pouncing on the detail.

'Most women are married by the time they reach their late twenties,' Rutter pointed out.

And thoughts of Monika Paniatowski flashed through both their minds.

'Since you haven't asked, I assume you've already got all the details you need on the murder,' Rutter said.

'Far from it,' Woodend told him. 'But bein' at the scene, I probably know more about the death of Harry Dimdyke than you do, sittin' on your arse in Whitebridge.'

'Harry Dimdyke?' Rutter repeated, puzzled.

'Yes. That's the victim's name, lad.'

'I wasn't talking about the most *recent* victim.'

'What?!' Woodend exploded.

'I'm sorry, sir, but since you *are* already at the scene, I assumed somebody would already have briefed you on the Stan Dawkins case.'

Woodend gripped the phone receiver so tightly it was a wonder it didn't shatter.

'They're buggerin' me about, aren't they?' he said furiously.

'Well, it does seem strange that you haven't been told,' Rutter admitted.

'*You* tell me, lad,' Woodend said. 'You give me all the details that I should, by rights, have had since this mornin'.'

Seventeen

It had been a long night for Constable Thwaites – long *and* troubled. He had tossed and turned. Several times a raging thirst had forced him from his bed. He had knocked back a pint of water each time, but it had done no good. Sleep would not come, and the thirst would not go away.

Finally, when dawn had broken, he'd got dressed in his uniform and gone downstairs to his office. And there he sat, waiting for he knew not what, but knowing that he was waiting for *something*.

When he saw the Wolseley draw up outside, he finally understood what his vigil had been about – realized that he had cast himself in the role of sacrificial lamb, and had been preparing himself for the arrival of the high priest without whom the sacrifice could not be made.

The high priest was wearing his customary hairy sports jacket. He looked very angry as he climbed out of his car, and seemed even more enraged to see the gate barring his path to the police house office. He wrenched at the latch, swung the gate open, and marched up the path with furious – almost giant – strides.

Watching his progress through the window, Thwaites shuddered. He had known it was going to be bad – but he'd never imagined it would be anything like as bad as this.

When Woodend opened the door, Thwaites jumped to his feet and gave a clumsy salute. If he had hoped that would serve to propitiate the angry gods, the look in Woodend's eyes quickly assured him that it wouldn't.

'I thought I might just calm down overnight, but when I woke up this mornin' I was as angry as I'd been when I went to bed,' the Chief Inspector said. 'Now why do you think that is?'

'I ... I don't know, sir,' Thwaites said.

'You're either a bloody liar or a bloody fool,' Woodend told him. 'An' I'm beginnin' to suspect you might be both. Am I hurtin' your feelin's, Constable Thwaites?'

'Well, sir—'

'Because this is nothin'! Nothin' at all! I haven't even got in my stride yet!' Woodend glanced down at the chair the constable was standing next to. 'I'd take the weight off my feet if I was you,' he advised. 'Because for the kind of bollockin' you're goin' to get, you'll need to be sittin' down.'

Thwaites sank heavily into the chair. 'What

have I done wrong, sir?' he asked.

'What have you done wrong?' Woodend replied, sitting down opposite him. 'You've been holdin' back information that just could be vital to my investigation into the murder of Harry Dimdyke.'

'I never—'

'You remember that theory of yours – the one that the fairground people might have had a grudge against this village?'

'Yes, sir?'

'Can you think of any reason *why* they might have had a grudge?'

Thwaites shrugged. 'They're funny folk, fairground workers. You never know what's goin' to upset them.'

'Tell me, Constable Thwaites, does the name "Stan Dawkins" mean anythin' to you?'

'It's got a familiar ring to it,' Thwaites said.

'Stan Dawkins was one of the workers on the fairground that visited this crappy little village for the last Witch Burnin'. An' do you know what happened to him?'

'He got killed?'

'He got killed,' Woodend agreed. 'The mornin' after the Witch Burnin', he was discovered on the edge of the village. He'd been beaten to death.'

'I remember now,' Thwaites admitted.

'It took you long enough,' Woodend said. 'Now let me ask you this, Constable – don't you think it's just possible that Stan Dawkins' death could have been connected with Harry Dimdyke's death?'

'How, sir?'

Woodend slammed his fist down on the desk, and the whole room seemed to shake.

'For God's sake, Thwaites, isn't it obvious?' he demanded. 'Harry Dimdyke could have been killed in revenge for what somebody in this village did to Stan Dawkins twenty years ago!'

'But the village had nothin' to do with this feller Dawkins' death,' Thwaites protested. 'It was one of the other carnival workers who killed him. The inspector in charge of the case said so.'

'Accordin' to the research *my* inspector's just done, the officer in charge of the investigation had *no idea* who'd killed Dawkins. Yes, it could have been one of the carnival workers. But I don't think it was. An' can you guess *why* I don't think it was?'

'No, sir.'

'Because *you* don't think it was.'

'Have you started readin' minds now, sir?' Thwaites asked, in a sudden burst of defiance.

'I've *always* read minds,' Woodend told him. 'It's part of my job. An' would you like to know what I've read in that slim, badly printed volume that makes up *your* mind?'

'You'll tell me, won't you, whether I want

to hear it or not,' Constable Thwaites said.

'Bloody right, I will,' Woodend agreed. 'If you'd thought one of the carnival workers had killed Stan Dawkins, you'd have mentioned it right from the start. "They're animals, sir," you would have said. "They killed one of their own the last time the funfair was here. Why wouldn't they have killed one of ours this time?" But you didn't say that – an' the *reason* you didn't is because you don't want the Dawkins investigation reopenin', in case I blunder across some evidence which points me to the killer.'

'So you're sayin' I know who murdered Dawkins, are you?' Thwaites demanded hotly.

'No,' Woodend told him. 'All I am sayin' is that you're pretty sure it was somebody from Hallerton.'

Thwaites' chin quivered slightly. 'I want to talk to a Police Federation lawyer,' he said.

'I wouldn't, if I was you,' Woodend advised him.

'Why? Because you're afraid it'll get you into trouble?'

Woodend smiled disconcertingly. 'Nay, lad. Not me. You! It'll get *you* in trouble.'

'I have the legal right to—'

'We're not talkin' about legal rights here. It's nothin' at all to do with the law. The reason I wouldn't do it if I was in your shoes is because *the village* wouldn't like you

131

bringin' in yet another bugger from outside!'

Thwaites said nothing, but it was clear from the defeated expression which came to his face that the argument had squarely hit its target.

'Somethin' else you forgot to mention was the suicides,' Woodend said. 'Now why was that?'

'They have nothin' to do with the murder.'

'Know that for a fact? Because if you do, you'll also know *why* those two women killed themselves, won't you?'

'Nobody can ever really know what goes on in the mind of somebody who takes their own life,' Thwaites said defensively.

'But you *think* you know, don't you? You think you've at least got an *inkling*?'

'No,' Thwaites said unconvincingly.

Woodend suddenly stood up – so violently that his chair toppled over and crashed to the floor behind him.

'I don't like frightenin' the men who serve under me,' he said. 'I don't like it at all – but I'll do it if I have to. An' *when* I do it, I make a pretty good job of it. You're frightened of me right now, aren't you, Thwaites?'

'I...'

'The problem is, there's somethin' that's frightenin' you even more. But this I promise you, Constable – once I find out what that somethin' *is*, you're finished in the Mid Lancs Police.'

132

The Chief Inspector turned and left the police house office, slamming the door behind him as he went.

For perhaps two minutes after he'd gone, Constable Thwaites sat there doing all he could to bring his trembling under control. Then he stood up on shaky legs and reached for his keys. He didn't want to go out – didn't want to leave the cosy safety of the police house. But there was no choice in the matter, because Tom Dimdyke needed to be told what was going on – and needed to be told *quickly*.

Eighteen

From the outside, the caravan had looked like an attractive prospect for someone – say a female detective sergeant – who suddenly decided to jack her career in and take to the open road. Once inside, Paniatowski quickly changed her view about it as a potential permanent home. She didn't like the metal walls, which clanged every time she inadvertently touched them with her elbows. She didn't like the fact that everything so obviously had to be in the place assigned to it, otherwise there would be no room to move. And she was not entirely happy about sitting on a bed, with only a fold-down table between her and Ben Masters.

Masters was around fifty-five, she guessed. He had the tanned skin of a man used to working outdoors, and the yellowing teeth of a man who had never availed himself of the facilities offered by the National Health Service. Two of his fingers were stained permanently brown by nicotine, and the bloodshot lining in the whites of his eyes bore testament to the fact that he liked a more-than-occasional drink. He wore a battered trilby hat on his head, and had a discoloured kerchief tied in a sloppy knot around his neck. He was not, Paniatowski thought, someone she would be delighted to be set up with on a blind date – though from the way *he* looked at *her* it seemed that he wouldn't have minded at all.

'So why are you here?' Masters asked, giving her what he probably considered to be an engaging smile.

'I told you that when we first met, Mr Masters. I'm Detective Sergeant Paniatowski and—'

'What I mean is, why has your boss sent a young woman like you, instead of coming here himself?'

Because I *am* a young woman, Paniatowski thought. Because Cloggin'-it Charlie thinks that fairground folk – who instinctively distrust the law – are more likely to talk freely to me than they would to him.

But aloud, she said, 'How do you know I've even got a boss?'

'I know you've got a boss because, as far as I can recall, detective sergeant isn't anywhere near the top rank in the rozzers.'

'What I mean is, how do you know I've got a boss *here in Hallerton*? How do you know I'm not in charge of this investigation?'

Masters flashed his teeth again. 'Except when we're doing business with it, we like to keep ourselves apart from the outside world. It's like water and oil, you see – we just don't mix well together. But that's not the same as saying we don't know what's going on out there.'

'I think I'm beginning to see that,' Paniatowski said.

Masters ran his eyes over Paniatowski's charcoal-grey jacket and skirt, but the lust he had made such a show of earlier seemed to be strangely absent from this new examination.

'Nice outfit you've got on,' he said. 'But it's deceptive.'

'Is it?'

'Yes. What you should really be wearing is a figure-hugging costume and sparkling tights.'

'And why's that?'

'Because you're not the star performer. That job's been given to the big bugger in the tweed jacket who came up from Whitebridge with you. You, my dear, are what we in the trade call "the beautiful assistant".'

He was playing a game – or perhaps a *series* of games – Paniatowski suddenly realized. He'd been doing it from the moment they entered the caravan.

First, he'd tried to intimidate her by pretending to fancy her. Now he'd changed gear, and was attempting to make her feel worthless. Well, if push came to shove, she was not a bad games' player herself.

'You must know all about the trade – and the *tricks* of the trade – because you've been with this funfair for a long time, haven't you?' she said.

A hint of caution crept across Masters' face, as if he understood that she was on to him.

'That's right,' he agreed. 'I've been with the fairground a *very* long time. Man and boy. I've been running it myself for the last fifteen years, and my old dad – may he rest in peace – ran it before me.'

'And this *is* the funfair which was here, on this same site, for the last Witch Burning?'

'Might have been,' Masters said reluctantly. 'Difficult to remember something like that, don't you think? We go to a lot of places up and down the country – and twenty years is a long time.'

'Where did the figure of twenty years come from?' Paniatowski asked innocently.

'You said—'

'No, I didn't. I took great care not to.'

Masters smiled again, and a hint of grudging respect was starting to creep into his expression.

'You've got more about you than most of the beautiful assistants have,' he conceded. 'I seem to recall, now I put my mind to it, that we *were* here at the last Witch Burning.'

'And do you also recall that one of your

workers – a man called Stan Dawkins – was killed while you were here?'

'Is *this* where Stan died?' Masters asked. 'I suppose it could have been, now you mention it.'

'Let's stop sniffing round each other's backsides to see what it smells like, shall we?' Paniatowski suggested. 'I know that you can help me if you really want to. And you know that, if I went looking for them, I could easily find enough breaches of the health and safety regulations to close this place down.'

Masters shook his head admiringly. 'You don't pull your punches, do you?' he asked. 'You'd make a first-class barker at one of our sideshows. Let me know if you ever consider changing careers.'

'Tell me about Dawkins,' Paniatowski said.

'What's to tell?'

'I don't know. That's why I'm asking.'

'He was raised in a children's home. In Southampton, I think. We get a lot of orphans working in our business.'

'Why's that?'

'Maybe it's because they want to taste a bit of freedom after years of being cooped up in an institution.'

'Or maybe it's because most of them have very little training, and have to take work where they can get it,' Paniatowski suggested.

Masters chuckled. 'Oh, you're a hard one,

all right.'

'So Stan Dawkins didn't have any family?'

'None that I know of.'

'But he must have had friends.'

'Not that I can remember.'

'That Big Wheel really *doesn't* look very safe to me.'

'It's not even properly up yet!'

'It still doesn't look safe. And I've got my doubts about the bumper cars as well.'

'I'm telling you the truth,' Masters protested. 'Carnival folk are very clannish. Dawkins might have made mates – given time – but he wasn't with us long enough for that. He'd only been working here a few weeks when he was killed. Believe me!'

Paniatowski smiled charmingly. 'I'm not sure I'd believe you if you were on fire and said you were feeling quite hot.' She paused. 'What can you tell me about the night of the murder?'

'Nothing! Really!'

'I find that hard to believe.'

'What do you think happens when the fairground closes down for the night?' Masters asked.

'Everyone has a cup of tea, says their prayers, and then is tucked up in bed by the Bearded Lady?' Paniatowski asked facetiously.

Masters threw back his head, and laughed with what seemed like genuine amusement.

'Not exactly,' he said. 'It's bloody hard work running the attractions, and when they've finished, the lads want to wind down a bit. So what they do is, they go to one of the caravans and crack open a bottle of whisky.'

'And Dawkins did this?'

'Usually.'

'I thought you said he didn't have any friends.'

'You don't have to be bosom buddies to get drunk together. We depend on each other on the fairground. It's us against the world. So even if we're not all exactly friends, we're certainly comrades.'

'I see,' Paniatowski said. 'I take it, from what you've already implied, that Dawkins wasn't in the "drinking" caravan that night?'

'Correct. Nobody saw him from the time the fair closed down for the night till the time my dad, as the boss of the place, was called in by the police to identify the body.'

'The villagers thought someone from the carnival killed him.'

'They would!'

'Well, you can't really blame them, can you? I mean, it does seem the most likely explanation, doesn't it?'

Masters' fists clenched, and his face darkened, 'Of course it does!' he said angrily. 'More than likely! Almost a dead cert, in point of fact. You can't trust any of these carnival people, can you? They're all thugs and robbers. It's well known. Well, let me tell you something, Detective Sergeant Paniatowski, we've got our share of villains working on the fairground – but it's no bigger a share than you'll find on the outside.'

Paniatowski chuckled. 'I got right up your nose, didn't I?' she asked. 'I never thought I'd be able to, but I did.'

Masters hesitated for a moment, then joined in her amusement. 'You're all right, Sergeant,' he said. 'And like I told you – any time you want a job on the fairground, just come and see me.'

'So what do you think *did* happen?' Paniatowski asked, growing more serious.

'I honestly don't know.' Masters admitted. He fell silent for a moment, as if considering all his options. 'But I suppose I could make a good guess, if you wanted me to.'

'Feel free.'

'Where are you from, Sergeant?'

'Whitebridge.'

'Big town. Lots going on. But imagine if you'd spent your girlhood in a place like this. Doesn't bear thinking about, does it? It's so boring that even pulling your own head off could pass for entertainment. And the only lads these girls get to know are yokels who suck on straws and smell of cow shit. Then the girls come to the fair. That, on its own, is more fun than they normally get from one

141

year's end to the next. But as a bonus, there's the lads who work on the attractions. They may not hold much glamour for a city girl like you, but to these lasses they're as exotic as the Sheikh of Araby.'

'You're saying that the local girls make a play for your lads?'

'It happens all the time. And our lads are only human. They know they'll be gone the next day or the day after, so what harm is there in grabbing a bit of pleasure while they can? You see where I'm going with this?'

'Yes, I think I do,' Paniatowski admitted. 'But I'd still like you to spell it out for me.'

'It's my guess that Dawkins hit it off with one of the local girls when she was at the fair, and arranged to meet her later. That's why he didn't join the rest of the lads in the drinking caravan. Anyway, he goes to the village, and after he's got what he went for – or even *before* he gets it – he runs into some of the local hayseeds. They know why he's there – and they don't like it. So they decide that they're going to teach him a lesson he'll never forget. Only they go too far, and they kill him. It's as simple as that.'

'Did you mention this theory of yours to the police at the time?'

'What! And draw attention to myself? No chance!'

'So you didn't really care. You just sat back and let the killers get away with it.'

142

'If anybody let them get away with it, it was the local rozzers.'

'What makes you come to that conclusion?'

'The rozzers could have worked out what had happened, just like I did. And they'd have known where to look and who to talk to – if that was what they really wanted. But they didn't do any of that. After all, why should they upset people they'd known all their lives, just because some toe-rag of a carnival worker had got himself murdered? The way they probably saw it, by being in the village at all he was asking for what he got.'

Paniatowski lit up a cigarette, inhaled, and studied the fairground manager for a few moments.

'What a jaundiced view on life you really do seem to have, Mr Masters,' she said, blowing smoke out of her nose.

'What a jaundiced world I have to live in, Detective Sergeant Paniatowski,' the funfair manager replied.

Nineteen

The general store in Hallerton was located further down the main street than the pub. Thus, while the Black Bull had a view – of sorts – over the Green, all that could be seen from the store was a seemingly endless row of grim stone cottages.

The store was no more than a stone cottage itself, Woodend noted. And a badly neglected one, at that. The paintwork around the door and window frame was cracked and blistered. The window itself was streaked with dirt. And though the man who ran it was a widower, the sign over the door announced that it was owned by Alfred and Doris Raby.

The Chief Inspector stepped closer to the window, and peered inside. There wasn't much to see. Central to what could only *charitably* have been called a window display was a jumbo-sized cardboard model of a brand of cigarettes which Woodend was sure the manufacturers had stopped producing shortly after the war. This sad, fading and dusty relic was flanked by an advertisement for a chocolate bar that virtually no one ate any more, and a haphazardly arranged set of mugs celebrating the coronation of the Queen, eleven years earlier.

It was true that the whole village had stood still in time, Woodend thought, but most of it did not seem to have actually *decayed*, as this place so obviously had.

He lit up a cigarette, knowing as he did so that he was only stalling – putting off the moment when he would force himself to do something which was probably going to be as unpleasant as it was necessary.

An old man – heavily muffled despite the warmth of the day, and leaning heavily on a stick – came out of one the houses opposite. At first he was too busy watching where he put his feet to notice anything else, and it was only when he was sure he was firmly anchored to the pavement that he looked up and saw Woodend standing there on the other side of the street.

The effect of his discovery was instantaneous. He twisted arthritically around and, using his stick, hammered on the door he had just come out of. A woman – who looked young enough to be his daughter, and probably was just that – opened the door. The old man spoke urgently to her, they both looked across at Woodend, then the woman helped the man back into the house.

So you've started scarin' granddads now, have you? Woodend asked himself. Well, that's *certainly* somethin' to be proud of!

He flung his cigarette to the ground, stubbed it out with the toe of his shoe, and opened the shop door. A brass bell just inside it whimpered a cry of metallic desperation to announce his arrival.

The man standing behind the counter fitted in perfectly with his surroundings. He was wearing a knitted cardigan. It hung loosely on him, and had gone at the elbows, so his shirt sleeves stuck out through the holes. His jaw was slack; his eyes were watery. He was probably not that old in actual years, Woodend thought – he was possibly still even in his early forties – but his face held the expression of a man who had long since wearied of life.

'Mr Raby?' Woodend asked.

'That's me,' the other man replied, in a voice which was little more than a whisper.

'My name's Woodend. Chief Inspector Woodend. I'm here to investigate the death of Harry Dimdyke.'

'Yes?' Raby replied dully, as if the subject could hold no possible interest for him.

'And I was wondering if I could ask you a few questions.'

'I know nothing about Harry Dimdyke's murder. How could I? I hardly ever leave the shop.'

'It wasn't actually his murder I wanted to ask you about,' Woodend said awkwardly.

'Then what is it you want?'

'I ... er ... I know it's probably still very painful for you, but I was wonderin' if you'd be willing to answer a few questions about your wife's suicide.'

'You want to ask me about my wife's suicide?' Raby repeated.

Under the circumstances Raby would have had a perfect right to be angry, Woodend told himself. But that wasn't what the man was! The tone in his voice was not one of rage, but of incredulity. It was almost as if he'd passed beyond anger – had reached a point at which such heavy and expressive emotions were well outside his emotional range.

'I'd really appreciate it if you could spare me a few minutes, sir,' Woodend said.

'But what would be the point?'

What indeed? Woodend wondered.

Looked at coldly, he could argue no clear link between the unusual number of suicides in the village and the murder of Harry Dimdyke. On the other hand, he reminded himself, he could name half a dozen cases he'd worked on in which a series of abnormal – but apparently unconnected – occurrences had turned out to have a common thread running through them.

'It wouldn't take long,' he coaxed. 'And I

promise you that we'd stop immediately you found it was becomin' too much of a strain.'

'There's the shop to look after, you see,' Raby said, looking helplessly around him. 'I was expectin' somebody to come in an' take over from me, but they haven't.'

He was speaking now with the voice of a man who is never disappointed because he never has expectations, Woodend thought – the voice of a man who accepted misery as his lot with an almost gloomy satisfaction.

The door open, the bell emitted its mournful peal, and a small, round woman entered the shop.

'Sorry I'm late, Alf,' she began, 'but what with the bobbies swarmin' all over the place and—'

Then she saw Woodend, and bit back the rest of her words.

'Are you Mr Raby's assistant?' the Chief Inspector asked.

The woman seemed to take it as a personal slight. 'No, I'm not his *assistant*,' she said.

'Then...?'

'I just help out. A lot of us do. That's what it's like in this village, not that you'd know anythin' about that. And what are *you* doin' here?'

'He wants me to talk about—' Raby began.

'Shall I go an' get Tom Dimdyke?' the woman interrupted him. 'Is that what you'd like me to do, Alf?'

Panic crossed Raby's face. 'No, I—'

'Because it won't take me a minute to go up to the barn, you know, if you think it's for the best.'

Raby waved his hand weakly in protest. 'I wouldn't want ... You can't go and...' He took a deep breath. 'Would you mind lookin' after the shop for a few minutes, Emily?'

'Of course I'll look after the shop,' the round woman said. 'That's what I'm here for.'

'An' if *you* wouldn't mind comin' into the back...' Alf Raby said to Woodend.

He doesn't want to talk to me, Woodend thought – it's just that he'd rather do that than have a visit from Tom Dimdyke.

The Chief Inspector followed the shopkeeper through a door into the back parlour. It was a joyless room – a shrine to the 1950s, but a shrine which had been very much neglected.

Raby sank into a heavy, overstuffed armchair, and indicated to Woodend that he should take the one opposite.

'Emily's been very good to me,' the shopkeeper said. 'She looks after me. They all do. I don't know how I'd manage if they didn't.'

'Could we talk about your wife?' Woodend asked gently.

'The one thing I'm grateful for is that Doris didn't hang herself, like Beth Thompson did,' Raby said. 'Her goin' at all was bad enough, but if I'd found her hangin' in the lavvy, like Jed found Beth—'

'How *did* your wife kill herself?'

'She took sleeping pills. They said at the hospital that she must have swallowed at least a hundred of them.'

'Where did she manage to lay her hands on so many? Did they ever find out?'

'She'd been saving them up. The doctor gave her a few every week, an' she hid them until she had enough.'

So she didn't do it on impulse, Woodend thought. She must have been very unhappy – and very desperate – for quite a while.

'She wasn't ill, was she?' he asked. 'She didn't have some sort of terminal disease?'

'No, she'd never had a day's sickness in her life. She was as strong as a horse, physically. But she didn't have the *mental* strength of the other women.'

'What other women?' Woodend asked, mystified. 'The other women who killed themselves?'

Raby looked puzzled by the question. 'No,' he said. 'The ones who didn't.'

'Sorry?'

'She couldn't take it any more, you see.'

'Couldn't take what?'

'The pressure. The strain of it all. She just couldn't convince herself that she was doin' the right thing. I tried to tell her it was the same for everybody in the village – that we

150

all did what we had to do – but ... but ... she just wouldn't see it.'

The man's mental balance was on a knife-edge, Woodend thought. He had to be handled with extreme care, or he would go to pieces before his very eyes.

'This pressure?' he said softly. 'This strain that the other women could handle, but your wife couldn't? Would you like to tell me what it was?'

The bell in the shop rang again. Woodend cursed the interruption, but decided that it was probably just a customer. Well, fat Emily was there, and she could handle whoever it was.

'If you could give me some idea of what this pressure was,' Woodend cajoled. 'Just a hint will do.'

'It's always been the same,' Alf Raby said. 'Ever since we burned Meg Ramsden. I should have known Doris wasn't strong enough. But even if I had, what could *I* have done about it?'

The parlour door crashed opened, and a furious Tom Dimdyke stormed into the room.

'What the bloody hell's goin' on here?' he demanded of Woodend. 'You're supposed to be investigatin' my brother's death, you bastard, not persecutin' a poor widower.'

Woodend rose from his chair. Previously, he'd only seem Dimdyke bent over the

Witch. Now they were facing each other, he could fully appreciate what a big hard bugger Dimdyke actually was.

'I *am* investigatin' your brother's death,' he said. 'Not that I'm gettin' much cooperation from his immediate family. But leavin' that aside for a moment, Mr Dimdyke, what business of yours is my conversation with Mr Raby?'

'I didn't tell him anythin', Tom,' Raby bleated pathetically. 'He asked me, but I didn't say anythin'.'

'You'd better leave while you still can,' Dimdyke told Woodend.

The Chief Inspector shifted his weight slightly. 'That's the second time in two days you've threatened me, Mr Dimdyke,' he growled. 'It didn't work the first time, and it's not working now. You may be an important man to this village, but don't let that fool you into thinkin' you can have your own way with me.'

Though they'd never been intended to, Woodend's words seemed to have a calming effect on Dimdyke. His face relaxed a little, and a look that was a mixture of pity and amusement came to his eyes.

'Me! An important man!' he said. 'I count for nowt! None of us do. Don't you realize that, Mr Chief Inspector? There's only one feller in this village who matters – an' that's the Witch Maker.'

'Who, now that your brother's dead, happens to be your son,' Woodend pointed out.

'Wilf *may have been* my lad before, but he isn't now,' Dimdyke said. 'The Witch Maker isn't *anybody's* son.'

'Then what is he?'

'He's the one who has been chosen to carry the heaviest burden.'

'And who chose him?'

'Do you want a name?' Dimdyke asked, incredulously. 'Do you actually want me to say it was me – or Alf here – who made the decision?'

'Yes, that's what I'd like,' Woodend agreed.

'Well, it's not that simple. It doesn't work that way at all. He wasn't chosen by a *person* – he was chosen by what happened all those years ago.'

'You're not makin' any sense.'

'Maybe I'm not – to you.' Dimdyke's expression softened. 'Look, I'm sorry if I came on all heavy-handed. I'm sorry if I seemed to threaten you. It's been a terrible couple of days for all of us, an' I probably said things I never intended to say. But there's no point in makin' matters any worse, now is there? Alf's upset. Don't you think it might be best if you just left him alone?'

'Yes, I think it might,' Woodend agreed.

But probably not for the same reasons Tom Dimdyke thought it best. Woodend would agree to leave Alf Raby alone because there would be no point in doing anything else – because even applying thumbscrews wouldn't make the shell of a shopkeeper say any more now.

Twenty

Mary Dimdyke sat on the orange crate – her elbows resting on her knees, and her chin resting on her hands – while Wilf worked slowly and patiently on the modifications to the left foot of the effigy of Meg Ramsden.

She seemed to have spent half her lifetime watching her brother at work, Mary thought. And, in a way, she had.

Wilf had become the Assistant Witch Maker when he was ten and she'd been eight. He'd been so excited about it, she remembered. And because she'd adored her big brother, she'd been excited too. So she'd taken her place on the orange crate – her little legs so short back then that they hadn't even reached the packed-earth floor – and watched as Wilf had been initiated into the skills which had been passed down from generation to generation.

Through her young eyes, she had witnessed the change that had gradually come over Wilf. The excitement had faded – worn away by the endless sanding and polishing –

155

and had been replaced by gravity and earnestness.

Wilf never joked with her any more. He never enjoyed the things they used to enjoy together. The Witch Maker's Assistant, it seemed, had far too many responsibilities to be allowed to behave like a normal growing boy. And because of that, his sister had lost something too.

The door swung open, and their father entered the barn. He was red in the face, Mary noticed, and looked both troubled and angry. She wondered what had happened in the time between Constable Thwaites' urgent visit to the barn and that moment.

Tom gave his son a nod which came close to being a bow. Then he turned to his daughter.

'It's been all arranged,' he said.

'D ... Dad...'

'It's all been arranged, our Mary, an' there's no point at all in arguin' about it.'

Mary glanced at her brother, but he was still working away as if he'd heard nothing.

He'd tried his best to defend her the previous day, she thought, but then the mantle of his new post had only just been placed on his shoulders, and he had not yet fully understood how heavy a burden it was. Now he did, and with that knowledge he had ceased to be her protector.

He didn't belong to her any more. That

was long and short of it. He belonged to the village.

'You're to be there at eight o'clock,' her father told her, and when she said nothing, he added sharply, 'Did you hear me?'

'Y ... yes, Dad.'

'Well, don't be late.'

'Who'll be d ... doin' it?' she asked, feeling her lower lip start to tremble.

'Lou Moore,' Tom Dimdyke said.

It could be worse, she tried to reassure herself. Lou Moore was a nice man – a kind man. He would do his best to make the whole thing as painless as possible. It might be just about bearable, if only...

'There d ... doesn't have to be anyone else there watchin', d ... does there, Dad?' she pleaded.

'You know there does.'

'But you'll g ... get what you want. You'll *all* g ... get what you want. Why d ... does it have to...'

'The sacrifice must be witnessed, just as it has always been.'

Mary turned towards her brother. Once, long ago, he had fought the biggest boy in school, merely because that bully had pulled his little sister's hair. Surely the obvious distress in her voice would awaken some of that old feeling now, even if he *was* the Witch Maker.

It had to! It just *had* to!

Wilf, as though he had heard nothing of the exchange – nothing of his sister's pleading and his father's determination – went calmly on with his work.

Hettie Todd and her mother sat on the steps of their caravan, shelling fresh green peas into an enamel pan full of cold water. They could have gone inside to do the work – the seats were more comfortable in the caravan, and the weather was not yet hot enough to make it particularly stuffy. But it was not the way of fairground folk to be enclosed within walls when there was no need to be.

'I saw you talkin' to your mate Pat Calhoun yesterday, Mam,' Hettie said conversationally.

'Did you, pet?' her mother asked, with seeming indifference.

That was not what she should have said *at all*, Hettie thought. It simply wasn't like Zelda to miss the chance to bring Pat into their conversation.

'I wondered if it was me you were talking about,' she said.

'Well, of course it was you we were talking about,' her mother said. 'We're always talking about you. What else *would* we be talking about?'

She was lying, Hettie thought. 'The thing is, you weren't looking at me – you were looking towards the village,' she persisted.

'And is there any law that says that when we're talking *about* you, we have to be looking *at* you?'

This approach was getting her nowhere, Hettie decided. It was time to try another tack. 'You like Pat, don't you?' she said.

'He'd make you a good man,' her mother replied, evasively.

'That's not what I meant, Mum. I meant that you *respect* him – that you *trust* him.'

'I should hope that I would trust and respect any man I'd want to see my daughter paired off with.'

'And if you had a problem, would you go to him with it?'

'*If* I had a problem – though I can't think of any problem I might have – then I probably would go to Pat. What makes you ask?'

'You looked like you had a problem yesterday afternoon.'

'You're imaginin' things, child.'

Hettie nodded, convinced she was now on the right lines – because her mother only ever called her 'child' when she was starting to feel defensive.

'Do you know anythin' about the man who was killed in the village yesterday mornin', Mum?' she asked.

Zelda shrugged. 'How could I? As you know well enough yourself, we only got here the night before.'

'But it's not the first time you've been here,

159

is it?'

'Possibly not.'

'Does that mean that you think you *have* been here before, or that you think you *haven't*?'

'If you're so interested, you'd better ask Mr Masters,' her mother said. 'He's the boss. He's the one who keeps a record of where we go and where we don't.'

'Did anything unusual happen the last time you were in Hallerton?' Hettie asked, taking her mother's refusal to neither deny or confirm as a confirmation in itself.

'Like what?' Zelda asked.

Hettie frowned. 'I don't know,' she admitted.

'Well, then—'

'But I think that *you* do.'

Zelda Todd placed the bowl she'd been holding on her knee down on the step. Then she stood up.

'You can finish the peas on your own, can't you?' she asked.

'I could if you wanted me to, but I don't see why—'

'Good. Because I've got other business to deal with.'

'What kind of business?' Hettie asked.

But she was talking to her mother's already retreating back.

Twenty-One

Standing in the centre of the field where the funfair was sited, Woodend looked around with frank admiration at what had been achieved. The previous morning it had all seemed so haphazard that it could have been dropped where it stood by some unfriendly and disorganized giant. Now, less than thirty hours later, a definite order had been imposed. The caravans had been parked neatly in one corner of the field, the trucks which had pulled the heavy trailers in another. And in the middle of the field, the very heart of the funfair was very nearly completed.

With a nostalgia for his lost childhood, Woodend let his eyes rove over the attractions.

There was the Caterpillar – that grown-up version of a kids' merry-go-round – which first shrouded its passengers under a dark-green canvas and then took them on an un-dulating, sick-inducing journey into mock-terror, before finally depositing them safely right back where they had started from.

There were the bumper cars, which served no other function than to allow lads like the young Charlie Woodend to demonstrate how much they fancied young girls by crashing into them – and gave the girls, in return, the opportunity to either giggle seductively or to break hearts with their looks of disdain.

There were the stalls, offering fabulous prizes to anyone who could actually make a blunt dart stick in a specially hardened board or defy the laws of physics by getting one of the hoops to land where it needed to.

And there were the sideshow tents, which promised a myriad of delights: wrestlers who staged fights in which the clean-living lad always beat the masked bone-crusher; strippers, well past their prime, who shed far less of their clothing than the garish pictures outside might have suggested; freaks who owed their grotesque appearance more to bits of wire and plaster of Paris than they did to nature.

Once the customers poured in, it became a fantasy land, Woodend thought. But before then, it was something else entirely. Though it might not look like Hallerton or any of the other places it visited, it was still every bit as much of a village as they were.

The 'village' headman, Ben Masters, was sitting on his caravan steps, picking his yellowed teeth with a matchstick. He seemed totally unaware of either the Chief Inspector's arrival on the scene or any of the construction work that was going on around him.

Which was, of course, total bollocks, Woodend told himself.

Villages like this one were not created by chance. There was a driving force behind all the hard graft which was taking place. There was a keen intelligence watching for any intruders who might threaten the community. And both that driving force and that intelligence were concentrated in the body of the man sitting on the steps.

It was only when Woodend was almost close enough to touch him that the fairground manager looked up and said, 'Where's the Beautiful Assistant this afternoon?'

She was talking to the widower of the second of the most recent suicide victims, Woodend thought, but he was damned if he was going to tell Masters that. So instead, he just shrugged and said, 'If I know women, she's probably off somewhere repairin' her make-up.'

Masters laughed disbelievingly. 'Sergeant Paniatowski doesn't seem to me like the kind of woman who'd waste a lot of time paintin' herself, even if she needed to – which she doesn't.'

'Fancy her, do you?' Woodend asked.

'I'd have to be either a fool or a blind man

not to,' Masters replied easily. 'But I like to keep my admiration at a distance.'

'An' why's that?'

'I'm older than I look,' Masters said. 'At least, I am inside here,' he continued, tapping his head. 'There's a lot of effort goes into bringing pleasure to folk. It ages you. I haven't felt the need of a woman for years.'

'But when you did, where did you go to find one?'

Masters chuckled. 'Not only has Sergeant Paniatowski told you what passed between us this morning, but you actually bothered to listen to her.'

'Aye,' Woodend agreed. 'Unlike some chief inspectors I could mention, I happen to think that *my* sergeant might have somethin' useful to say now an' again. So where *did* you find your soldier's comfort when you still felt up to it? In the arms of the lasses who were workin' on the fairground? Or from the girls who lived in the towns an' villages you visited?'

'Maybe a bit of both,' Masters said cautiously.

'An' what about Stan Dawkins? Where did he choose to sow his wild oats?'

'I was wondering when we'd get around to that.'

'I'm sure you were,' Woodend agreed. 'An' what's the answer?'

'He was seeing a girl who worked on the

fair,' Masters admitted, 'but that's not to say he couldn't also have gone into Hallerton on the night he was killed, looking for a bit of fresh.'

'This girl on the fair he was seein'? Is she still around?'

'Now that'd be unlikely, wouldn't it?'

'That's no answer, an' you know it as well as I do.'

'I feel responsible for all the people who work for me,' Masters told the Chief Inspector. 'It'd probably be stretching things a bit to say I'm like a father to them, but I sometimes see myself as a bit of a kindly uncle.'

'But a kindly uncle who couldn't stop Stan Dawkins gettin' killed,' Woodend pointed out.

Masters looked at him thoughtfully. 'You're not above putting the boot in, are you?'

'Only when it's necessary,' Woodend said. 'Speakin' of which, I expect my sergeant's threatened you with findin' all kinds of safety violations on the fairground if you don't cooperate with us.'

'But just in case she forgot to, you'd like to make the same threats now?'

'That's right. But there is a difference.'

'What kind of difference?'

'She'd have to get clearance to carry out *her* threats, an' *I* don't. I could have you closed down in ten minutes.' Woodend paused. 'What did you say that girl Stan

Dawkins was seein' was called?'

'I didn't.'

'But you will, won't you?'

'Don't have much choice, do I? Her name's Zelda Todd.'

'An' is she still with you?'

'What do you think?'

'I think that if she'd been long gone, it wouldn't have been half so difficult to prise her name out of you.'

'You've got your answer, then, haven't you?'

Woodend took out his packet of cigarettes, offered one to Masters, took one for himself, and lit them both up. 'I'm goin' to want to talk to her, you know,' he said.

'I suppose you are,' Masters said fatalistically. 'Thing is, she's not here at the moment.'

'No? Then where is she?'

'Gone into Preston, with one of our drivers. It's where we have to shop, you see – because the buggers in this village won't sell us *anything*.'

'Aye, I've seen that for myself,' Woodend agreed. His eyes narrowed suspiciously. 'She's not done a runner, has she?'

Masters laughed. 'If you knew Zelda like I do, it'd never occur to you to even ask that question. Zelda's not one to run. Never has been.'

'So how long do you think she'll be?'

Masters shrugged. 'Not long.'

'There's other things I can occupy myself with for an hour or so,' Woodend said. 'But then I'll be back, an' if Zelda's not here by then I might just take it into my head to wander around the fairground lookin' for some of them safety violations we talked about.'

'You're a hard man, Chief Inspector,' Masters said.

Woodend grinned. 'I get the distinct impression you're not so soft yourself, Mr Masters,' he countered.

'You'll be wantin' a cup of tea,' Jed Thompson said, as he showed Monika Paniatowski into his front parlour.

Paniatowski weighed up her options.

She probably had no more than half an hour before word of what she was doing got back to Tom Dimdyke – and once that had happened, he'd come storming in on her and Thompson as he had stormed in on Woodend and Raby. That definitely argued for refusal.

On the other hand, she'd often found that drinking tea with the person she was questioning helped to create an intimacy between them – an intimacy which often led to that person saying more than he or she had ever intended to say.

On balance then, the tea won out.

167

'I'd love a cup,' she said.

Thompson disappeared into the kitchen. For the next five minutes Paniatowski was assailed by the sound of china banging and water running, but there was still no sign of the promised tea.

She glanced down at her watch. The half an hour she'd allowed herself was rapidly ticking by. She couldn't wait much longer for Thompson to complete his simple task.

She rose from her seat and went to the kitchen. The place looked like a disaster area. Loose tea was spread all over the counter, and was starting to mingle with a pool of spilled milk. A saucer and cup lay smashed on the floor. The kettle was whistling furiously as it boiled itself dry. And standing in the middle of all this chaos was Jed Thompson, with clearly no idea of what to do next.

'Why don't you go and sit down in the parlour, Mr Thompson?' Paniatowski suggested.

The man waved his hands helplessly in the air. 'But what about the tea?' he asked. 'Who'll make the tea?'

'I'll make it. It's more woman's work anyway,' Paniatowski told him, hating herself even as she uttered the words.

Thompson returned to his parlour, Paniatowski cleaned up the mess in the kitchen, and within a couple of minutes they were sitting facing each other, cups and saucers resting on their knees.

The records said Thompson was in his mid-forties, Paniatowski reminded herself, but if she hadn't known that, she could have taken him for twenty – or perhaps even thirty – years older. During the war, as she and her mother had wandered about a devastated Europe, she'd seen plenty of men burned out before their time – but she didn't think she'd ever seen a worse case than this one.

'You're the local postman, aren't you?' she asked, wondering how he ever found the strength to lift his leather post bag, or the concentration to sort through his letters.

Thompson nodded weakly. 'Yes, I'm the postman.'

'I don't envy you your job,' Paniatowski said breezily. 'Getting up so early in the morning! Covering the whole of the village in all kinds of weather. I tell you, I don't think I could do it.'

'Neither could I, if people didn't help out.'

'That *is* kind of them,' Paniatowski said, continuing her impersonation of a little ray of sunshine while recalling that it was illegal for anyone but an authorized postman to handle the mail. 'A couple of your mates, are they?'

'Are who?'

'The people who help you out. Are they a couple of your mates?'

169

'No.'

'They're *not* your mates?'

'It's all kinds of different people who help. They just come here for the sack. I don't know who's doin' the job from one day to the next.'

Paniatowski nodded understandingly. 'I know this is painful for you, but would it be possible to talk about your wife?'

'She hanged herself, did my Beth,' the postman said mournfully. 'In the lavvy. I found her myself. It was so hard, so very, very hard. I really did love her, you know.'

'I'm sure you did,' Paniatowski agreed. 'Did you ever wonder why she did it?'

'I *know* why she did it,' Thompson said, with a fierceness and sudden strength which took the sergeant completely by surprise. 'She did it because she didn't believe. But I believe. I *have* to believe. It's the only thing that stops me from goin' completely mad.'

'Believe in what? In God?'

'God!' Thompson repeated contemptuously. 'God – if there is one – is on the side of *them*!'

'Them?'

'The squires who ride round on their fine horses an' watch us breakin' our backs labourin' in the fields. The priests who collect their tithe whether we can afford to give it to them or not. Aye, an' them judges in Lancaster, who don't know what it's like

170

to live Hallerton, but who slip the black caps on their heads anyway, an' tell two poor souls that they'll be hanged by the neck until they're dead.'

'I'm sorry?' Paniatowski said, completely taken aback.

'You think I'm rantin', don't you?' Thompson demanded.

'No, I—'

'You think them squires an' priests an' judges are all a thing of the past. But they're not. They may wear different clothes these days. They may talk different. *But they're still out to get us.*'

'Out to—?'

'You asked me what I believe in. Well, I'll tell you, Miss. I believe in the village.'

'But what exactly does that mean?'

'It means the village is my world. I'd die for it if I had to. We'd all – each an' every one of us – die for it if we had to.'

'But what about the *wider* world?'

'*What* about it?'

'You can't just ignore it,' Paniatowski said. 'You can't just pretend it isn't there.'

'Why not?' Thompson asked her. 'It's what we've doin' for the last three hundred an' fifty years.'

Twenty-Two

Wilf Dimdyke looked down at his Witch, and frowned. There was something missing, he told himself. He had got her right *physically* at last, but the *essence* of Meg Ramsden was still not quite there – and without that essence he had produced no more than an artfully constructed dummy.

His Uncle Harry would never have noticed the difference, he thought, but the Witch Maker before him – Great-Uncle George – would have seen it right away. He found himself wishing his great-uncle was still around to advise him, but George, like so many Witch Makers of the past, had completed his life's work and then simply faded away to an early grave.

When the barn door swung open, Wilf expected either his father or his sister to walk in. But it was neither of them. Rather, it was the big bugger from Whitebridge.

Woodend looked across at the young man, standing over the Witch with his chisel in his hand, and the expression of great concentration – and obvious artistic distress – on his face. He had expected to find Tom Dimdyke standing guard over the new Witch Maker, but luck was on his side for once, and the other man was absent.

'Dad isn't here,' Wilf said curtly.

'An' why would you assume it's him I want to talk to?' Woodend asked mildly.

'Well, because...'

'Because he *is* your dad? Because he's the head of the family?'

'I suppose so,' Wilf said.

'But you're the head of the whole *village*, aren't you?' Woodend asked. 'The monarch of all you survey?'

'I wouldn't put it quite like that,' Wilf said, sounding confused.

'Wouldn't you?' Woodend responded interestedly. 'Why not?'

It was strange to be talking to this outsider, Wilf thought. Part of the strangeness, he supposed, came from the fact that he didn't normally talk to any outsiders at all. But there was more to it than that. Woodend was the enemy – at least, that was how his dad saw the man – yet he seemed very kindly for an enemy. There had been no challenge in his questions, merely a curiosity. It was almost as if he really *did* want to understand what was going on in the village.

'Cat got your tongue?' Woodend asked amiably.

'No, I...'

173

'So what's the problem, lad?'

'I was just thinkin' about what you said. I'm not like a king at all. A king can do what he wants. There are so many things I *can't* do.'

Woodend chuckled. 'You shouldn't believe everythin' you read about the royal family in the papers, you know.' He paused. 'Although, of course, you probably don't read the papers anyway, do you?'

'No. None of us do.'

There was no need to ask who 'us' was, Woodend thought. Wilf was talking about the whole village.

'When people talk about the monarch havin' freedom, they're missin' the point,' the Chief Inspector continued. 'Can you imagine the Queen goin' down to the Black Bull on Saturday night for a few pints an' a bit of a knees-up?'

Wilf grinned. 'Not really.'

'If truth be told, she probably doesn't even want to. But if she *did*, she still couldn't. There's hundreds of things she's constrained from doin'. But she *is* still the Queen, an' – in certain matters – if she says jump, then everybody round her leaps into the air. An' I imagine it's pretty much the same for you.'

'Maybe,' Wilf said dubiously.

'When did they first tell you that you were goin' to be Witch Maker?' Woodend asked.

'I've ... I've always known,' Wilf said, with

174

a wonder in his voice which came from the realization that he'd never really thought about the matter before.

'*Always?*' Woodend asked.

Wilf frowned. 'I can remember my mum's funeral,' he said, almost as if he were slipping into a trance. 'I wasn't more than three or four at the time. We were standing by the grave – me an' my dad. Mary wasn't there. She was too young.'

'I understand.'

'I ... I wanted to cry, but just before I did, Dad squeezed my hand very hard. I don't think he meant it to hurt, but he sometimes doesn't know his own strength.'

'Aye, he's a powerful feller, all right,' Woodend agreed.

'Then he bent down an' whispered somethin' in my ear.'

'What did he say?'

'He said, "You can't cry now, son. Not while you're on show. Save it till later. Once we're back in our home, we'll *both* have a bloody good bawl." An' we did. We were up half the night, sobbin' away.'

'I'm sure you were,' Woodend said. 'I was a grown-up when my own mam died, but it still hit me harder than I'd ever imagined it would.'

'That's not the point,' Wilf said impatiently.

'Then what is?'

'I knew what he meant when he said I couldn't cry. I knew *why* I couldn't cry. Do *you* know?'

Woodend nodded gravely. 'Because even then you understood that you were goin' to be the Witch Maker – that one day you'd wear the crown.'

'I'm not a king!' Wilf said angrily. 'I'm *not*. I'm just the lad who knows how to make the Witch.'

'You don't really believe that, do you, lad?' Woodend asked. 'That you're no more than the lad who knows how to make the Witch?'

'Why shouldn't I believe it?'

'Because if all you were doin' was makin' a dummy, it wouldn't take so much out of you. Buildin' the Witch isn't just a mechanical experience, is it? There's somethin' *religious* about the whole process.'

'We don't believe in religion in Hallerton,' Wilf said.

'I know that,' Woodend said. 'So maybe "religious" isn't the right word. Would you be happier if I called it a *spiritual* experience?'

The bobby was getting too close to the truth, Wilf thought – too close to what he thought himself.

'My thoughts are my own business,' he said.

'Aye, so they are,' Woodend agreed. 'But would you mind if I asked your *opinion* about somethin' that's been puzzlin' me?'

'You can *ask*,' Wilf said, not yet ready to give an inch.

'I was thinkin' about the Witch Maker an' how he's selected,' Woodend said. 'I never knew your Uncle Harry, but I've seen enough of your dad to be able to form an impression of him, an' it seems to me that—'

'Don't go attackin' my dad!' Wilf said with new fierceness. 'Don't you *ever* dare do that. He's the best man who ever walked this earth.'

'I wasn't goin' to attack him,' Woodend responded. 'Like I said, I was just thinkin'.'

'Thinkin' about what?'

'That he really cares about this village, an' what it stands for.'

'He does.'

'An' that he'd have made a perfect Witch Maker.'

'He would. He'd have put his heart an' soul into it.'

Woodend pulled out his packet of cigarettes and offered it to Wilf, and when the young man shook his head, he lit up one for himself.

'So what I don't understand,' the Chief Inspector continued, after he'd inhaled deeply, 'is why it wasn't your dad who was chosen. What's the answer?'

'I don't know,' Wilf admitted.

'But surely you must have asked yourself the question?'

Wilf shook his head. 'In this village you don't ask questions – you accept things as they are.'

'I wonder how your dad felt about it,' Woodend pondered. 'Do you think he resented not bein' Witch Maker?'

Wilf laughed hollowly. 'Why should he have? It's not much of a prize.'

'Not to you, maybe, but, as you've already pointed out, he'd have put his heart an' soul into it.'

Wilf's fingers tightened around the chisel in his right hand. 'What are you suggestin'?' he demanded, furious. 'Are you sayin' my dad killed Uncle Harry because he was jealous of him?"

'No,' Woodend said. 'But I rather think you are.'

'My dad's the gentlest man alive!' Wilf screamed. 'An' if he was goin' to kill Uncle Harry because of jealousy, wouldn't he have done it years ago? When they were both still kids? When there was still a chance of him becomin' the Witch Maker himself?'

'There was *never* any chance of him becomin' the Witch Maker,' Woodend said.

Both the words themselves and the certainty with which he had expressed them came as a surprise to him – such a surprise that he felt a shiver run down his back.

'*There was never any chance of him becomin'
the Witch Maker,*' he'd said.

But he hadn't always thought that way. Indeed, at the start of the investigation he had automatically assumed that Tom *would* replace his brother. So what had brought about this change in his way of thinking? What had made him so convinced that Tom had never had a chance?

The impression had to have come from the man himself, he decided. Not so much from what he had said, as from how he had acted. There was an aura about Tom Dimdyke which suggested that he knew that the one thing he desperately wanted – desperately *craved* for – had been denied him from the very start. He was not to be Witch Maker, and he had understood that from much the same age as his son had understood that he *would* be.

Twenty-Three

If Woodend had had to choose one word to describe Zelda Todd's caravan, that word would have been 'cosy'. But it was not cosy like some of the gypsy caravans he'd seen – all exotic hangings and bright wood carvings. No, this was cosy in a front-parlour-in-Whitebridge way, with its Boots' prints hanging on the metal walls, and its shelves of knick-knacks which would surely have to be carefully stored in cotton wool every time the fair moved on.

Zelda herself was in her late thirties. Her hair was set in a sensible salon perm, and she was wearing a cardigan and skirt which could have been bought from any of the high-street chains. The only things which distinguished her from an ordinary house-wife were a number of large and elaborate rings on her fingers, and the fact that when the sunlight caught her at the right angle, it gleamed on her three gold teeth.

'You know why I'm here, don't you?' Woodend asked, settling himself down as comfortably as he could on the narrow bench which ran along one side of the caravan.

'You're here to ask me about Stan Dawkins,' Zelda said.

'That's right, I am.'

'Well, I'm not sure there's much I can tell you. He was only with the fair for a few months before he was killed.'

'Yet even in that short time, accordin' to your boss, you got to know him quite well,' Woodend countered.

Zelda sighed. 'We were both young,' she said. 'It was all very romantic – almost innocent.'

'*Almost* innocent?' Woodend asked, pouncing on the word. 'It seems to me that means that it wasn't innocent at all?'

Zelda shrugged. 'You can believe what you like, Chief Inspector. Whatever it was, it's long past now.'

'So are you sayin' you *didn't* sleep with him or that you *did*?' Woodend persisted.

'You wouldn't have been quite as blunt as that if you'd been talking to a middle-aged woman back in Whitebridge, would you?' Zelda asked. 'If I'd lived in a semi-detached house – rather than been a traveller – you'd have found a much nicer way to say it.'

Woodend couldn't remember the last time he'd blushed, but knew that he was blushing now.

'You're right, of course,' he admitted. 'I

made an assumption you wouldn't be offended by my comin' directly to the point. But it was an assumption I had no right to make – an' I apologize for it. Still, you do see my dilemma, don't you?'

'No. But maybe I will if you can be bothered to explain it to me.'

'I'm tryin' to find out what happened twenty years ago. I'm tryin' to get into the mind of a man who's been a long time dead. An' part of understandin' what made him think like he did – an' act like he did – is your relationship with him. If you were keepin' company together in a serious way...' He paused and smiled. 'Is that tactful enough for you?'

Zelda smiled back. 'It'll do.'

'If you were keepin' company in a serious way, he might have acted differently to if you'd only been at the pressed flowers an' love notes stage. Do you see what I'm sayin'?'

'No.'

Woodend wasn't sure she was being entirely honest with him. In fact, he suspected that she was using his early insensitivity as a weapon with which to keep him on the hop. This was a very intelligent woman he was dealing with here – and if he didn't watch himself, she'd run rings round him.

'Perhaps it would help if I told you what I felt like when I was Stan's age,' he suggested.

182

'Perhaps it would,' Zelda agreed.

Woodend sighed. 'I was brought up in a different world to the one that the lads growin' up now know. In my day, you didn't "keep company in a serious way" with the lass you were plannin' to marry until you *were* married – an' that meant waitin' while you'd come out of your apprenticeship an' were earnin' a decent wage, so you could rent a house of your own.'

'Go on,' Zelda encouraged.

'Well, when a lad's eighteen or nineteen, he wakes up in the mornin' with a hard ... he wakes up feeling amorous. There's nothin' he can do about it. It refused to go away. An' somehow, for the lads of my generation, that seemed to make all the waitin' until we could afford to get married even more difficult to take.'

'So what was the solution?'

'There were always a few girls in any town who didn't want to wait for the weddin' ring to be placed on their fingers, an' if you bought them a few port an' lemons on a Friday night, there was the chance they'd "keep company in a serious way" with you on a purely temporary basis.'

'Is that what you did, Chief Inspector?' Zelda asked.

For the second time in just a few minutes, Woodend felt himself starting to flush, which – he was well aware – was exactly what she'd

183

intended.

'I ... er ... considered it,' he said.

'But you didn't follow it through?'

'Well, no, I didn't,' Woodend admitted, almost as if he were ashamed of himself.

'I didn't think so,' Zelda Todd told him. 'Can we get back to Stan Dawkins now?'

'Aye, we'd better,' Woodend agreed. 'You see, the way my mind is workin' is that Stan might have gone in the village in search of one of them port-an'-lemon girls an'—'

'He didn't.'

'...an' that the local lads might have given him a worse beatin' than they intended to, and killed him.'

'That's certainly what Mr Masters thinks,' Zelda said. 'And it's what the police *probably* thought at the time, though they'd never have admitted it. But it's not what happened.'

'How can you be so sure.'

'I just am,' Zelda Todd said evasively. 'Anyway, what's that got to do with the murder of the man yesterday?'

'I'm not sure it's got *anythin'* to do with it. I'm just makin' general inquiries.'

'No, you're not,' Zelda Todd contradicted. 'Shall I tell you what you're *really* thinking?'

'Will that involve readin' my palm, or takin' out your crystal ball?' the Chief Inspector asked.

'This is what you're really thinking,' Zelda

said, ignoring the comment, and making Woodend feel ashamed of himself all over again. 'You're thinking that Stan was murdered by some of the lads in Hallerton, and it's been a festering wound in the side of this funfair for twenty years. So when we finally come back, some of our lads decide they've finally got an opportunity to take their revenge. Now, they either think they know who killed Stan, or they decide that – on the principle of an eye for an eye and a tooth for a tooth – it doesn't matter which of the villagers is killed, as long as it's one of them. How am I doing?'

'You're nearly right,' Woodend admitted. 'Except that if it did happen that way, I don't think the killer necessarily had to be someone who was with the fair the last time.'

'No?' Zelda Todd asked, expressionlessly.

'No,' Woodend said. 'Most violent killers are youngish men, an' anybody who was here the last time must be well into middle age by now.'

'So?'

'So fairground folk are a tight bunch – an' they have what might be called a collective sense of honour. Somebody wanted Harry Dimdyke killed – but that doesn't have to be the same person who actually carried out the murder. In other words, one of the older folk might have talked one of the younger folk into doin' the killin' for him. Or for *her*.'

'You think I arranged it?' Zelda Todd asked.

'I didn't say that. But if the theory that Harry Dimdyke was killed by somebody from the funfair is correct, then that certainly makes you one of the main suspects.'

'I swear on my daughter's life that if anybody from the fair was involved, I know nothing about it,' Zelda said.

'An' I'm *almost* certain I believe you,' Woodend said. He rose to his feet, being careful not to bang his head on the caravan roof. 'It's been nice talkin' to you, Mrs Todd.'

'*Miss* Todd,' Zelda corrected him.

'*Miss* Todd,' Woodend amended.

Head bent, he made his way to the door. On the threshold, just before stepping out into the bright sunshine, he stopped and turned around. 'By the way, there is one more thing.'

'Yes?'

'I asked you if you were keepin' serious company with Stan.'

'I remember.'

'But somehow, you managed to avoid answerin' one way or the other.'

Zelda Todd laughed, and the sunlight caught her gold teeth again. 'Yes, I did, didn't I?' she said.

Twenty-Four

Even at that late stage in the afternoon, the light which flooded in from outside was almost blinding. So for a few seconds after the barn door swung open, all Wilf Dimdyke could make out were two dark shapes – one broad and solid, the other slimmer and almost insubstantial. Then the two figures advanced into the barn, and Wilf saw the new arrivals were his father and a young woman.

Tom Dimdyke had his hand on the woman's shoulder. There was nothing sexual about the contact – but neither was it entirely casual. There seemed, in fact, to be both avuncular concern *and* a certain amount of control in the way that the large palm rested on the slim shoulder.

The woman herself seemed a little unsure of how to react. Her stance suggested, if anything, that while she was not exactly reluctant to be there, she was not quite sure that she wanted to be, either.

Wilf thought about saying something, then decided against it. Instead, he picked up his chisel and mallet again, and began to gently shave the edge of Meg's thigh bone.

'You'll know Lizzie Philips, won't you?' his father said.

Of course he knew her. How could he *not* know her? They were from the same village – which was the only village in the world which mattered to either of them. They had gone to the same village primary school. And when age – and the law of the land – had forced them to attend an alien secondary school in the nearest small town, they had spent their breaks huddled together in the playground – along with all the other children from Hallerton.

'Lizzie's gettin' married soon,' Tom said, with a joviality which didn't quite work.'

'Is she?' Wilf asked.

'She is indeed,' his father replied, as if answering an eager enquiry rather than an indifferent one. 'She's gettin' wed to your cousin Sid – so she'll be part of the family!'

If an outsider – Woodend, for example – had been listening, Wilf thought, he'd have assumed from Tom's enthusiasm that Sid was his nephew, and that the two families were never out of each other's houses. But that wasn't the case at all. Sid Dimdyke wasn't a *first* cousin. He wasn't a *second* cousin – or even a *third* cousin. Part of the clan, certainly, but definitely not part of the family. So why was his dad getting so worked up about this marriage?

'Well, what have you got to say about that, son?' Tom asked.

Not a lot, Wilf told himself. But aloud he said, 'Congratulations, Lizzie.'

'It's Sid you want to be congratulatin', not Lizzie,' Tom Dimdyke said. 'Like I said, he's a lucky man. There's plenty of lads in the village who wish they were in his shoes on his weddin' night.'

Lizzie giggled. 'Oh, do be quiet, Mr Dimdyke,' she said.

'I'm only speakin' the truth,' Tom Dimdyke said firmly.

At school, Sid had always been a bit of a drip, Wilf remembered – the sort of lad the playground bullies would naturally have picked on even if he *hadn't* come from Hallerton. But if Lizzie was marrying him, there had to be a reason for it. So maybe, while he himself had been totally absorbed in the Witch, Sid had grown up a little.

'Aye, they're gettin' married in October,' Tom Dimdyke said.

Why had his father brought this girl to the barn? Wilf wondered. Didn't he realize that was this was a crucial stage of the process – that the trap being almost finished, it would soon be time to lure the spirit of Meg into it?

'Aye, October,' Tom said. 'That's only four months away, you know.'

'I can count,' Wilf told him, sounding surly

189

– and not caring.

'It'll be gone before we realize it.'

Wilf looked down at the Witch and stretched his free hand so that his fingers were brushing against the mallet.

'I've got work to do,' he said.

'We know that, lad,' his father said understandingly. He turned to Lizzie. 'Well, I expect you've got things you should be gettin' on with yourself, lass.'

Lizzie blinked. 'What?'

'With gettin' married in only a few months, you'll have a lot to do.'

'Oh, yes, I have,' Lizzie said, unconvincingly. 'I've got *a lot* to do.' She fell silent for a moment, then said, 'Well, it was nice talkin' to you, Wilf.'

'An' I'm sure he found it nice talkin' to you,' Tom Dimdyke said. 'Didn't you, lad?'

Wilf made a grunt which may have passed as a 'yes', and Lizzie, nodding nervously, turned and almost *fled* the barn.

'What's the matter with you, son?' Tom Dimdyke asked when the girl had gone.

'Nothin',' Wilf replied.

'She's a nice lass, you know,' his father persisted. 'A good lass from good stock.'

'I'm sure she is – if you say so.'

'Then why weren't you nicer to her? Is it that you don't fancy her? Are her legs too skinny for your taste? Does she not have enough bosom for your liking?'

190

'Why are you askin' me all these questions now?' Wilf demanded. 'Look at this.' He pointed down to his workbench. 'This is *my* Witch! My moment! She has to be perfect. That's what you've always told me, isn't it? So I've no time for anythin' else at the moment.'

Tom nodded sympathetically. 'You're right,' he agreed. 'You're the Witch Maker, an', of course, you're right. We can leave most things till after Sunday. But there's one matter we have to deal with before then.'

'An' what's that?'

'The bobby from Whitebridge. He's pokin' his nose into things that are no concern of his.'

'Is that what he's doin'? I thought he was tryin' to find out who killed my Uncle Harry.'

'An' so he is. An' I'll be very glad if he does.'

'Glad!' Wilf repeated. 'You'll be *glad*! Is that all?'

Tom sighed. 'I want the killer caught. Of course I do. But let's face it, your Uncle Harry should never have been the Witch Maker in the first place.'

'Then who should have been?' Wilf demanded. '*You?*'

'I wasn't chosen, an' I played the part that was given me with no regrets an' to the best of my ability,' Tom said. 'But yes, I think I'd

191

have made a better Witch Maker. Your Uncle Harry had a wilful nature. He could have destroyed everythin'. He very nearly did. An' even now he's dead, we still have to live with his legacy. But you'll be different. You'll be a fine Witch Maker. They'll be holdin' you up as an example two hundred years from now.'

'An' supposin' I don't want to be held up as an example two hundred years from now?'

Tom laughed. 'What a lot of nonsense you talk sometimes. Don't want to be held up as an example! Of course you do. It's every Witch Maker's dream.' His face grew more serious again. 'But to get back to the matter of this bobby. He's been to the funfair. He's been askin' questions about that feller who got killed the last time it was here. Somethin' has to be done about him.'

'Like what?'

'That's what I'm here to ask you.'

'Kill him, then!'

Tom Dimdyke looked thoughtful for a second. 'Is that what you really want?' he asked.

'Of course it's not what I want!' his son said exasperatedly. 'Only a lunatic would want that. An' only another lunatic would take the suggestion seriously.' Then he saw the look of hurt which had come to his father's face, and felt instant regret. 'Look, Dad,' he continued, 'I don't *know* what to do. In case you hadn't noticed, I'm not much more than a kid. I shouldn't be makin' big decisions.'

'I was, at your age,' his father said reprovingly.

'Then maybe you were more of a man then than I am now,' Wilf said. 'Maybe you were more of a man then than I'll ever be. I don't know. It's hard growin' up as I did – with a dark shadow hangin' over you. You can never work out what you're really like as a person – because your eyes are always fixed on what you're intended to be. On what *the village* wants you to be.'

'You think about things a lot more than your Uncle Harry ever did,' Tom said. 'He was a fine craftsman – no doubt about that – but that's all he was. That's why I believe you're goin' to be one of the greatest—'

'Shut up! Bloody well shut up!' Wilf said – and was amazed when his father meekly did as he'd been instructed.

The silence which followed was intolerable for the both of them, but in the end it was Wilf who broke it.

'What do you want from me, Dad?' he asked.

'I didn't like it when you said I should kill that bobby, you know.'

'I know you didn't.'

'But if you'd told me that's what *you* wanted doin', I'd have done it – because

193

you're the Witch Maker. An' however much you may not want to give me a decision, you must – because it can only come from you.'

It was just as Woodend had explained earlier, Wilf thought. Like the Queen, he had so much power in some areas – and so little in others.

He looked down at the chisel he was holding in his hand. If he decided to attack his father with it, the older man would just stand there and take it – because he was the Witch Maker!

Yet at the same time, he could order Tom to leave the barn and the other man would simply refuse to go until he'd been told what to do about Woodend.

Wilf took a gulp of air.

'A general back at headquarters can make all the sweepin' decisions in a war,' he said, 'but the little ones – the ones made in the heat of the moment – have to be taken by the men on the ground. That's what dealin' with this bobby will be – a decision made in the heat of the moment by the men on the ground.'

'So you're sayin' that you're leavin' it up to me?'

'I'm sayin' I have no choice,' Wilf replied.

'You've worked it all out, haven't you?' Tom said, giving his son a nod of what could only be called frank admiration. 'When I look at things, I can only see what's goin' on close to me. I'm like a worm, peepin' out of the ground. But you – you're like a hawk. Hoverin' above it all. Seein' the whole picture.'

No, no, no! a voice in Wilf's head screamed. It's not like that at all, Dad. I've duped you. Can't you see that? I've talked you into makin' choices I was *born* to make. I'm lettin' you do the dirty work because I'm just not brave enough to do it myself.

He wanted to say the words out loud, but he couldn't. Because the only way he could avoid deceiving this good, honest man further would be by admitting that he'd already made a fool of him – that he'd already *betrayed* him.

So he simply said, 'I have to get back to the Witch, Dad.'

'Aye, you get back to the Witch, son,' his father agreed. 'That's the important job, an' it couldn't be in better hands. For the rest, don't give it a moment's thought. I'll do whatever else has to be done.'

Tom Dimdyke turned and left the barn.

Wilf watched him go, his heart almost bursting with love. Tom had been both a father and mother to him. Nothing had ever been too much trouble. Nothing had ever been skimped on.

And *this* was how all his care and attention was to be rewarded! He was being sent out on to the front line because a younger, more able, man didn't have the guts to go there himself.

The chisel dropped from Wilf's hand, and he burst into deep grieving sobs.

Twenty-Five

When Hettie thought about her childhood, it was usually the conversations she'd have with other funfair brats on the subject of parents which first came to mind.

'I wish I had a mum like yours,' the kids would say to her.

But what they'd actually meant was: 'I wish *your* mum was *my* mum instead.'

She hadn't needed the envy of others to make her aware of how lucky she was. She'd always known that if she'd been given the choice of all the mothers in the world, she'd have chosen the mother she already had.

It wasn't that her mother was particularly indulgent – other mothers often let their daughters get away with far more than she was ever allowed to. It wasn't that her mother was particularly easy to live with – there were few mothers who tried to steer their daughters' lives in the way Zelda tried to steer hers. Yet those things were merely a minor irritation. What really mattered to her was that, despite their difference in ages, she and her mother were real *friends*. They laughed at the same things, they were serious about the same things – and they could say what they liked to each other without worrying that it might wreck their relationship.

Or at least, that was the way that things *had been* until they'd come to Hallerton!

Now, a fence had suddenly been erected between them – a very high fence with cruel strands of barbed wire running along its top.

Her mother had thoughts she didn't want to share. Her mother had conversations with good-looking fairground workers – and with senior police officers from Whitebridge – which she chose to keep to herself. Well, that state of affairs could not be allowed to continue, Hettie resolved. Which was why, when she saw her mother enter their caravan, she followed her and closed the door behind her.

Zelda Todd was startled to hear the metal door clang so forcefully, but all she said was, 'Don't shut out the sunlight, girl. We get little enough of it in this cold wet country.'

'Sit down, Mum,' Hettie said firmly.

'Why should I want to—?'

'Just sit down.'

Zelda lowered herself on to one of narrow benches which pulled out at night to make a bed. Hettie sat down opposite her. There wasn't much space, and their knees touched.

'Well, isn't this cosy?' Zelda said.

'I want to know what it was all about, Mam,' Hettie said.

'What *what* was about?'

'Why did that bobby come callin' on you this mornin'?'

'Maybe we're old friends,' Zelda suggested innocently. 'Maybe he just came to renew our acquaintanceship.'

'Don't try that line on me,' Hettie warned her.

'What's the matter? Can't I *have* old friends?'

'You can have as many friends as you like, Mum. You've got scores of them. But they're all either part of this funfair or part of one of the others. You don't have friends from the outside world. None of us do. That's just the way things are.'

'There's always an exception to every rule, you know, Hettie.'

'And even if you *did* have friends from the outside, they wouldn't be bobbies. Bobbies and funfairs just don't mix.'

Zelda reached up to the shelf above her head. Like a blind brown mouse, her hand groped around for her packet of Player's Navy Cut and her box of matches. When she'd located them she pulled them down, extracted a cigarette from the packet, and lit it up. Hettie couldn't be sure, but she thought she saw a slight tremble in her mother's hand.

'All right,' Zelda conceded, when she'd taken a long drag of her Player's. 'The bobby wasn't an old friend. He was asking about a murder that happened a long time ago.'

'Whose murder?'

'You wouldn't have known him. How could you have? He was killed before you were even born.'

'But *you* knew him?'

'There'd have been no point in that bobby asking me about it if I *didn't*, now would there?'

Hettie sighed. The problem was, she thought, that she was trying to *interrogate* her mother – and the other woman was so much better at playing the game than she was.

'The bobby didn't want to know anything about the murder that happened the other night, by any chance, did he?' she asked.

'I expect he did. That's probably the main reason he was here. But he didn't ask me about it.'

The words were a little too glib, Hettie thought. A little too casual. It was not often her mother overplayed her hand like this – she must really be feeling under pressure.

'I want to know what you've been talking so earnestly to Pat Calhoun about,' Hettie said.

Her mother hesitated. 'Private matters,' she said finally.

'Private!'

'Yes, private. Don't look so surprised, Hettie. There are some matters which need to be kept private, even from you.'

'I can't imagine what they might be,' Hettie said, in a voice which was almost sulky.

'No, I'm sure you can't,' her mother agreed. 'And as far as I'm concerned, it's best kept that way.'

'I need to know,' Hettie insisted.

Her mother reached above her head again, found the ashtray – a souvenir from Scarborough – by touch, and stubbed out her cigarette in it.

'Pat's not like most men,' she said. 'He's wise beyond his years. In some ways, he's almost like a woman. I can tell him things, and he'll listen and understand. He so reminds me of...'

'Of who?'

'Of whom!'

'Who does he remind you of?'

'Of ... of an older, wiser woman. That's why I like talking to him. And that's why I'd like to see the two of you paired off – because I know he cares for you, and I know he'd *take care* of you.'

'I've told you before, I'm not ready for a man,' Hettie said. 'And when I am ready, I'll—'

She stopped suddenly. She'd been sidetracked by the idea of herself and Pat getting together, she realized – just as her cunning mother had intended that she should be.

'What's the secret you're sharing with Pat

that you're not willing to share with me?' she demanded.

'Does it matter, when there are so many secrets I share with you that I'd never share with him?'

'It matters.'

Zelda lit up another cigarette, and this time her hand was definitely shaking. 'I'll make a deal with you,' she said.

'What kind of deal?' Hettie asked suspiciously.

'I won't tell you what I told Pat, but I *will* tell you about something I never talked to you about before – something I've never told *anybody* about before. And in return, you'll stop pestering me. Is that fair?'

'It's not a trick, is it?'

Zelda shook her head. 'It's no trick.'

'All right,' Hettie agreed. Then, just to show she wasn't a complete pushover, she added, 'What thrilling subject do you have in mind?'

Zelda took another long drag of her cigarette. 'Your father.'

The dark area! The one thing that – until now – Zelda had never been prepared to open up on.

'My father!' Hettie gasped.

'That's what I said.'

'*What* about him?'

'What do you want to *know*?'

There were so many questions Hettie had

wanted to ask – so many she knew she *should* ask. Yet now the moment had come – now she had her opportunity – she couldn't think of a single one of them.

Zelda was waiting patiently for her to speak.

This *was* another trick, Hettie thought. Another way of getting her off the subjects of the policeman and Pat Calhoun. Yet this time it was worth it. This time the bait was irresistible.

'Who is my father?' she asked breathlessly. 'Where does he live? What does he do?'

Zelda thought back to the last time she had seen Stan Dawkins alive. She had watched him leave the funfair and walk towards Hallerton. He had seemed so strong. So graceful. What a fine man he had been. What an upright man. What a *beautiful* man.

'Well?' Hettie demanded. 'Tell me. Have I ever met him? Is he with one of the other funfairs? What does he do?'

'He doesn't do anything any more,' Zelda said.

'What's that suppose to mean?' Hettie asked aggressively.

And then she noticed the tear that was running down her mother's cheek – a tear so large and so perfect that it seemed to encompass a whole world.

'He doesn't do anything because he's *dead*,' Zelda sobbed. 'He was murdered.'

Twenty-Six

They didn't welcome his custom in the Black Bull. Woodend was well aware of that. And, as a matter of fact, he didn't particularly feel like drinking there himself. But he was buggered if he was going to let a bunch of inbred locals dictate his actions, and so before driving back to Throckston for the night he decided he'd pay the Hallerton pub a visit.

He bought a pint and took it with him into the corridor, where the public phone was located. After setting his drink down on the shelf provided and lighting up a Capstan, he fished in his pocket for change, dialled Whitebridge headquarters, and was connected to Bob Rutter.

'Got anythin' for me, Inspector?' he asked hopefully.

'I'm not sure of how much use it's going to be to your actual investigation, sir,' Bob Rutter told him, 'but I have found the answer to your little war memorial teaser.'

'An' that answer is...?'

'There's no war memorial because there

are no dead from Hallerton to commemorate.'

Woodend remembered film footage he had seen of the First World War. Wave after wave of men urged on by the commanders into the hail of deadly enemy machine-gun bullets. Thousands upon thousands of brave soldiers falling in a single day's fighting. And if he needed any further confirmation, he had the war widows he'd known in his own street, when he was growing up. There'd certainly been more than enough of them!

'What you've just said isn't possible,' he told Rutter. 'There isn't any way that men from Hallerton couldn't have been called up an' sent to France.'

'You're half-right,' Rutter said. 'Several of them *were* called up, but they were never sent to fight.'

'An' why's that?'

'Because just before they were due to be shipped to the Front, they all deserted.'

It made sense, Woodend thought. 'Country' didn't mean anything to the men of Hallerton. Bloody hell, *county* didn't mean anything to them. Of course they would have deserted. But they would have been captured again almost immediately. The lucky ones would have spent the rest of the war – and beyond – in a military stockade. And as for the *unlucky* ones – the ones who the court martial decided were the ring leaders...

'How many of them were shot for treason?' he asked.

'None!'

'None?'

'Oh, they probably would have been, if they'd been caught. But they weren't. They seemed to have completely disappeared off the face of the earth. The military police went to Hallerton to look for them – in ninety-nine cases out of a hundred, apparently, deserters would head back for their own village – but there was no trace of them there. The files are still open, of course, but fifty years is a long time, and nobody seriously expects any results now.'

Fifty years might be a long time in the rest of the world, Woodend thought, but in Hallerton it was the mere batting of an eye.

'What about Hallerton men in the Second World War?' he asked. 'Did *they* desert, an' all?'

'No,' Rutter said. 'But apparently there was no attempt to post them abroad, either.'

No, there wouldn't have been, Woodend told himself. By then, the military authorities would have understood that this place was different to every other village in the country – and, knowing the effect that desertion could have on the morale of the soldiers left behind, they would have done nothing to provoke the men from Hallerton.

'Thanks, Bob,' he said.

'Was that any help?' Rutter asked.

'Buggered if I know,' Woodend admitted.

The first thing that Woodend noticed when he returned to the bar was that the eyes of all the locals were fixed on the table in the corner, and turning towards it himself, he understood why. Who, after all, could *not* look at the graceful woman in the colourful sari and sheepskin jacket who was sitting there?

The Chief Inspector made his way across to the table, and sat down opposite Dr Shastri.

'I thought I'd find you here, Chief Inspector,' the doctor said. Then she held up her hands to her mouth in mock horror. 'No criticism intended. I was not suggesting for a moment that you are an alcoholic. Far from it. I am well aware, as a qualified medical doctor, that you are a special case – that you suffer a rare physiological complaint which means that your brain simply does not work effectively without sufficient lubrication from best bitter.'

Woodend grinned, but said nothing.

'I am afraid I can be of little help on your current murder,' Dr Shastri continued. 'Indeed, my detailed examination has revealed no more than the information I gave you at the scene of the crime, which was that Harold Dimdyke was first rendered unconscious by a powerful blow to the back of the head, then was tied to the post at which he was garrotted.'

'You've got something else for me though, haven't you, Doc?' Woodend said.

Dr Shastri smiled. 'What makes you say that, Chief Inspector?'

'Because if your findings on Harry Dimdyke were *all* you had, you'd have given the details over the phone. Instead, you drove all the way here to see me personally. Now why was that?'

'You tell me.'

'Because you've got a bit of a bombshell to drop – an' you wanted to see the look on my face when you dropped it.'

The doctor raised one eyebrow. 'Perhaps you are right,' she agreed. 'And what do you think this small bombshell of mine might concern?'

'My guess is that it's about the death of the other murder victim – Stan Dawkins.'

Dr Shastri laughed delightedly. 'Then you are guessing up a blind alley. Though I do have a *little* information about Mr Dawkins.'

'And that little information *is?*'

'The speculation of the medical examiner of the time was that Dawkins was beaten to death by a gang. I have examined the gruesome black and white photographs that your police photographer so lovingly took at the scene of the crime, and from the nature and angle of the bruisers, I would guess they were all delivered by a single assailant. Of course, I could be wrong.'

Woodend nodded thoughtfully. 'Let's have the bombshell now, shall we?' he suggested.

'As I told you, it is the tiniest of bombs. Possibly no bigger than a hand grenade.'

Woodend grinned again. 'Let's see you pull the pin on it, then.'

'I examined the post-mortem reports on the women who most recently committed suicide. The two deaths were quite different. In one case, the liver was completely destroyed by an overdose of sleeping pills. In the other, death was caused by a blocking of the breathing passage, which thus denied blood to the brain. But there was one feature they had in common – both of the women had suffered quite heavy vaginal bruising.'

'They'd been raped?!' Woodend asked, astonished.

Dr Shastri shook her head. 'No, I do not think so. If they'd been raped, there'd be other indications.'

'Like heavy bruising to thighs, and bruises on the arms where they'd been restrained.'

'Exactly. And there is no evidence in the reports of that kind of thing.'

'So what—?'

'My conclusion is that shortly before their deaths, they'd both indulged in energetic – almost brutal – sexual intercourse. It was almost certainly voluntary, but I would be very surprised if it were not also quite painful. And there had been anal penetration, which I would imagine is a dangerous and forbidden novelty, not often practised in darkest Lancashire.'

'Bloody hell!' Woodend said.

'That one of the women had undergone such indignities is scarcely worth comment,' the doctor continued. 'But I did find it strange that both of them should have borne what might be called the same "signature" of sexual abuse. I may be quite wrong, of course. Perhaps these two women did not see it as abuse at all. Perhaps the men in this village do have a different approach to love-making from men in the rest of the county.'

Perhaps they did, Woodend thought. But he still couldn't imagine Alf Raby, the shell of a village shopkeeper, treating *his* wife in the way that the doctor had just described.

Twenty-Seven

There were two pubs in Throckston and, for the sake of variety, Woodend suggested that that night he and Paniatowski should try the Red Dragon instead of the Wheatsheaf.

He knew he had made a mistake the moment he walked through the door. The pub had retained its old oak beams and horse brasses, but – in a crime almost as horrendous as murder in Woodend's book – the wall between the public bar and the saloon had been knocked through to make one big room.

Paniatowski caught the expression on her boss's face and laughed. 'The trouble with you, sir, is that you don't like progress,' she said.

'Progress!' Woodend snorted, walking over to one of the round, copper-topped tables. 'You don't know what you're talkin' about. It's not *progress* to go meddlin' with things that were perfectly all right as they were. It's not *progress* to change things just for the sake of change.'

Paniatowski's grin widened as she sat

down. Pushing Woodend's buttons and releasing the inevitable tirade was not something she did often – but it was certainly fun once in a while.

'The thing about a decent pub is, it's organic,' Woodend continued, not seeing the trap he was walking into. 'It's as natural to a village as the hills which surround it, or the stream that runs through it. It's taken hundreds of years of slow development to get it how it is. Then some smart alec in a pink shirt comes in from the brewery in Manchester or Preston, an' decides that he knows more about how the pub should look than the people who actually use it.'

Paniatowski lit up a cigarette. 'It seems to me as if you think Hallerton is the ideal community,' she teased.

The remark had more of an effect on Woodend than she'd ever intended it to. Because perhaps she was right, he thought with a sudden mental jolt. Maybe he had got his gaze fixed too firmly on the past. Maybe he was more like the narrow-minded, tunnel-visioned inhabitants of Hallerton than he'd care to admit.

'Not all changes are bad,' he said gruffly.

'For instance?'

Woodend struggled to find an example of one that wasn't. 'Well, Whitebridge Rovers got promoted to the First Division last season,' he said finally. 'Now *that* was a good thing.'

Except of course, that now the team would have more money to play about with, it could bring in players from outside the county, he added mentally. Except that success would probably mean the end of the Rovers as a local institution, and the start of its metamorphosis into a big sporting *business*.

'Perhaps I should move with the times a bit more,' he suggested. 'How do you think I'd look in one of them new collarless Beatle jackets?'

'Ridiculous,' Paniatowski said, without hesitation.

'Aye, that's what I suspected,' Woodend agreed.

They gave the waiter the order for their drinks, then Paniatowski said, 'There's something I've been meaning to bring up, sir.'

'Go on, then.'

'I think I've been followed around Hallerton.'

'Who by?'

'An old man.'

'Not an old man with a black an' white check cap an' green muffler, by any chance?' Woodend asked, thinking of the one he'd seen when he'd been knocking on the shopkeeper's door. 'Leaned heavily on a stick?' he elucidated. 'Dived for cover when you noticed him?'

Paniatowski shook her head. 'No, this man wore a trilby and didn't have a stick at all. In fact, mine was very nippy for his age. But there was definitely something furtive about him.'

'Maybe Tom Dimdyke's hired him as a private eye, an' his job is to trail you,' Woodend suggested.

'Not likely though, is it?' Paniatowski asked.

'I suppose not,' Woodend agreed.

And since there seemed to be nothing more to say on the subject, he found himself looking around the bar and examining the customers. They were a mixed bunch, he decided. Some – going by their flat caps and wellington boots – were obviously farm hands, snatching a pint between the last milking of the day and their suppers. Others, wearing jackets and cravats, were equally obviously office workers of some kind – part of the new generation of townees who had moved their families into the countryside. And standing at the bar, looking questioningly at him, was a man wearing a check shirt and brown knitted tie.

Woodend signalled that the man should join them. 'This is Mr Tyndale,' he told Paniatowski. 'He's somethin' of a local historian.'

'So you know all about Meg Ramsden?'

Paniatowski asked.

Tyndale smiled diffidently. 'I've read all the available records. And I suppose I know as much about the way her mind worked – and the way the minds of the villagers worked – as any modern man possibly can.' He gave a lopsided grin. 'Of course, if you ask the folk in Hallerton, they'd say that since I wasn't born there, I know nothing at all.'

'Tell us somethin' about Meg,' Woodend said. 'Do you think she *was* a witch?'

'Are you asking me if she really had magical powers?' Tyndale said, his smile transforming itself into an amused grin.

'No. Since I don't believe in magic myself, there'd be no point. What I am askin' is whether *she* thought she could perform magic.'

'Absolutely not. She was far too level-headed a person for that. The power that Meg worshipped was much more tangible. And that's where the real problem was.'

'Would you care to be a bit more specific?' Woodend asked.

'Meg was no witch, and everybody in the village knew it. But what they also knew was that she had the ability to make their lives a total misery – and very often did.'

'An' how did she manage that?'

'Meg inherited a fair amount of money from her father. Enough to live comfortably on. But she didn't just sit on it – she put it to

215

good use. Villages like Hallerton always exist on the edge of disaster, and when times are particularly hard, the people who live there have no choice but to borrow money.'

'An' Meg became the village money-lender?'

'She did indeed. And a particularly harsh one she was. In those days, villages were real communities. Everybody supported everybody else. But Meg was having no truck with that. A debt was a debt, and if it couldn't be paid in cash, then it had to be paid in some other way. There are at least three or four documented cases of Meg calling the bailiffs in to evict families that had fallen behind with their payments. By the time she died, she owned half the village.'

'Can't have made her popular,' Woodend said.

'But there was one way in which she was generous,' Tyndale continued. 'She was very free with what we used to call "her favours".' He turned to Paniatowski and blushed slightly. 'Sorry if this is getting a little indelicate for you.'

'I'm a detective sergeant in the Mid Lancs Police,' Paniatowski told him sweetly. 'It comes as no news to me that there are some women who never wear knickers.'

'I see,' Tyndale said, still not sure of how to take her. 'Well, anyway, if you took Meg's fancy, she'd soon let you know it, if you

216

understand what I mean.'

'Sounds like a woman who'd be on top more often than she'd be underneath,' Paniatowski said.

Tyndale coughed awkwardly. 'Exactly,' he agreed. 'It's not known how many of the men from the village she took to her bed – they weren't going to admit it, were they? – but it is absolutely certain that any good-looking traveller who was passing through Hallerton would soon fall prey to her.'

And they probably wouldn't have put up much of a fight, Woodend thought, remembering the portrait – the one which looked so much like Mary Dimdyke – that hung in the Meg Ramsden Museum.

'Anyway, then the witchcraft trials started in Lancaster, and that was just the excuse the villagers had been looking for. As you know, they tried her themselves, and then carried out their own execution.'

'But was it *just* an excuse?' Paniatowski asked. 'Didn't they really believe she *was* a witch?'

'Perhaps a few of them might have pretended they did. But even by the standards of the time, there was very little of what you might call "evidence" of witchcraft. Oh, a couple of children died in the village, but infant mortality was very high in those days. And a few sheep went sick – but shepherds back then were too good at their job not to know the cause, even if they didn't know the cure. So while they might have said they burned her as a witch, they actually burned her for being Meg Ramsden.'

'You mentioned she had no kids of her own,' Woodend said.

'That's right. And I might further have suggested that was part of the problem. If Meg had been able to fulfil herself in the way most other women did, she may have been less interested in money and adultery. I believe the contemporary phrase for what she did is "displacement activity".'

Paniatowski bridled. 'You mean that if a woman doesn't have kids to tie her down, she's bound to turn into a first-rate bitch!' she demanded.

Tyndale gulped. 'No, I wasn't meaning to suggest—' he began.

'Of course you weren't,' Woodend said, attempting to rapidly smooth over the cracks.

But Paniatowski didn't *want* them smoothing over. 'And why is it always the wife's fault?' she asked. 'Maybe her husband had no lead in his pencil. Maybe the reason she took her pleasure elsewhere was because he wasn't enough of a man for her.'

'I ... er...' Tyndale said, helpless in the face of this fresh onslaught.

'From what Mr Tyndale's just told us about her sleepin' around, she'd have been almost bound to get pregnant if she'd been able to,' Woodend said.

'Besides, her husband *did* have a child,' Tyndale said, in an attempt to insert himself back in the conversation. 'He married again, before Meg's ashes were even really cold. Of course, he never actually saw the baby, because, by the time it was born, he was dead himself, but—'

'It's all so very convenient, isn't it?' Paniatowski interrupted. 'Meg was a strong woman, so there must have been something wrong with her. And from that it's only a short step to saying that everything that happened to her must have been *her* fault!'

Woodend stood up. 'Let's go an' get a breath of fresh air, Monika,' he said in a tone which made it plain that he was issuing an order.

Paniatowski followed him through the door. A chill breeze was coming in off the moors, and when it hit her, she shivered.

'Now what the bloody hell was that all about?' Woodend asked.

Paniatowski shrugged. 'I just get sick of people – men especially – assuming that—'

'Listen, Tyndale's not a criminal,' Woodend said harshly. 'He's a member of the public, who's tryin' to help us as best he can, an' I will *not* tolerate him bein' spoken to in the way you just have.'

Paniatowski looked down at the ground.

'Sorry,' she said.

'An' so you bloody-well should be,' Woodend told her. 'We're goin' back in there, an' when we do, you'll treat the man with the respect he's entitled to. Understood?'

'Understood,' Paniatowski muttered.

Tyndale was still sitting at the table where they had left him, though from the look of apprehension as he saw Paniatowski approach, it was plain that he had at least *considered* flight.

Woodend and his sergeant resumed their seats. 'So Meg's husband remarried straight away, did he?' Woodend said, as if there had been no gap at all in the conversation.

'That's right,' Tyndale confirmed.

'I suppose it's hardly surprisin' that he didn't spend long in mournin' after the way Meg had humiliated him,' Woodend continued. He paused, and gave his sergeant a warning look, but Paniatowski seemed completely wrapped up in her own thoughts. 'I shouldn't imagine Mr Ramsden did a great deal to stop the trial and burnin', either.'

'Mr Ramsden?' Tyndale repeated, mystified. 'Her father? I thought I'd already told you that he was dead.'

'Not her father,' Woodend said. 'He wouldn't have been called Ramsden, would he? It's her husband I'm talkin' about.'

'Ah, I see what you mean,' Tyndale said. 'You're wrong, but that's probably my fault for explaining it badly. Her husband wasn't a Ramsden at all.'

'Then why was *she*?'

'Strictly speaking, she wasn't. But that's the way things were in villages. Whoever they were married to, women were habitually called by their maiden name until the day they died.'

'Which, in Meg Ramsden's case, was probably long before she would have gone naturally,' Woodend said. 'Anyway, I take it that this husband – whatever his name was – didn't do too much to stop her being burned.'

'Far from it,' Tyndale told him. 'In fact, he was one of the main instigators of it.'

'Along with the Dimdykes.'

'I really have made a mess of explaining things, haven't I?' Tyndale said. 'He didn't *help* the Dimdykes. He *was* a Dimdyke. Harry Dimdyke. The man who tied her to the stake.'

Twenty-Eight

Mary Dimdyke, the nineteenth virgin since the death of Meg Ramsden to go through the ritual, took a deep breath at Lou Moore's front door before knocking. When the door swung open, she slipped off her shoes and stepped through the gap.

It was a warm evening, but the inside of the cottage had none of the heat of the air outside, and Mary felt a chill on the soles of her bare feet. She looked around her. She couldn't see much. The electric light had been switched off, and the room was lit by half a dozen tall candles in the centre of the floor.

The people sitting beyond these candles were no more than dark shapes. Mary wondered for a moment if her brother was there – but then realized, of course, that he was not. This was a vital part of the process, but it was not one that the Witch Maker had a role in.

'Art thou Mary Dimdyke?' asked a deep voice from beyond the circle of light.

'I am,' Mary said.

'Dost thou know why thou art here?'

'I h ... have been called by the sp ... spirit of Roger Tollance.'

And around the room, her words were echoed by everyone gathered there. 'The spirit of Roger Tollance ... the spirit of Roger Tollance ... the spirit of Roger Tollance...'

Mary knew the whole story of Roger Tollance, of course. *Everyone* in Hallerton knew the story.

Roger Tollance had been nothing when it all began. Less than nothing. A shell of a man who had once been a priest but had lost his faith in God and replaced it with a faith in drink.

For a while he had fallen in with a group of strolling players who, their own theatre in London having been closed due to outbreak of the plague, had taken to touring the provinces to make a living. They had been hard-drinking men themselves, but in the end even they had not been able to take Roger's excesses, and when the company had moved on from Hallerton, they had simply left him behind.

That he had remained had been due less to his desire to stay than a lack of will to go on. A man could scrounge as easily in Hallerton as he could anywhere else, he had probably told himself – easier, since there was no competition.

For years, children had pointed at him

scornfully as he lay drunk in the street. Adults, feeling pity for him, had offered him a space in their barns, where he had lain down in the straw with the beasts of the field. Sores had covered his face and body. He stank. No one had ever imagined that he would become a great man – the saviour of the village. No one had thought, in those long-gone days, that his spirit would still be being invoked nearly four centuries later.

'Dost thou come here of thy own free will?' a disembodied voice in the corner of the room asked Mary.

No! she wanted to scream. *I come because it is expected of me. I come because even my own father and my own brother will not protect me from this.*

But aloud, she said, 'I do c ... come of my own free will.'

'And why dost thou come?'

'Because I must pl ... play my p ... part. We must all pl ... play our p ... parts.'

'We must all play our parts,' Roger Tollance said, standing on the Green on the blackened spot where Meg Ramsden had been burned.

And people were listening to him! For the first time since he had cast off his cassock and left his church for ever, people were listening *to him.*

There had been great changes in the village since Meg had been killed. Tom and Harry Dimdyke had been arrested and tried, and were soon to be executed. The rest of the village had been denounced from the pulpits and in the countless broadsheet ballads.

Hallerton was an evil place, full of evil folk, it was said. The villagers were beyond redemption for what they had done. They would burn in hell, just as Meg had burned on the Green. Though it was not visible to the naked eye, the Mark of Cain was on them, and would go with them to their graves. They were less than human – less, even, than animals.

The villagers had ignored such rebukes at first. They had done right, they claimed. Anyone who had known Meg Ramsden would have done the same. But then the weeks passed and the rebukes continued – and slowly the dam of reassurance had begun to crack.

Perhaps there had been another way, people began to say.

Perhaps, despite her evilness, Meg had not deserved the fate the village had inflicted on her.

Doubts spread. Could the rest of the world be so wrong? people began to ask themselves.

Soon there were some who openly admitted that they had sinned. Children would suddenly burst out weeping. Grown-ups would strike their own heads with their bunched-up fists. The blacksmith mutilated his own hand with a red-hot iron, to show that he was penitent. A farm labourer hanged himself from an old oak tree next to his cottage. The village was dying of guilt and self-loathing. And then Roger Tollance – a dead soul himself for so many years – had spoken.

'We must all play our parts,' he repeated to those assembled on the Green. 'We must unite again, as we were united once before. We must reaffirm our moral purpose – must show that justice is on our side.'

'And how will we do that?' one of the crowd asked.

Roger Tollance's eyes blazed with his new-found fervour.

'We must not deny this thing that we have done,' he said – although, after denouncing Meg, he himself had done very little.

'Not deny it?'

'No! Rather, we must celebrate it. We must be defiant in the face of the Devil and those who follow in the wake of his forked tail. If all of England says that we are wrong, we must show them by our actions that we know we are right!'

'What actions dost thou speak of, Roger?'

'Jesus Christ died even before your grand-fathers' grandfathers were born, yet every day his priests re-enact His triumph over death. Why then, should we not re-enact our triumph over evil?'

'But how?'

'The Witch is dead – her body turned to ashes. But were she amongst us once more, would we not burn her again? And this is the message that we must proclaim to all who will listen. We will suffer – we will all become martyrs if need be, as

226

Tom and Harry Dimdyke will soon become martyrs – but we will not recant. We will never recant! And though those chosen to follow in the footsteps of Tom and Harry will have the greatest role to play, no one – from the tiniest child to the most aged amongst us – will be excluded. We all have our parts to play.'

'Dost thou see the chair, Mary Dimdyke?' asked the voice in the shadows.

How could she fail to see it, surrounded, as it was, by candles rendered down from sheep fat by the faithful? And how could she look at it – how could any of them look at it – without seeing Meg Ramsden sitting there, as she had sat there on the last day of her life?

'I s ... see it,' Mary said.

'And wilt thou now sit in that same seat, as it is written thou *must* sit?'

What choice did she have? she asked herself.

There had been those, over the years, who had fled the village. But what had become of them? They had been swallowed up by the wicked world outside – a world in which darkness was allowed to prevail because none of those who inhabited it had the courage to fight back. They had – so deep village rumour proclaimed – rolled around in the sinfulness of that world, and died in misery.

Sacrifices must be made – that was what

Roger Tollance had taught. And those who carried the blood of the Ramsdens and the Dimdykes must always pay the heaviest price.

'Wilt thou sit, Mary?' the voice asked again.

'I will s ... sit,' Mary replied.

She stepped between the candles, and lowered herself on to the chair. And immediately, as her own arms made contact with chair's arms, she felt a strange power – which both revolted and attracted – begin to flow into her.

She wanted to move, but she could not.

She wanted to say that this was all a mistake – but she knew that it was not possible for her to be right, and for generations of villagers to be wrong.

The man stepped from out of the shadows, and she could now see that it was Lou Moore – and that he was holding some kind of metal instrument in his hand.

'Wilt thou submit, Mary Dimdyke?' he demanded.

She lowered her head, so that her eyes fixed on the flagstones which made up the floor.

'I w ... will submit,' she said.

Twenty-Nine

It was the morning of the last full day before the Witch Burning, and a beautiful morning it was. The sky was blue, save for a few of those tiny, fluffy clouds which always rush about trying to look busy on even the slightest excuse of a breeze. In the fields rabbits scuttled and hares lazed, while up above them skylarks and swallows swooped and glided. Gorse popped, and buttercups basked in the sunshine. Insects chirped cheerfully and even the croaking frogs managed to give the impression that they were glad to be alive. There was a feeling of total well-being in all the air which surrounded Hallerton, though none of it, of course, dared to enter the village itself.

Mary Dimdyke sat on her orange crate, watching her brother at work on the Witch. Today, despite the mild weather, she was wearing a knitted woollen cap on her head. It was the same cap – they *said* – that Roger Tollance himself had commissioned all those years ago.

'*For thou must go out into the fields and find the ewe which is the whitest of the white,*' he had told the village women. '*And from the wool that thou obtainest, thou must knit the cap that the virgin shall wear.*'

Could it really *still* be the same cap? Mary wondered. Could it actually have survived that long?

Yes! she decided, answering her own question. In this village, it could! But not by magic, as outsiders might think. If it had survived, it had done so because the collective mind of the village had *willed* it to.

The cap itched. She could have removed it if she'd wished. Because even though this was the most restricted of all societies, just about to enter the most restrictive of all its cycles, there existed no rule – amazingly enough – which said she *had* to wear it.

Yet despite the fact that she could have shed it with one rapid movement of her hand and arm, she did not. She couldn't – somehow – bring herself to.

Was it shame that prevented her taking off the cap? she asked herself.

If it was, it was shame without cause – for despite her proclaiming that she had submitted willingly, it had not been her choice.

Besides, shame was something the villagers had been told they should *never* feel. If they did what they should do – what they had to do – how could there be any shame at all?

Yet shame there had been, she thought.

Doris Raby had felt shame.

Beth Thompson had felt shame.

Her brother, Wilf, did not know about Doris and Beth. She should not have known about them herself until she was older. But she was a woman, and women shared their secrets, even when they were not supposed to.

Mary scratched her head through the cap.

'Try not to think about it, our Mary,' Wilf said, looking up briefly from his work.

'Who's speakin'?' Mary demanded.

'I am.'

'An' who are you? The Witch Maker? Or my brother?'

'Your brother,' Wilf said. 'I'll always be your brother, Mary, whatever happens.'

'You weren't my brother last night!' the girl said with a sudden fury. 'You could have stopped it if you'd wanted to!'

'I tried,' Wilf said. 'You heard me.'

'You should have tried harder!'

Wilf shook his head. 'It wouldn't have done any good. I *used* to think it might stop one day – but I don't believe it any more.'

'How can you say that?' Mary asked.

'Because it's obvious,' Wilf said, angry himself now. 'If it wasn't obvious, I wouldn't be the Witch Maker, would I?'

Monika Paniatowski stood in the Meg

Ramsden Museum, enthralled by the portrait of Meg.

There was real character – real force – in that face, she thought.

And though there was very little similarity between herself and the woman who had been burned for witchcraft – apart from their both having blonde hair – she liked to think that when she looked in the mirror she could see a similar strength and determination to Meg's staring back at her.

But were there other ways in which she was just like Meg, too?

'*If Meg had been able to fulfil herself in a way most other women did, she may have been less interested in money and adultery,*' Tyndale, the 'so-called' local historian had said the previous night. '*I believe the contemporary phrase for what she did is "displacement activity".*'

'Displacement activity!' Paniatowski repeated to herself, with disgust.

How like a man to produce an impressive-sounding phrase to explain away something he didn't even begin to comprehend. Only a bird with damaged wings could possibly know what it felt like to no longer be able to fly. And only a woman who was brought up believing that it was natural to have children could know what it was like to find out that, in her case, that simply wasn't true!

There have been so many changes in her life

232

*recently. She is a WPC. She's finding it tough –
very tough – but she is confident that, in the end,
she will succeed. And she seems to have overcome
her aversion to men, an aversion dating back to
a dark period in her childhood that she doesn't
even want to think about now.*

She's dating a man. She's even sleeping *with
him. She doesn't love him, but she likes him –
and the sex is good. And then one morning, she
realizes that her monthly period is several days
late.*

*Could she be pregnant? She must be! She waits
for the shock – the horror – to hit her. But it never
comes. Instead she is consumed by a calm which
is almost beautiful.*

*She considers the implications. She will have to
leave the police – give up the job which she is
learning to love. She will have to endure the
pointing and the scorn which all unmarried
mothers must endure. But she doesn't care about
that! She really doesn't care!*

*She goes to the doctor's surgery and submits to
all the usual tests. A few days pass, and she goes
to see him again. He looks serious.*

Well, Mrs Paniatowski ... he begins.

Miss *Paniatowski, she corrects him firmly.*

*Well, Miss Paniatowski, he continues, I have to
tell you that you're not pregnant –* and it's
highly unlikely that you ever will be.

*At first she is totally devastated, but then she
tells herself that she will soon get over it. She and
her mother survived years of being chased round*

233

Europe during the bloodiest war the world had ever seen. Compared to that, this bit of news is a doddle to handle.

She throws herself into her work. Her arrest rate is the highest on the Force. She is promoted. She quickly becomes the only female detective sergeant in the whole of Lancashire. And there are the affairs. Plenty of them. She is careful to promise nothing to the men she goes to bed with. She holds out no hope for them that there might be a longer-term relationship, and if it cuts them up when she drops them, then they only have themselves to blame. And then she falls for a colleague – something she'd sworn she'd never do.

And not just any colleague.

A man with a wife.

A blind wife.

A man with a baby.

And though he may think that it is he who has seduced her, she knows that it is she who has seduced him.

Monika gazed up at Meg's portrait again.

'It's not the same at all,' she told the painted woman gazing complacently down at her.

It wasn't even close, she argued to herself.

Meg had taken her rage at her infertility out on the only world she knew – had revenged herself for her fate by making others suffer. She, on the other hand, had chosen to do something positive with the freed energy that her infertility had brought her. She served justice. And not for the sake of the power it gave her over others, but because justice needed to be served.

Falling for Bob Rutter was never intended to be a punishment on his wife, who, despite being blind, had been able to do something she could not do herself. How could it have been, when she had gone out of her way to make sure that Maria Rutter never learned about the affair?

She was not guilty, she told herself.

She was weak, as humans often are.

She was sometimes foolish – which made her far from unique.

But she was *not* evil. She had earned herself no place at the stake, and if hell existed, she had every hope of avoiding it.

So that was it! That was settled! And now it was settled, she could leave the portrait of Meg Ramsden behind her, and go about her work.

Yet still she had an uneasy feeling that everything was not quite as clear-cut as she was trying to assure herself it was.

She opened the door of small chill museum – a museum which had seemed to grow ever more chilly and constricted as she had run her life quickly through her mind.

She stepped out into the light and breathed the gentle morning air deeply into her lungs.

And then she saw it! Her car! Her precious

little MGA, for which she would have sacri-ficed almost any other comfort to maintain.

She'd had it sent up from Whitebridge the day before, but now she realized that had been a mistake.

True, it was parked just where she had left it – outside the museum – but there was no air left in the tyres. Worse still, someone had desecrated it! Defiled it! The bright-red bonnet gleamed in the sunshine, but that only served to highlight the two words which had been crudely scratched into the cherished paintwork in letters a foot high.

Paniatowski read the words once, twice, a third time. Her heart was beating furiously. She found herself wondering – irrationally – whether whoever had committed this act of vandalism had also been able to read her mind as she stood in front of the portrait of Meg Ramsden.

She wouldn't cry, she promised. She *refused* to cry.

She took another deep breath and forced herself to look at the bonnet again. She had hoped the words would have miraculously disappeared in the few seconds it had taken her to fight off the tears. But they hadn't gone. They were still there for her – and the rest of the world – to see.

One of the words was 'SLUT'.

The other was 'HARLOT'.

Thirty

Anger did not come anywhere near describing her boss's mood, Monika Paniatowski thought, as she did her best to keep up with Woodend's long, furious strides through the village. The Chief Inspector had gone beyond that. He was like a boiler which had built up so much pressure that it was on the point of exploding.

'It doesn't matter, sir,' she said breathlessly.

Woodend looked down at her. 'Shut up, Monika!' he said.

'It's only a car, when all's said and done. The insurance will cover the cost of respraying it.'

'It isn't the damage to the bloody car that I'm worried about,' Woodend told her.

They reached the Witch Maker's barn. Woodend, not standing on ceremony, pushed the heavy door open as if it weighed nothing at all, and stepped inside.

Wilf Dimdyke was standing over his bench, just as Woodend had expected him to be. Tom Dimdyke was watching his son work, and had an expression on his face which could only have been described as awed.

Tom swung round to see who had dared to intrude on his son's task. When he realized it was Woodend, he scowled. 'Do you have a search warrant to come in here?' he asked.

'You're all for hidin' behind the law when it suits you, aren't you?' Woodend asked mockingly. 'It's only when it gets in the way of what you want to do that you decide it doesn't really matter any more.'

'If you don't have a warrant I'll—' Tom Dimdyke began.

'If I don't have a warrant, you'll *what?*' Woodend interrupted him jeeringly. 'Call your solicitor? No, you can't do that, can you, because you don't have one. Because lawyers are outsiders, an' you'd never allow an outsider to poke his nose in the affairs of your precious village.'

'I—'

'So you'll have to find some other way to get at me, won't you, *Mr* Dimdyke? An' maybe this time you'll have the guts to go for me directly, instead of attacking my sergeant.'

'I don't know what you're talkin' about,' Tom Dimdyke said.

And he didn't! Paniatowski thought.

He really didn't!

It was obvious from his face that he had no idea of what was going on, and if Woodend would only calm down for a second, he would see it too.

But Woodend had no intention of calming down.

'What did you hope to achieve?' he demanded. 'Did you really think a bit of vandalism would have us slinkin' back to Whitebridge with our tails between our legs?'

'Vandalism?' Tom Dimdyke repeated.

'Even with your limited vocabulary, you had the choice of thousands of words you could have chosen to scratch on to the bonnet,' Woodend said scathingly. 'But what *did* you choose? "Slut" an' "Harlot". You like to fight dirty, don't you? Well, that's fine with me, because I can fight dirty too.'

'You're makin' a mistake,' Tom Dimdyke said.

'No, you're the one who's made the mistake,' Woodend countered. 'Because Monika's not just any old bobby. She's *my* sergeant – an' I'd go to the wall for her, if I had to.'

'I didn't do it,' Tom Dimdyke said firmly. 'I might have done – if I'd thought it would help – but I didn't.'

'Bollocks!' Woodend strode to the door, then swung round and pointed an accusing finger at Dimdyke. 'I'll have you for this, you bastard!' he promised. 'If it's the last thing I do, I'll have you for it.'

They had not gone more than a few yards from the barn when they saw a red-faced Constable Thwaites coming towards them at as much of a trot as his corpulent frame allowed.

'Well, if it isn't the friendly local bobby,' Woodend said. 'But just whose friend are you, Thwaites? The law's? Or Tom Dimdyke's?'

'Tom didn't damage the sergeant's car, sir,' Thwaites said, gasping for breath.

'Of course he didn't,' Woodend agreed sarcastically. 'He's a pillar of the community. Bloody hell, he *is* the community, as far as I can tell.'

'You've got it all wrong, sir.'

'That's what everybody keeps tellin' me. Are you sayin' that Tom Dimdyke *wouldn't* vandalize Monika's car if it suited his purpose?'

'No, sir. I'm not sayin' he *wouldn't* – I'm just sayin' that he *didn't*. I'm the local bobby. I'd have known if he'd done it.'

'It's a funny thing, selective knowledge,' Woodend mused. 'I ask you if Harry Dimdyke had a bit on the side, an' you've no idea. But when it comes to the question of Monika's car, you're absolutely certain that his brother Tom is in the clear.'

'I'm telling you the truth, sir.'

'Then who *did* do it?'

'I don't know.'

'Find out!'

'It's not that simple.'

'*Make* it that simple,' Woodend told him. 'I'm tired of bein' buggered about by the people in this bloody village. I want answers – an' more specifically, I want answers from *you*. So within the hour I'll expect a piece of paper in my hand. An' written on it there'd better be one of two things – the name of the guilty party, or your resignation.'

Thwaites gulped. 'You can't ... you can't force me to resign if I don't want to, sir.'

'But I can, laddie. An' if you won't go, you can be pushed. There's a couple of stolen radios sittin' in the boot of my car. I was goin' to hand them in, but I never got round to it. Now I've got a better idea. I might just find them in the Hallerton police house.'

'But—'

'But nothin'! There's only two fellers know about them – me an' the toe-rag who nicked them. An' he's not going to open his mouth, now is he?'

'But Sergeant Paniatowski's just heard you say—'

'Sergeant Paniatowski will back me up, like she always does. Isn't that true, Monika?'

'I see what you tell me to see, and hear what you want me to hear,' Paniatowski

241

confirmed.

'Besides,' Woodend continued, giving Thwaites what – in other circumstances – could have been called a smile of encouragement, 'it's not a Herculean task I'm settin' you. Any local bobby worth his salt should be able to find out what I want to know in half the time I'm allowin' you.'

'But, sir—'

'Do it!' Woodend said, and then his mouth snapped shut with all the finality of a steel trap.

The walk back through the village calmed Woodend down a little, but it was not until he spotted the old man with the check cap and the muffler that the red mist finally cleared away, and he began to see things through a policeman's eyes again.

The old man had seen him, too, but age had slowed down his reactions, and he was still contemplating what avenue of escape to choose when the Chief Inspector and the sergeant drew level with him.

'Good mornin', sir,' Woodend said pleasantly. 'Do you happen to know the time?'

The old man's mouth fell open, but he seemed to have difficulty getting any words out.

'About half past ten, would you say?' Woodend asked.

'Yes, I ... I think it is about that.'

'Which is just when the pubs round here open their doors. An' by some happy quirk of fate, we're not more than a few steps away from the Black Bull, which is one of them pubs. I think we should take advantage of those two facts, an' go have a drink. Don't you?'

'I'd ... I'd rather not,' the old man said.

'An' *I'd* rather we did,' Woodend replied, putting his hand on the old man's shoulder and gently steering him towards the pub door.

Thirty-One

Hettie Todd was sitting on the steps of her caravan, looking across the fairground at the Big Wheel.

It had taken a long time to put the Wheel up. It always did. And when the carnival was over, it would take a long time to take it down again. Which was why the men in charge of its construction and dismantling were famed for their complaining.

'It's a grand little earner,' they'd admit, 'but then all the attractions are grand little earners – and most of them don't take *half* the effort. We'd be better off without it.'

They didn't mean a word of what they said, Hettie thought. If there'd been a move afoot to scrap the Wheel, they'd have been the first to oppose it. Because they knew – as everybody else who worked for the fair knew – that without the Big Wheel they had nothing.

It wasn't just that the Wheel towered over the surrounding area like a colossus. It wasn't that it brought people scurrying to the fairground even before it had opened. It wasn't even that at night, when it was lit up, it was pure magic. There was something more basic – something almost *primeval* – about it.

The Wheel was the heart of the fairground, and just as it revolved itself, so everything else revolved around it. It was like life – it took you on an exciting journey, let you see the wider world, and then returned you to the ground from whence you came.

'You're turning into a bit of a poet on the quiet,' Hettie rebuked herself, 'and there's no room for poets at the fair. Because the fair *is* poetry.'

She grinned. She was getting worse and worse, and if it went on, they'd be sending in the men in white coats to calm her down and then take her away to a nice padded cell.

She watched as two people walked slowly up to the Big Wheel, then came to a halt in front of it. She recognized them both. One was her mother. The other was the handsome Irishman whom her mother was always trying to persuade her to get friendlier with.

Hettie sometimes thought that the only reason Zelda wanted to see her daughter paired off with Pat was so she could be close to him herself. But, she had to admit, the two of them didn't seem to be getting on well at that moment. Quite the contrary, in fact.

Zelda was standing rigid, with her hands

on her hips. Pat kept shifting position and stance, now looking apologetic, now defiant.

Hettie took a sudden decision – one she would not have believed herself capable of the day before.

She would spy on her own mother! Since Zelda seemed unwilling to tell her what was going on, she would just have to find out for herself.

She should feel guilty about her decision, she thought – she'd fully *expected* to feel guilty. Yet she didn't. Perhaps the reason was that there was a part of her which recognized she needed to know what was going on – perhaps a part of her which even believed that it was *vital* she found out.

The old man wrapped his hands around his glass of Guinness, though whether he thought he was protecting his drink – or his drink was protecting him – was difficult to say.

'It's quite a novelty to be stalked by old-aged pensioners,' Woodend said jovially. 'I can't remember anythin' quite like it ever happenin' before.'

'I wasn't stalkin' you,' the old man protested.

'No, you weren't,' Woodend agreed. 'In fact, you've done your best to steer clear of me. But at least one of your mates has been stalkin' my sergeant. Now why do you think

men were sitting.

As Woodend turned his attention back to Paniatowski, there was a broad smile on his face.

'Well, that's one mystery cleared up, at least,' he said.

Thirty-Two

It had taken Hettie five minutes to get to the far side of the Big Wheel without being noticed by either Pat or her mother. She'd been hoping that once she'd reached the point she was at now, she'd have been able to hear everything that the two of them were saying. And maybe she could have – if they'd been shouting at each other through megaphones. But they weren't. However emotional their conversation might be, they were arguing quietly, and she wasn't getting a word.

She sighed.

Well, there was nothing for it but to risk exposure, she told herself, though she could only guess what her mother would say if she caught her at it.

She reached the rim of the Wheel, then took one more cautious step, so she was now on the same side of it as her mother and the Irishman. She saw that they were looking intently at each other. That was a good thing. As long as they stayed like that, they were unlikely to spot her.

She strained her ears, and was rewarded with the sounds of a conversation which was just about as loud as if it were coming from a radio in another room.

'Are you crazy, Pat?' her mother was asking. 'Have you completely lost your mind?'

Calhoun shrugged. 'We've been through this a dozen times, Zelda,' he said. 'What's the point of coverin' the same ground again?'

'Who do you think you are?'

'I'm—'

'Are you a bank manager? Or a teacher?'

'No, I'm—'

'You're a fairground worker, and you're Irish. That means you're doubly suspicious. That means you have to make twice the effort to keep your nose clean that anybody who sleeps under a roof would have to make.'

'Some risks *are* worth takin',' Calhoun replied. 'If they're for you! If they're for Hettie.'

If they're for *me*? Hettie thought, feeling her heart suddenly start to beat a little faster.

What risk – what possible risk – could Pat have run for *her*?

'Once Harry Dimdyke was dead, it would have been better to have done nothing,' Zelda said. 'It would have been better to lie low, and hope the whole thing would blow over.'

'But I could see it wasn't *goin'* to blow

over,' Calhoun argued. 'How could it, after the murder? How could it, with that sharp copper from Whitebridge here, askin' all his questions? He'll uncover the truth. He's bound to – unless I can do something to stop him.'

For a moment, Hettie contemplated striding up to the two of them and demanding to know what the hell was going on. Then she saw the man in blue who was making a beeline for them, and decided that her best course of action would be to beat a hasty retreat.

Woodend took a sip of his pint, then glanced down at his watch. Fifty minutes had ticked by since he'd issued his ultimatum to Constable Thwaites. That left only another ten.

What would he do if Thwaites either refused to meet his demands or was unable to? He certainly wasn't going to fit the constable up on criminal charges, as he'd threatened. So he'd lose face – he'd lose some of what little authority he seemed to have in this village – and that was fatal for a bobby in charge of a serious investigation.

He asked himself why he'd taken the risk.

Was it that the obscenities scrawled on Monika's car had got to him almost as much as they'd got to her?

It had to be. There was no other explanation.

He wondered when it was that he'd grown almost as fond of Monika as he was of his own daughter. But such speculation was pointless. What had happened had happened. He *did* feel protective towards the woman – and he'd just have to learn to live with it.

The pub door opened, and Mary Dimdyke stormed in. Her face was grim. Even so, her expression might have been softened by her wonderful golden hair, had she not chosen to tuck it all under the plain woollen cap she was wearing.

She walked directly over to Woodend and Paniatowski's table, and glowered down at them.

'You're t ... tryin' to blame it on my d ... dad, aren't you?' she demanded. 'You're t ... tryin' to say that he d ... damaged the car.'

'An' didn't he?' Woodend asked mildly.

'No, he bl ... bloody didn't.'

'He's been doin' his best to obstruct the investigation ever since we got here,' Woodend pointed out. 'You've seen him do it yourself. An' let me ask you one question, Mary. If your dad didn't do it, then who did?'

'When I first saw you, I th ... thought you might be different,' Mary said. 'I th ... thought *you* might understand. But you don't. You're like everybody else who c ... comes in from the outside. You always blame

253

the D ... Dimdykes.'

'Do we?'

'You d ... didn't understand about Harry an' Tom. How could you have, when you'd never l ... lived in this village? Yet you c ... came in, an' you took them away to Lancaster Gaol – an' you h ... hanged them!'

'That was over three hundred years ago.'

'It was *y* ... *yesterday*. An' it will be *t* ... *t* ... *tomorrow*. You'll never stop, because you d ... don't understand us.' Mary paused to catch her breath. 'I used to think my dad was wrong. I used to think it was all pointless. But he said that once I'd made my s ... sacrifice, I'd see what it was all about. An' he was right! I do!'

'What sacrifice?' Paniatowski asked.

'None of your bl ... bloody business!' Mary Dimdyke told her.

But Woodend thought he already knew. He was thinking back to the Witch Burning he had seen as a young man – to the horribly realistic Witch and her beautiful blonde hair.

'Take your cap off, Mary,' he said.

'Why sh ... should I?'

'Why shouldn't you? Unless, of course, you're ashamed.'

Mary reached up, and snatched the cap free. There was hardly any hair under it. Her head looked like a wheat field just after the harvest.

The girl stood there for a moment, staring

254

at him defiantly. Then the mask cracked, tears began to run down her face, and she turned and fled.

'Dear God, what kind of place *is* this?' Paniatowski said, more to herself than to Woodend.

Nine more minutes ticked by on the pub clock.

Thwaites wasn't going to come through with the information, Woodend thought. He'd been a fool to ever imagine the local constable would. It simply wasn't possible to put pressure on a man who was already burdened beyond endurance by the weight of history.

The phone behind the bar rang, and the landlord picked it up.

'Yes?' he said. 'Yes, he's here.' He held out the receiver across the counter. 'It's for you,' he told Woodend. 'Constable Thwaites.'

The Chief Inspector picked up the phone. 'Where are you?' he demanded.

'I'm at the police house, sir.'

'Why didn't you come to the pub, like I told you to?'

'Because I didn't want to leave my prisoner unattended.'

'Your prisoner!' Woodend repeated. 'What prisoner?'

'The bugger who vandalized Sergeant Paniatowski's car. I arrested him not ten minutes ago.'

Thirty-Three

Constable Thwaites met Woodend at his front gate. The local bobby was looking inordinately pleased with himself, the Chief Inspector thought. It was as if – after years of merely *playing* the part – he was finally coming to learn what it felt like to be a real policeman.

'I've put the suspect in the detention cell, sir,' Thwaites said.

'I didn't know there even *was* a detention cell in the police house,' Woodend replied.

'Well, there isn't exactly,' Thwaites admitted. 'I suppose what it is really is just a storeroom. But it's only got one small window, which makes it almost as good as a cell. And I've put a table an' chairs in it, so you can sit down while you're interrogatin' the prisoner.'

He really was like a kid with a new toy, Woodend thought. And it suddenly occurred to him that he might have hit on the big problem in this village – that it had never developed because it had never allowed itself to play with the new toys that the advancing world offered it.

Thwaites led him into the house and down a corridor. He stopped at a door at the end of it, and extracted a set of keys from his pocket with great solemnity. Then he opened the door and stepped to one side in order to allow Woodend to enter the 'detention cell' first.

The normal contents of the room – temporary traffic signs, bollards and posters warning of the dangers of foot and mouth disease – had been hastily pushed to the edges, and in the centre was a battered table and two chairs. Sitting on one of the chairs was a well-built young man with red hair.

'Name?' Woodend said.

'Patrick Michael Calhoun.'

'Hang about a minute,' Woodend told him. 'That's not a local accent you've got, is it?'

The Irishman gave him a strained smile. 'Well spotted,' he said, trying to sound more relaxed and at ease than he obviously felt.

'So where *are* you from?'

'County Cork.'

'An' you don't live in this village?'

'Never been here in my life until a couple of days ago.'

With growing fury, Woodend turned to Thwaites. 'Outside, Constable!' he said. 'Now!'

'Sir?'

'I'll talk to you out-bloody-side.'

The two men stepped into the corridor, and Woodend closed the door behind them. 'Is this some kind of joke?' he demanded. 'Or do you just think that I'm so bloody thick that you can fob me off with anythin' you feel like.'

'I've no idea what you're talkin' about, sir,' Thwaites protested.

'Whoever vandalized my sergeant's car was local, an' did it for a specific purpose. What possible reason could this Calhoun feller have for doin' it? Come to that, how did he even know the car belonged to Sergeant Paniatowski?'

'Maybe he'd been watchin' her.'

'An' why should he have been doin' that?'

A slight, almost superior, smile crossed Thwaites' lips. 'Because if he's the murderer, he'll have been followin' anybody involved in the investigation as closely as he could.'

He was right, Woodend thought. The bloody local yokel bobby was right. It was perfectly possible that there was some connection between what had happened to Paniatowski's car and the murder.

So why hadn't he come to the same conclusion himself? Because, he supposed, he was angry – angry about what had been done to Monika, angry about what had been done to Mary Dimdyke. And his brain didn't do its best work under those conditions.

He forced himself to focus.

'Is there any special reason you've pulled this particular lad in, Constable?' he asked. 'Or were you just workin' on the theory that anybody with red hair an' an Irish accent is automatically a villain?'

'It was certainly his red hair that put me on to him in the first place, sir,' Thwaites said.

'Would you care to explain that?'

'Several people in the village noticed a red-headed man close to the museum at roughly the time of the attack on Sergeant Pania-towski's car. One of them even saw him bending over the bonnet, though he couldn't swear that the man was tryin' to do it any damage. Well, nobody in Hallerton has red hair, so I went up to the funfair, an' talked to the manager. A Mr Masters, as it turned out.'

'I know his bloody name,' Woodend said, bad-temperedly. 'Go on with what you were sayin'.'

'He – that's Mr Masters – told me the only redhead he's got workin' for him is this Calhoun feller, an' so I brought him in.'

'Did you caution him?'

'Yes, sir.'

'An' what did you say?'

'That I was arrestin' him on the charge of damaging a red MGA, licence number...' Thwaites pulled his notebook out of his pocket and read the licence number out. 'That he was not obliged to say anythin' but anythin' he did say would be taken down an' might be used in evidence against him.'

'An' that's *all* you said.'

'Yes, sir.'

'You didn't give him any more particulars?'

'No, definitely not, sir.'

'An' he said?'

'Not a sausage.'

'Well, I'd better go straight back in there an' talk to him, hadn't I?' Woodend said.

He opened the door again, and stepped into the storeroom. He didn't invite the constable to join him, and Thwaites made no move to follow.

'Ever been in trouble with the police before, son?' he asked the man sitting at the table.

'I'm not entirely sure I'm in trouble with the police now,' the Irishman replied.

Woodend sat down. 'You do know what you've been arrested for, don't you?'

'The copper who brought me in mentioned somethin' about vandalizin' a car in the village.'

'Not just any car. A bright-red MGA. A classic, in its way. The owner's very cut up about it.'

Calhoun nodded. 'I can imagine. But there are worse things you can do to people than vandalize their cars.'

'Like what?' Woodend asked, sounding genuinely interested.

'Like...' Calhoun began, then, realizing he was in danger of saying too much, shook his head and fell silent.

'Like what?' Woodend persisted. 'What's the matter, lad? Afraid to give me an example?'

The remark stung. 'Like ... like takin' advantage of them,' Calhoun said. 'Like really hurtin' them.'

'So you're usin' that as an *excuse*, are you?'

'It's no excuse.'

'I can just see you in court, lookin' up at the bench and tellin' the Beak there's lots worse you could have done,' Woodend said. '"I could have broken her arm, Your Honour",' he continued, in a deliberately bad Irish accent. '"I could have smashed her jaw. So why don't you let me off with a caution for just *scratchin'* her car?"'

Calhoun let another slight smile play on his lips. 'You're very good at this, so you are,' he said.

'Aye, I know,' Woodend agreed. 'It's my job. I've done hundreds of interrogations in my time. But there are a couple of things which have got me puzzled about this particular one.'

'An' what might they be?'

'First off, you're not reactin' like the usual suspect does.'

'Am I not?'

'No. There's two ways he can go, you see –

the loud way an' the quiet way. The loud way is he protests his innocence at the top of his voice. You've not done that, have you?'

'No, I haven't. An' what's the quiet way?'

'The quiet way is to mumble that yes, he did do it, he's never done anythin' like it before, he doesn't know what came over him, an' if I'm prepared to turn a blind eye to it this time, he'll never do it again. But you haven't tried *that* either. I wonder why.'

'Maybe I think there's no point in pro-testin' my innocence in front of an English policeman.'

'Oh, I get it,' Woodend said. 'You're playin' the Irish card – all English bobbies are bastards, so they'll bang up any poor bloody Irishman whether he's guilty or not.'

'It's been known to happen,' Calhoun pointed out.

'You're right,' Woodend agreed. 'But it's not happenin' here. All I want is the truth.'

'You want to know if I did it?'

'I want to know *why* you did it.'

'An' if I said I'd never touched your sergeant's car? Would you believe me, an' let me go?'

Woodend shook his head, almost despair-ingly. 'Grow up, lad. We both know you're guilty. So why don't we just get the for-malities over as quickly an' painlessly as possible?'

Calhoun folded his arms. 'I have nothin'

more to say.'

'Right, that's it, then,' Woodend said.

'What's it?'

'If you've no more to say, then I've no more time to waste buggerin' about tryin' to get you to say it. I'm investigatin' a murder, an' this is no more than a local crime. I'll get the constable to make arrangements to hand you over to the bobbies in Lancaster.'

Calhoun laughed.

'Did I say somethin' funny?' Woodend asked.

'You were doin' very well, but now you've reverted to type,' Pat Calhoun said.

'Have I? In what way?'

'In the way you make your threats.'

'I wasn't aware I had made any threats,' Woodend said innocently.

'Oh, but you did, an' you were. You said you weren't one of them coppers who fits up a feller just because he's Irish, an' then you tell me you're goin' to hand me over to just the sort of coppers who will. Is this the point at which I break down in gratitude at you bein' so understandin', and confess all?'

'You've got it wrong, lad,' Woodend told him. 'We *might* both be playin' games here – as you seem to think we are – but we're certainly not playin' the *same* game. I meant what I said about havin' no more time to waste, an' I meant what I said about handin' you over to Lancaster. You don't have to believe me – you probably don't – but in a few hours' time, when you're sittin' in a cell in Lancaster Gaol, you'll be forced to accept the fact that I was tellin' the truth.'

The Chief Inspector stood up, and walked over to the door.

'What about the other thing?' Calhoun asked, intrigued.

'What other thing?'

'You said you'd done hundreds of interrogations, but a couple of things were puzzlin' you about this particular one. The first was that I was neither shoutin' my innocence nor whisperin' my guilt. What was the second?'

Woodend thought about it for a moment. 'Oh aye,' he said finally. 'I was wonderin' whatever possessed you to scratch the word "prostitute" across the front of my sergeant's car.'

'It wasn't "prostitute". It was...'

'"Harlot",' Woodend completed, when it was plain that Calhoun was not about to. 'I know. A quaint, old-fashioned term, isn't it? Do they still use it down in County Cork?'

'I wouldn't know,' Calhoun said, doing his best to stage a recovery, but not making a very good job of it.

'I'll just bet you wouldn't,' Woodend replied. 'An' incidentally, Mr Calhoun, it wasn't me who first mentioned the fact that the car in question belonged to my sergeant.'

'Wasn't it?'

'No, it wasn't. I was very careful when I was talkin' about the owner. All I said was "she". Yet you knew I was talkin' about Monika Paniatowski. Now where would an innocent man – who'd never set foot in the village until he was arrested – have got that particular piece of information from?'

Thirty-Four

Monika Paniatowski was walking round and round the edge of the Green. There was no particular reason for it. She wasn't there to observe the way in which the crime scene was being destroyed in order that the festival could take place – though that process was well under way, with uniformed constables removing the official barriers and villagers replacing them with barriers of their own. Nor was she there in the hope that her proximity to the spot on which the murder took place would stimulate her mind towards new lines of investigation. She was walking because she could think of nothing else to do – because since those words had appeared on her car, her mind had been in complete turmoil and she had begun to question the whole purpose of her life.

Under normal circumstances, she would almost immediately have spotted that she was being followed. Under *these* circumstances, it was little short of a miracle that she noticed it even on her third perambulation around the Green. But spot it she did, and *when* she did, her brain shifted a gear and she became *DS* Paniatowski again.

She stopped and turned around. The woman who was on her tail was in her late-thirties to early-forties, she guessed. She was no longer the slim creature she might once have been, yet, from the way she carried herself, it was plain she had no bitter regrets about the passing of her youth. Her face, though incredibly strained at that moment, looked both kind and understanding. Paniatowski caught herself starting to think that if she were in the market for a mother, this woman would be a very good choice.

The woman stopped when Paniatowski did. For a moment she hovered uncertainly, then she took a deep breath and closed the gap between them.

'Why were you following me?' Paniatowski demanded.

'I suppose I was getting up the nerve to talk to you.'

'What about?'

The woman hesitated again, then blurted out, 'Could Pat Calhoun go to prison?'

'It's possible,' Paniatowski replied, non-committally.

'Just for damaging a car.'

Not *a* car, Paniatowski though. Not *just* a car. *My* car. My precious little MGA.

'You can go to prison for stealing a sandwich, if your attitude's wrong,' she said. 'And his attitude is *definitely* wrong.'

'How?'

'We need to know why he did it, and he won't tell us.'

'No,' the other woman agreed. 'He wouldn't.' She paused for a moment. 'You're the injured party here, aren't you? What would happen if you dropped the charges?'

'He'd be released.'

'Then couldn't you do that? Couldn't you go to your boss and say you're dropping the charges?'

'Who are you?' Paniatowski asked.

'I ... Does it really matter?'

Paniatowski nodded. 'You want a favour. I need to know who's asking for it.'

'I'm ... I'm Zelda Todd. I work on the fairground. I'm in charge of the coconut shy.'

'And what's Pat Calhoun to you?'

'Nothing.'

'Nothing?'

'I mean ... I like him a great deal. And I'd be very happy if he and my daughter ... if they...'

'Is that why you want me to drop the charges? Because you think he'd make you a good son-in-law?' Paniatowski asked, noting, as she spoke, that she almost sounded bitter.

'Pat didn't mean any harm,' Zelda Todd said.

'You try telling that to my poor little car,' Paniatowski responded.

268

The remark seemed to take the other woman genuinely by surprise. 'You talk about it as if you were in love with it,' she said.

Yes, I do, don't I? Monika thought. Maria Rutter has Bob, Zelda's daughter will probably eventually have Pat Calhoun, and I have a red MGA I can scarcely afford to run.

'Why *did* he do it?' she asked.

Zelda Todd thought for a moment. 'Have you ever seen a magic act in one of the fairground sideshows?' she asked.

'No, I don't think I have.'

'You're probably too young. They don't do much of that kind of thing nowadays. But twenty years ago, there were almost as many magicians working the fairgrounds as there were in the music halls.'

'I don't see where you're going with this.'

'The magician usually had a girl with him. She would be young, reasonably pretty, and would wear a costume so skimpy that most girls wouldn't even think of wearing it on the beach.'

'The beautiful assistant,' Paniatowski said, thinking of the fairground manager's words.

'That's right,' Zelda Todd agreed. 'The beautiful assistant. Why do you think she was there?'

'To help the magician with his tricks?' Paniatowski guessed. 'To add a bit of glamour to the show?'

'To distract!' Zelda Todd said. 'I was a beautiful assistant once – and that was my downfall.'

Zelda, only nineteen years old, and pretty as a picture, is standing on the rickety stage next to the Magnificent Antonio. Antonio – real name, Archibald Hicks – is fifty-three years old. He is long past his best as a magician, and – even more damaging – he has been drinking quite heavily before the show. He is going to fumble his tricks – she is sure of that – and if they are not to get booed off, she will have to work extra-hard tonight.

They are reaching the crucial point in the trick, the moment when Archibald-Antonio must accomplish a very complex sleight of hand, and the chances are that he'll mess it up. Zelda counts slowly to three, then takes a step forward. It is only a slight step, yet she manages to imbue it with a sexuality made all the more potent by the fact that she is still so obviously a teenage virgin. The eyes of the men in the audience are all on her, as she'd known they would be, and the eyes of the women are all fixed, resentfully, on the men. Perhaps the kids will see Archibald-Antonio fumble the trick, but kids don't matter, because nobody will listen to them anyway.

Archibald-Antonio has got through the difficult moment. Zelda gives one more little shimmer – her young breasts wobbling invitingly – then steps back to her original position. The magician bows, the hayseed audience applauds – and Zelda begins to feel a pair of eyes burning into her.

The next trick is so simple that even a drunk like Archibald can perform it without a hitch. Zelda lets her eyes wander, and locates the man who has been looking at her so intently. He is older than she is – but not that much older. He is stocky and not particularly handsome, yet there is a power emanating from him which quite over-whelms her. She already has a boyfriend – Stan Dawkins – and though they have not yet pro-gressed beyond the slap and tickle stage, she knows that she loves him and will eventually allow him to go further. So she has no interest in any other man. No interest at all. And yet ... and yet she still feels herself irresistibly drawn to this stranger.

Archibald-Antonio produces a scabby pigeon, masquerading as a pure white dove, from inside his top hat. The unsophisticated audience claps furiously.

The man looks down at his watch, flashes the fingers of his right hand three times, and then points to the area beyond the roundabout. The message is clear. She is to meet him in fifteen minutes at the edge of the fairground. She doesn't want to – she knows she shouldn't – but she finds herself nodding her head anyway.

'Your downfall?' Paniatowski repeated. 'Just what do you mean by that?'

271

'We're not here to talk about me,' Zelda tells her. 'Pat is the one who matters now.'

'Then tell me about Pat,' Paniatowski said. 'Tell me about the distraction he hoped to create by attacking my car. What was he trying to distract us *from*?'

'I can't tell you that,' Zelda said, still hoping that she could find a way to keep the past buried.

'Why can't you?' Paniatowski demanded.

'Because – don't you see – if I tell you, then Pat might as well not have done it at all.'

'If you won't talk, then I can't help you,' Paniatowski said. 'But perhaps Pat will talk – when he's been in gaol for a few days. Of course, by then we might not need the information, so it won't do his case any good anyway.'

A feeling of unworthiness began to fill her even as she was speaking the words. She was using a trick of the trade which was perfectly legitimate with hardened criminals, she told herself. But what possible justification could she have for employing it with this obviously well-meaning middle-aged woman?

'Please!' Zelda Todd said.

Paniatowski steeled herself. She was dealing with a murder case here – possibly even *two* murder cases. There was no room for sentiment. No room for understanding.

'I have to know,' she said.

'All right,' Zelda Todd agreed reluctantly.

'But you must promise me you won't draw the wrong conclusions.'

'I won't draw the wrong conclusions,' Paniatowski promised, adding a mental note to herself that Zelda might well find the *right* conclusions just as unpalatable.

Thirty-Five

Zelda meets the man at the edge of the fair-ground, just beyond the reach of the lights. She can't see him very clearly, but he has made such a big impression on her already that she can picture him even in the dark.

'I was watchin' you up on that stage,' he says.

She giggles. 'I know you were.'

'I can have any woman in the village I want, you know. But the one I want is you.'

He obviously means it as a compliment, but she is not flattered. Stan may be uneducated but he is not crude like this man is, and she is starting to feel sorry that she came.

'I have to be getting back,' she says.

'What do you mean?' he asks, obviously puzzled.

'You asked me to come and see you, and I have,' she says, noting the tremble in her voice. 'Now I have to be getting back.'

'You think I wanted you to come here just to talk?' he asks.

'I didn't know what you wanted,' she says.

She's lying. She knew what he wanted and thought she didn't mind. But now she does. Now

274

she minds very much.

'Come here!' *he says.*

It is the voice of a man used to being obeyed, and despite herself, she takes a step closer to him. She has been expecting him to try and kiss her, but he doesn't. Instead, he reaches out and grabs her breasts. And twists them! As if they were not attached to her at all! As if they are there only for his pleasure, and he doesn't care how she feels.

'You're hurting me!' *she gasps.*

'You know you like it.'

'No, I—'

'All women like it – however much they shout an' squeal.'

He has a firm grasp of her now, and is pulling her down to the ground. She doesn't scream at first – because she doesn't want the other people from the fairground to know what she has done – but when she feels her back press against the grass, a scream does begin to form in her throat.

It never gets out. It is never allowed to get out. The man clamps his left hand over her mouth, while his right hand is exploring under her skirt. She wants to get away, but his body is pressing down on her, his knees forcing her legs apart.

She tries to struggle free, but the hand which has been under her skirt reaches up and slaps her. Once, twice, three times. She is crying, but she knows he doesn't care. She wishes she was dead.

He enters her roughly, tearing her hymen, bruising her insides. It does not last long – though to her it seems to last for ever. He grunts, rolls off her, stands up, and buttons his trousers.

'I'll bet you've never had a seein' to like that before,' he says.

And then he disappears into the night, leaving her lying there, sobbing softly to herself.

'Who was this man?' Paniatowski asked.

'I don't know,' Zelda said, sobbing again as she had sobbed on that night all those years ago. 'He didn't tell me.'

A lie!

He had told her his name, right enough. Had not just told her, but actually *boasted* about who he was.

As if he thought she should have known it already!

As if he had failed to understand that however celebrated he might be in his own village, the name meant nothing to those people who came from outside it.

So she knew who he was. But Pat was in enough trouble already, without her passing the information on to this policewoman.

'Do you know *anything* about him?' Paniatowski asked. 'Do you know if he came from this village?'

'Stan thought he did.'

'Stan? Stan Dawkins? You told him about it?'

'I didn't mean to. I just couldn't hide it from him.'

276

She has no idea how long she has been lying there, but she can see the funfair is closing down and knows she must get back to her caravan. It hurts to stand up, but she forces herself. She finds walking painful, too, and despite the need to get cleaned up before her mother sees her, she has to stop and rest at several points in her journey.

It is during the last stop before her caravan that Stan finds her. He doesn't ask her what has happened. He doesn't need to. All he wants is the name, and she – so weak she cannot think ahead, so weak she cannot even imagine the consequences – gives it to him.

'So Stan didn't come into the village to look for girls, as people at the time thought,' Paniatowski said. 'In fact, he had quite the opposite purpose – he wanted to avenge you.'

'Yes.'

'And got himself killed in the process.'

'I didn't know that would happen. I never *thought* it would happen.'

'But after it *did* happen, you didn't even bother to tell the police about it! Why?'

'It wouldn't have made any difference if I had. *We* didn't matter. We were all just no-good gypsies as far as the police back then were concerned. They'd never have arrested anybody "respectable" for killing one of *us*.'

'That's not true at all!' Paniatowski said. 'If

you'd told them what you've told me, they'd have taken you into the village and asked you to point out the killer for them.'

'And how could I have done that – when I didn't even know who he was myself?'

'But of course you knew! The man who killed Stan must have been the same man who raped you.'

'He wasn't.'

'And how can you possibly be so sure of that?'

'Because, just after Stan had set off for the village, he came back.'

She is still standing where Stan left her when she sees the man has returned. She wants to scream, but he puts his finger to his mouth to silence her, and somehow she cannot bring herself to disobey him.

'I don't want to hurt you,' he says.

'You've already *hurt me,' she tells him.*

He looks down at the ground. 'I know,' he mumbles. 'It's been pointed out to me.'

She can't believe what she's hearing. It's been pointed out to him. *It shouldn't have needed to be* pointed out *to him. What kind of a man was he? What kind of world did he live in where he didn't know he'd done wrong until it had been* pointed out *to him?*

'Who told you you'd done wrong?' she asks. 'Your dad?'

'No, not my dad.'

'Who then?'

'It doesn't matter.' He takes a step closer to her, and when she instinctively shrinks away, he says, 'I told you, I don't want to hurt you. I'm here to give you somethin'.'

He holds out his hand. There is just enough light for her to see the small piece of brown paper which it contains.

'A ten bob note,' she says, hardly able to believe it.

'It's a lot of dosh, is ten bob,' he answers. 'It'd take you a while to earn ten bob, an' now it's yours after only ten minutes' work.'

So that is the price of her humiliation, she thinks. Ten shillings.

'I don't want your money,' she tells him.

'He said I should make sure you took it.'

'Who *said*?'

'My ... Look, I don't want it.'

'And I don't want it either.'

She makes a dash for her caravan, and he doesn't try to stop her.

But he does not go away, either. Not then – and not later.

He stays standing in the shadows, watching her caravan. Nobody else notices, because if you're not looking for him, you can't see him. But she is looking. Several times during the night, she peers through the window and sees the dark form standing there. It is only just before dawn breaks that he finally disappears.

Why did he stay so long? she wonders to

herself, when he has finally gone. Not because he was sorry. Not because he wanted to apologize for what he had done. He'd made it quite plain he had no regrets.

So why then?

Because somebody – perhaps the man who gave him the money – had told him to stay away from the village in case there was any trouble. In case someone from the funfair came looking for him.

And somebody had! Stan!

'I still don't understand,' Paniatowski said.

'Pat did what he did because he was trying to protect my daughter – the girl he loves.'

'But what has she—?' And suddenly Paniatowski understood. 'The man who raped you also made you pregnant!' she said.

Zelda nodded. 'Yes.'

'And you never told your daughter about it?'

'I've never told her who her father was, but I've always let her think that I was in love with him. I was terrified that you and your boss were going to accidentally uncover the truth, and then Hettie would find out. I didn't want her to know she had the blood of a brutal rapist running through her veins. And neither did Pat. He thought ... he thought you'd think it was somebody from the village who'd damaged your car, and that would mean you'd stop looking so closely at *us* and start looking more closely at *them*. It seems like a mad idea now, but it made sense to me when he explained it to me back then.'

'Why those words?' Paniatowski said, knowing she was asking more for her own sake than for the sake of the investigation. 'Why "slut"? Why "harlot"?'

Zelda looked at her strangely – questioningly.

As if I've suddenly shown her my secret self, Paniatowski thought. And perhaps I have!

'There was nothing personal in it,' Zelda said.

Paniatowski knew she should leave it there – but couldn't. 'It *felt* personal,' she said.

'What did you want him to write?' Zelda asked. ' "Bent"? Anyone can see you're not, so that would have had no effect on you. "Ruthless"? You'd have taken it as a compliment. He knew he had to knock you off balance, so he used words that would have worked in his village back in Ireland. But he was wrong. You should never call a woman that – just as you should never *treat* a woman like that. So can you forgive him? Can you let him go?'

'It's not up to me,' Paniatowski told her. 'I really think we have to go and talk to my boss.'

Thirty-Six

Two hours in the police house storeroom had eroded some of Pat Calhoun's jaunty self-confidence, and he looked distinctly unsettled by the fact that Woodend had not returned alone but had brought his sergeant with him.

'Do I need to introduce her?' Woodend asked. 'Or have you already met the Harlot?'

Calhoun reddened. 'I'm sorry, Miss,' he said. 'I didn't like writin' what I wrote, honest I didn't, but it seemed the best way to—'

'Not so much an apology, more a self-justification,' Woodend said dryly. 'Still, we've other fish to fry at the moment.'

'Are you really goin' to have me locked up in Lancaster Gaol?' Calhoun asked.

'Oh yes, the car's on the way to pick you up even as we speak. The only thing that's changed is what we're goin' to charge you with.'

'I don't understand,' the Irishman said.

'Could you hold out your hands, please, Mr Calhoun? I need to handcuff you.'

'Handcuff me!' Calhoun repeated incredulously. 'What for? All I did was vandalize a car!'

'That's where we disagree, you see,' Woodend told him. 'Hold out your hands, Mr Calhoun. It'll be a lot easier than puttin' up a struggle – an' findin' yourself on the sharp end of the Harlot's nasty temper.'

Calhoun sighed, and held out his hands. Woodend clicked a set of cuffs on to his wrists.

'That should be enough restraint for the present,' the Chief Inspector said. 'But if you start makin' things difficult for us, we'll have to cuff your hands *behind* your back. Understood?'

'Understood,' Calhoun said defeatedly.

'Right then, now we're all sittin' comfortably, we can begin. When exactly did Zelda Todd tell you the name of the man who had raped her?'

'She never told me.'

Woodend turned to Paniatowski. 'Now why don't I believe him, Monika?' he asked.

'Possibly because he's lying through his teeth?' Monika Paniatowski suggested.

'Possibly because he's lying through his teeth,' Woodend agreed. 'Shall I tell you *why* we both think that, Mr Calhoun?'

'I don't care whether you do or not,' the Irishman replied, with a casualness which was clearly forced.

'All right, you don't care, so I'll do it purely for my own amusement,' Woodend said. 'Will you at least agree that you're aware of the fact that twenty years ago Zelda Todd was raped?'

'Why should I agree?'

'Because it would be pointless not to. Because you've already blown your chance of pleadin' ignorance.'

'Have I indeed?'

'Yes, you have. If you were goin' to deny knowledge of it, you should have done so when I asked you if you knew the rapist's name. "Raped!" you should have said. "Was she raped? How shockin'!" But it wasn't a shock, was it?'

Pat Calhoun smiled sadly. 'We're never quite as smart as we think we are, are we?'

'What did you hope to achieve by vandal-izin' my sergeant's car – by writin' "harlot" on it?'

'Isn't that obvious?'

'Maybe. But us bobbies still like to have things spelled out for us.'

'I hoped it would divert your attention from the fairground an' towards the village. I didn't want you to find out that Zelda had been raped, because then there was a danger that Hettie would find out, too.'

'Was that your only motive?'

'What other could there have been?'

'Let's go back a few days, shall we?' Woodend suggested. 'Zelda's a worried woman when the fair arrives in Hallerton. An' what's she worried about? She's worried that her rapist will come to the fair – probably drunk – and say somethin' so indiscreet in Hettie's hearin' that the girl might put two an' two together, an' work out that he's her father.' He shook his head. 'Imagine that. Suddenly learnin' that you weren't born out of an act of love, but out of an act of violence. It would have been devastatin' for the poor girl.'

'It would,' Calhoun agreed.

'So how is Zelda to prevent it happenin'? By goin' to her mate, Pat Calhoun, an' tellin' him all about it, of course. By askin' him to make sure that the rapist never gets anywhere near the fairground. But how could her mate Pat have done that if he didn't even know the rapist's name?'

A small smile came to the Irishman's lips. 'It seems I'm not the only one who's not as smart as he thinks he is.'

'Would you like to explain that?'

'Zelda wasn't worried about the man comin' to the fairground at all,' Calhoun said. 'She knew he'd be far too busy with the—'

Only now did he see the trap he had been walking into. A look of horror came to his face, and he closed his mouth.

'He'd be far too busy with what?' Woodend

asked.

'Nothin'.'

'With the Witch Burnin'?'

'I've said all I'm goin' to say.'

Woodend turned his attention to Paniatowski. 'Mr Calhoun was tellin' the truth when he told us he vandalized your lovely red car to distract our attention away from the fairground,' he said.

'But he was lying when he said he didn't know the rapist's name, wasn't he?' the sergeant responded.

'Of course he was,' Woodend agreed. 'Zelda told him. Zelda would *have* to have told him in order for him to be able to do what he did the other night. As I see it, Harry Dimdyke wasn't killed to protect Hettie from finding out about her father at all. He was killed to *avenge* Zelda for the rape.'

'You ... you can't think...?' Pat Calhoun gasped.

'Oh, but I can,' Woodend assured him. He cleared his throat. 'Patrick Michael Calhoun, I am chargin' you with the murder of Harold Dimdyke. You do not have to say anythin', but anythin' you do say may be taken down an' used in evidence against you.'

Thirty-Seven

It was nine o'clock in the evening, just thirteen hours before the first Witch Burning in twenty years. Woodend and Paniatowski sat opposite each other in the public bar in the Wheatsheaf in Throckston, he drinking pints of bitter, she sipping at neat vodka. It was almost the end of a case and it should have been a celebration – but neither of them felt as if they had much to celebrate.

'You're not going to charge Zelda Todd for any part in the murder, are you?' Paniatowski asked.

Woodend shook his head. 'Maybe she intended Calhoun to kill Dimdyke, or maybe she just intended him to beat him up. Either way, we don't have enough evidence to arrest her.'

'We haven't even got enough evidence to convict *Calhoun* yet,' Paniatowski pointed out.

Woodend nodded sombrely. 'I know we haven't,' he agreed, 'but he did it, an' we *will* have enough evidence by the time he comes to trial. Every killer makes mistakes, an' the

287

chances are that Calhoun made more than his share. Now they know what they're lookin' for, the boffins from the lab will probably be able to find some forensic evidence to link him with the barn.'

'And if they can't?'

'If they can't, somethin' else will turn up. One of the villagers will have got up in the middle of the night, for example, looked out the window, an' noticed a red-headed man crossin' the Green. All we have to do is persuade that person to come forward. Anyway, after a night in Lancaster Gaol, Calhoun will probably save us the trouble an' confess.'

'You think so?'

'Why wouldn't he? He knows he's goin' to prison, but he won't serve a long sentence, because even the hardest-hearted judge is bound to see that Harry Dimdyke *needed* killin'.' Woodend paused. 'I shouldn't have said that, you know,' he continued. 'No policeman should *ever* say anythin' like that. But it doesn't make it any less true.'

Paniatowski nodded. 'He thought he was God Almighty. And he almost was – as far as the village was concerned. Most rapists travel miles before they stalk their victims. Most rapists wear a mask, or put a stocking over their heads. But not Harry Dimdyke. He was so sure of himself – so sure he could get away with *anything* – that he never thought twice about raping a woman not more than a couple of hundred yards from his own home.'

'It's a pity Stan Dawkins didn't catch up with him the night it happened,' Woodend said. 'A pity Dawkins wasn't the one to finish him off – before he could do any *more* harm.'

'What harm are you talking about, exactly?' Paniatowski asked.

'I've got a theory that...' Woodend paused. 'No, now's not the time to talk about it.'

'Why not?'

'Because it's no more than a seed at the moment. It needs time to grow. If I expose it to the light now, it might just shrivel up an' die.'

'But it's about something you think Harry Dimdyke did?'

'Ask me somethin' else,' Woodend said impatiently. 'Ask me who killed Stan Dawkins.'

'All right,' Paniatowski agreed. 'Who *did* kill Stan Dawkins?'

'Tom Dimdyke, without a doubt. He had to – to protect his bastard of a brother.'

'It doesn't *have* to have been him,' Paniatowski argued. 'The retiring Witch Maker could have been the one who decided Stan had to die. Or maybe it was one of the other villagers who took the matter into his own hands. God knows, they *all* care enough about the Witch Burning to have killed to protect the man who makes it all happen.'

'It was *Tom*,' Woodend said firmly.

'That's your gut feeling, is it?'

'Yes, but there's more to it than that. If the position of Witch Maker had been an elected one Tom would have romped home well ahead of his nearest rival. He's a natural leader, an' – more to the point – he'll *always* have been one. So when there was trouble it would have been him that people turned to – him that sorted it out. Maybe he struck the blows that killed Stan Dawkins himself, or maybe he told somebody else from the village to, but whichever it was, it happened because he willed it to happen. Not that we'll ever be able to prove it after all this time.'

They lapsed into an uncomfortable silence in which Paniatowski found herself thinking about three hundred and fifty years of village history, about Meg Ramsden – and about herself.

She hated Hallerton more than she had ever hated any place she'd ever been to.

More than the shells of towns and villages she and her mother had wandered through in war-torn Europe.

More than her stepfather's house – which should have been the great escape, but wasn't.

Yet she dreaded the thought of leaving the village and going back to Whitebridge – returning to the problems she had left behind her and which she knew would only have festered further in her absence.

'Why did he kill him at the Witchin' Post?' Woodend asked suddenly, in a troubled voice.

'What was that, sir?'

'Why did Pat Calhoun take Harry Dimdyke to the Witchin' Post before he killed him?' Woodend lit up a cigarette, despite the fact that there was already one burning in the ashtray. 'Look, there's two possible ways the thing could have happened. The first is that Calhoun intended to kill Dimdyke all along, an' went to the barn with that purpose in mind. The second is that he *didn't* intend to kill him, but lost his temper once he was in the barn. In either case, we come back to the same question. Why not kill him then an' there? There were enough tools in the barn to serve as a murder weapon, an' since they all belonged to Harry, there was no way they could be traced back to Pat. So why not just pick up a hammer and turn his head into pulp? Why, instead, did he run the lunatic risk of transportin' Dimdyke across the village?'

'Because the Witching Post is symbolic?' Paniatowski suggested.

'You're right,' Woodend agreed. 'It *is* symbolic. Ask anybody in the village, an' they'll confirm that. But what possible significance could that symbol have for Pat Calhoun? He was brought up in an entirely different culture. Bloody hell, Monika, he was brought up in an entirely different *country*! An' until a few days ago, he'd probably never even heard of Hallerton. So I ask you again, why did he do it in the way that he did?'

Thirty-Eight

The roads leading towards Hallerton were jammed with traffic from just after dawn, and even the large number of extra police drafted in from Lancaster were finding it difficult to cope with the situation.

He supposed he should have expected it, the inspector from the traffic division thought grumpily, as he surveyed the growing chaos. Rarity always made the Witch Burning a big event, and that year there was the added spice that one of the folk most intimately involved in the whole process – the Witch Maker himself – had been brutally murdered only a few days earlier.

The inspector had positioned himself at what he considered the nerve centre of his whole operation – the boundary to the village itself. No cars were to be allowed beyond that point, he had decided. Anyone wishing to enter the village would have to park in one of the fields which had been specially opened up for the occasion and complete their journey on foot.

There were complaints, of course, but the

inspector had anticipated that. In his opinion, the general public had gone soft since the end of the war, and a lot of folk seemed to find it too much of an effort to wipe their own backsides, never mind walk the few hundred yards into the village.

But whatever the idle sods said – however much they protested and cajoled and wheedled – his lads stood firm. No one was to drive into the village, and that was that.

This was good policing, the inspector thought, watching his officers at work – the kind of policing that being in the Force was really all about. Oh yes, catching murderers was all very well in its place, he supposed. But homicides were few and far between in Lancashire – whereas traffic jams were a daily reality. The two flash, headline-grabbin' buggers who were in the village at the moment might do well to bear that in mind.

The 'two flash, headline-grabbin' buggers in the village' stood side by side outside the Black Bull and watched the unfolding events with a depression that neither of them seemed able to shake off.

The Green had been divided, for the purposes of the festival, into four distinct, roped-off areas. The one which dominated it – and would dominate the attention of everyone who had come to see the Burning – was the space around the stone Witching

Post. The second, a narrow strip, ran from the centre of the Green to the edge, and was obviously intended to serve as a passageway for the actors in the drama.

The other two sections were for the spectators. The larger of them stood directly behind the smaller. It had been filling up for nearly an hour, and now it had almost reached bursting point. The smaller enclosure was closer to the Witching Post – so close, in fact, that anyone standing against the ropes could almost have reached across and touched the Post itself. This one was still completely empty, but was watched over by two stern-faced village stewards, whose job it was to keep the general public out of it.

'Suppose we'd better get a bit nearer to the scene of the ancient crime, Monika,' Wood-end said, without much enthusiasm. He looked down at his sergeant's hand, and saw she was holding a cigarette in it. 'Better stub out your fag before we go. We don't want you startin' a fire, now do we?'

As jokes went, it really wasn't much of one, but Paniatowski still managed to respond to it with a weak grin as she ground the half-smoked cigarette under the toe of her shoe.

'Now where should we stand?' Woodend pondered. 'Just inside the Witchin' Post enclosure might be nice.'

They walked towards the roped-off corridor, and immediately found their way blocked by a second pair of stewards who looked as if they meant business.

'You can't go down there,' one of them said aggressively.

'Course I can, lad,' Woodend said easily. 'I'm the Filth. I can go anywhere I want to.'

The man tensed. 'This is a private affair.'

'Doesn't look very private to me,' Woodend replied, glancing across at the visitors' enclosure, which was now packed almost beyond endurance.

'They don't matter,' the man said contemptuously.

'Don't they?'

'No. They're nothin' but a mindless mob. This might as well be a circus, as far as they're concerned. They'll see what happens, but they won't understand what's *really* goin' on.'

'An' do you think I will?' Woodend ask, interestedly.

'It's possible,' the other man conceded.

'An' that bothers you, does it?'

'No, but...'

'I mean, I really don't see why it should – unless, of course, you don't want me to understand the Witch Burnin' because you're *ashamed* of it.'

The steward's fists bunched. 'We're not ashamed of it,' he said. 'The only reason we go through all this is to *show* we're not ashamed.'

'Well, then?'

The man unclenched his fists and stepped to one side. 'Don't get too close to the Witching Post,' he warned.

'Don't worry, we'll keep our distance,' Woodend assured him. 'We've no desire to go the same way Meg Ramsden did.'

The Chief Inspector and his sergeant walked down the roped-off corridor. Dozens of sets of eyes from the visitors' enclosure followed their progress enviously, but they were scarcely aware of it.

Piles of faggots had been stacked around the base of the Witching Post. Now there was less of it visible, it should have looked shorter and less impressive, Woodend thought. But it didn't. If anything the faggots seemed to make it loom even more ominously, as they transformed it from a simple stone column into the centrepiece of agonizing death.

The Chief Inspector wondered why he had felt a driving compulsion to attend the Witch Burning.

He knew he would not enjoy it. He was not one of those men who rush to see traffic accidents – and if he had been born in an earlier time, he was sure he would not have shared the general enthusiasm for public executions.

Nor would being there help to advance his case in any way. He already had his murderer under lock and key, and further additional evidence which the site of the murder might once have provided had long since been trampled underfoot, because – as the Chief Constable had informed him only a couple of hours earlier – it would have been very bad press indeed to have cancelled the event.

So just what *was* it that had brought him there?

Perhaps it was the Witching Post itself. Perhaps, by merely gazing at it, he would be able to get into Pat Calhoun's mind and understand why the Irishman had chosen it as the spot on which to enact his own personal brand of justice.

An excited murmur spread through the crowd of visitors, then swelled until it was almost a loud roar.

The villagers were coming! these visitors told each other. The villagers were coming! It was all about to begin!

The villagers approached in a column which was three people wide and stretched back beyond the edge of the Green. There was no discernible pattern in their deployment. They were led by three old men, but behind them came two women and a child, then one man and two children. Yet there was nothing haphazard about it, either. They walked with the determination of a peasant crusade which had finally caught sight of Jerusalem. There was a glint in their eyes –

even in the eyes of the kids – and a firmness in their bearing which said that nothing – not God Almighty Himself – would make them turn back now.

And they were dressed for the occasion, Woodend thought. Jesus, were they dressed for it!

They had abandoned their cheap chain-store jackets and off-the-peg frocks for the day. The men were wearing breeches and jerkins. The women wore long dark dresses, and had their hair tightly fixed under their white caps. Thus would their ancestors have been dressed when Scottish James ascended to the English throne.

The Chief Inspector studied the villagers closely, looking for an unintended flash of modernity. A zip fastener, perhaps. Or a recently manufactured hook. But he was not the least surprised when he found no such mistakes. These were careful people. This was their day, and they were determined to get things right.

But it was neither the villagers' clothes nor their sense of purpose which had really caught the spectators' attention. It was the fact that all of them – every man, woman and child – was carrying a pail.

And *pails* was what they were! Not modern buckets, made of galvanized iron or plastic. They were *wooden* pails, held together by iron hoops – pails the like of which it had not been possible to purchase in any shop for at least a hundred and fifty years.

Each pail was filled almost to the top with water. As the villagers walked, the water swilled back and forth, sometimes managing to slip over the edge of the pail and stain the grass as dark as if blood had recently been spilled there.

'Do you know why they're bringing the water with them, sir?' Paniatowski asked.

'Yes,' said Woodend, who had seen it all before, yet had somehow managed to forget just how primeval it was.

'Then what *is* the reason?' Paniatowski said.

'You'll soon see,' Woodend promised her.

Thirty-Nine

The villagers filed solemnly into their enclosure. It was a tight squeeze, but this – like everything else due to happen that day – had been carefully planned, Woodend thought. Because now they were inside the enclosure, all pressed together, these people had ceased to be individuals at all, and had become instead a single mass which was far greater than all its parts.

An old farm cart with huge thick wheels appeared at the edge of the Green. It was pulled by a powerful shire horse, and in the back of it were three figures. The two men – Tom Dimdyke and his son, Wilf Dimdyke – were wearing the same rough, hand-spun clothes as the rest of the village men had donned for this special day. The woman – the effigy – had nothing in common with the village women who were awaiting her arrival. Meg wore a scarlet dress which hugged her figure, and her beautiful blonde hair – which had once belonged to Mary Dimdyke – cascaded freely over her shoulders.

Had she really been dressed like that when

she met her end? Woodend wondered.

Yes, it was possible. It was *more* than possible.

Meg had been vain enough to have her portrait painted by an artist who had travelled all the way from York to do it. Wasn't it likely, then, that she had owned a dress such as the one her effigy was dressed in that day? And though she would not have been wearing such a fabulous garment when the village had tried her for witchcraft, Woodend could well imagine her husband – the Harry Dimdyke now long dead – forcing her to put it on for her execution. Because it was not what Meg *was* that had been important. It was what the village had wanted her to be – *needed* her to be, if it was to have a reason to take her life.

As the crude farm cart trundled its way across the village green – rattling her bones, bruising her soft, pale skin – Meg Ramsden could still not quite believe what had occurred.

She had the power, she told herself. She owned this village, just as she owned the people who scratched out a miserable existence from the poor land which surrounded it. This nightmare could, therefore, be no more than that. It was a troubled sleep brought about by eating too many green apples – and soon the bad dream would end.

But it did not end. The cart continued to trundle towards the ominous stone pillar.

She could see the freshly dug earth – dark and wet. She could see the heaps of faggots, neatly tied together, and stacked against the post. And she could see the people, their faces twisted into masks which reflected their hatred, fear – and now – their triumph.

She heard someone speak to the driver of the cart – and though the words were not ones she had ever thought to hear herself utter, though the tone was so new to her that it was almost as if some wandering spirit had taken over her body – she recognized that speaker as herself.

'Do not thee let this thing come to pass, Harold,' she pleaded. 'Thee and I have been to church together. We have trod the same path.'

'Thee hast trodden no path but thine own,' Harold Dimdyke told her sternly.

'I have not—'

'It is pointless to deny it now. Thee hast trod no path but thine own. Aye, and walked over the bodies of purer souls on thy route.' Harold paused for a moment. 'Yet, for what thee once were to me, I will show thee a mercy thou hast never shown to others.'

Meg felt the light of hope ignite inside her. 'Thee will help me to escape?' she asked.

'Nay, not that. I could not do it, even if I willed such a thing. It is the wish of the village that thee go the stake – and that will is not to be denied.'

'Then how can'st thou talk of mercy?' Meg demanded. 'What manner of mercy is it that will let thee stand and watch as I am consumed by

the hot flames of hell? What manner of mercy?
Tell me! I must know!'

'*When thou is touched by it, then wilt thou*
know it,' Harold Dimdyke told her.

The cart reached the Witching Post, and
Tom, who was holding the reins, brought it
to a halt. Wilf produced a broad wooden
board from the back of the cart, then laid it
across the faggots, so that one end was
touching the ground and the other resting
against the Witching Post. That done, he
returned to the cart, and he and his father
lifted the Witch off it.

From the way they were handling her it
seemed as if she weighed as much as a real
woman, Woodend observed.

And maybe she did. Maybe they had taken
as much care over this detail as they had
taken over all the others.

Midway between the cart and the ground,
the Witch slipped from their hands and fell
heavily. The visitors, who had not been
expecting this, let out a roar of surprise.

But it was not clumsiness which had
caused Tom and Wilf to drop her, Woodend
thought. It had happened because it was
intended to happen – because Meg Ramsden
had fallen at this point, and so her effigy
must fall too.

And he was prepared to bet that at the
moment she hit the ground one of her

carefully constructed wooden ribs had broken, in just the place where Meg's rib had broken over three hundred and fifty years earlier.

Carrying the effigy between them, the two men mounted the board.

Woodend examined the carved mask the dummy was wearing. It was hideous, he thought – a gross distortion of Meg's true appearance.

But it was no mistake!

No failed attempt to recreate life by the hands of a clumsy amateur!

Wilf Dimdyke was a skilled craftsman, and had been training hard for this one task for the whole of his young life. And while visitors to the museum might see a beautiful woman when they looked at the portrait of Meg, this mask – this grotesque, evil, leering face – was a perfect representation of what the villagers saw in that same picture.

The two men and the dummy had reached the top of the board. Tom took the Witch's arms and held them behind the post, while Wilf reached over and fastened them securely with a piece of twine. That done, the younger man bent down and tied the ankles to the post.

The blonde hair caught the breeze, and moved slightly. It would be beautiful hair wherever it was hanging, Woodend thought. But to do it full justice it should be on the head of a living girl with a hopeful future to look forward to – not attached to the carved skull of a dummy which symbolized only the hatreds of the past.

She was in pain. Incredible pain.

Some came from her body – the pain from the broken rib she had suffered when she had fallen from the cart in front of the post; the pain from the bonds which tied her wrists and ankles to the stone.

Some came from her mind. She could picture the fire slowly slithering up her legs like a hungry serpent. She could imagine the agony as it reached her midsection and consumed her barren womb.

And now, too, there was the spiritual pain. She knew that she was not guilty as charged, but that was not to say she would die innocent. She wondered if there really was a god, and – if He existed – He would cast her into the eternal fire, which would make the agony she was now to endure seem as nothing.

New actors appeared on the scene – two men who carried between them a metal brazier filled with glowing coals. Tom backed carefully down the board, took the unlit brand which one of the men offered him, and held the end of it over the brazier. It caught fire immediately, and he lifted it clear, so all those present could see the

306

bright red flame.

'Now you'll see why they're carryin' the pails,' Woodend whispered to Paniatowski.

But *why* was he whispering? he asked himself. Was he falling under the spell of this spectacle? Was he becoming as susceptible to its influence as the villagers themselves?

Tom Dimdyke strode to the edge of the villagers' enclosure and stopped directly in front of Alf Raby. The last time he had seen the village shopkeeper, Woodend recalled, the man had been a complete wreck, with a slack jaw, watery eyes and trembling hands. Now, dressed in breeches and jerkin, rather than worn woollen cardigan, he seemed to have regained a little of the dignity he might once have had.

Dimdyke thrust the burning brand forward, until it was inches from Raby's face. Even had they been expecting it, most men would not have been able to avoid flinching from the flame – but Raby didn't even blink.

'Wilt thou, with thy water, quench this flame?' Tom Dimdyke demanded.

Alf Raby shook his head with a decisiveness Woodend would never have thought him capable of.

'Nay, not I!' he said, in a loud, certain voice.

'Then let all men know that thou dost will this burning,' Tom Dimdyke pronounced.

He withdrew the brand a few inches, took

307

a step to the side, and thrust it towards the girl standing next to Alf, who, not by chance – for nothing here was left to chance – was Mary Dimdyke.

'Wilt thou, with thy water, quench this flame?'

'N ... nay, not I!' Mary said, with a fervour which matched Raby's.

'Then let all men know that thou dost will this burning.'

And on and on it went, all down the line. The same question, the same answer, the same warning.

'It's obscene!' Paniatowski gasped.

'Aye, that's the right word for it,' Woodend agreed.

As if responding to some secret signal – which he probably was – a small boy of three or four ducked under the rope.

'Burn the Witch!' he said, in a squeaky, but passionate voice.

'Aye, burn the Witch!' the rest of the villagers screamed. 'Burn her! Burn her!'

Tom Dimdyke nodded solemnly, turned around, and approached the Witching Post.

Thomas stepped forward, the burning brand held high for Meg to see. The woman bound to the hard stone post felt a little of her old spirit returning to her, and spat at her brother-in-law. And he laughed in her face – afraid of her no more.

Thomas bent, and held the brand against the heap of faggots. Smoke began to rise immediately, obscuring Meg's view of those she so despised – of those who hated her and wished her to die a painful death.

The smoke grew thicker. It insinuated its way into her nose and into her mouth. The burning process had begun in earnest. Yet the heat she felt was still no more than a distant rumour of the agony to come.

Around her, the villagers were chanting. 'Burn the witch! Let the witch burn!'

She felt a tightening in her throat. She fought against it harder than she had ever fought against anything before. She needed to keep her throat clear, she thought – for she had promised herself that in her last breath before the screaming took control of her, she would curse them all.

Then she realized that the tightening she felt did not come from within, but from without. And in the moments before she lost consciousness, she finally understood what Harold Dimdyke had said earlier about showing her mercy.

A slight breeze suddenly blew up. It was not strong enough to disperse the thick smoke, yet it did manage to rearrange it enough for Woodend to be able to catch sight of the dark shape standing on the pyre.

Wilf! It was bloody Wilf! The Chief Inspector had assumed that while everyone had been watching Tom and the villagers, the boy had climbed down. But the stupid young bugger was still there!

What was he doing? Didn't he understand – hadn't anybody told him – that if the smoke overcame him he would collapse into the fire and be badly burnt? How could he just stand there like that?

But he wasn't *just* standing there, Woodend realized with horror! He was *doing* something. He was strangling the Witch! Wilf had waited until the smoke had screened his actions from the other villagers – just as Harold, his ancestor must have done in his time – and now he was strangling the bloody Witch!

And it didn't matter that this witch was no more than a collection of cleverly contrived pieces of wood. It didn't matter that there was no life in her to be extinguished. Meg had been strangled, and so this Witch – the spirit of Meg – must be made to suffer the same fate.

The smoke thickened again, but not enough to hide the fact that the bright, greedy flames were climbing ever higher.

Jump for it! a voice in Woodend's brain urged the lad. Jump for it, you stupid young bugger!

And even as the thought was running through his mind, he found himself wondering why he was not saying the words aloud.

Wilf emerged from the thick black cloud, leaping clear of the conflagration and landing on the ground with practised ease. Behind him, the relentless flames continued to gobble up what had taken him a full ten years of his young life to produce.

Now fresh smells were starting to seep into the air: the wood smoke of the skeleton, which was quite different to the wood smoke from the faggots; the burning wool of the scarlet dress; the stink of the sheep fat as it bubbled and cooked. And overlying it all – though he told himself it was only his imagination – Woodend was convinced he could almost *taste* the incineration of Mary's beautiful golden hair.

The minutes ticked by, the fire died down, and all that was left was a blackened stone post and a heap of smoking ashes. But the performance was not over. Not quite yet.

Four men, mounted on black horses and dressed in the ancient livery of the High Sheriff of Lancaster, rode on to the Green and came to a halt before the Witching Post.

'Who hath done this?' their captain demanded.

'We have *all* done this,' Wilf Dimdyke answered.

And the villagers agreed.

'We have all done this! We have all done this!'

The captain shook his head – perhaps in

disbelief, perhaps in disgust.

'Who am I to take with me to Lancaster?' he demanded. 'Who will bear the guilt for this shameful act?'

'There *is* no guilt, for this was no shameful act,' Wilf said in a deep, confident voice which seemed to belong to a much older man. 'But if any men must die, then we – the Dimdykes – are more than willing to be those men.'

The captain thought for a moment, then nodded to two of his men-at-arms. The soldiers each reached for a length of rope which was wrapped around their saddle horns, dismounted, and walked over to where Wilf and Tom were patiently waiting for them.

'Put your hands together!' one of the soldiers barked. 'Put your hands together and hold them out!'

Father and son mutely obeyed, offering their clenched hands as if they were about to pray. One soldier wrapped and knotted the end of his rope tightly around Tom's wrists, the other around Wilf's. They tugged on the binding, to test that it was firm, then walked back to their horses, leaving a trail of rope behind them. Neither Wilf nor Tom moved so much as a muscle.

The soldiers remounted. Once in the saddle, they tied the other end of the ropes firmly around their saddle horns.

'Onwards!' the captain said.

The soldiers spurred their horses, and set off at a slow trot. The ropes which connected the Dimdykes to the saddle horns became taut, and Wilf and Tom were jerked forward. The procession made its way to the edge of the Green – the horses moving with graceful ease, Tom and Wilf running behind with all their might – then turned on to the street and was gone.

Now – finally – the Witch Burning was over. The visitors gave a collective sigh, and began to drift away. The locals waited until most of the intruders had gone, then started to leave themselves – slowly, as if even the simple act of walking were an effort after all they had been through.

'Very impressive,' Paniatowski said sombrely. And then, perhaps in an attempt to shatter the tension which she had felt building up in her during the performance, she added flippantly, 'Of course, they've taken a bit of a dramatic licence with the whole thing, haven't they?'

Woodend said nothing. Paniatowski waited for a moment, then decided the silence was becoming unbearable.

'I mean, it's a bit like a Hollywood film, isn't it?' she continued, knowing she was almost babbling, but not caring. 'You know what I mean, sir? They compress time. In a way, I suppose they have to – because if they didn't, the audience would get bored.'

There was still no response from Woodend.

'What I'm trying to say is that it couldn't have happened exactly like it's been played out,' Paniatowski persisted. 'We've just seen the sheriff's men ride up right after the burning, but we know that, before he was arrested, Harold Dimdyke had time to get married again and sire a child. So in practice, it must have been days – perhaps even weeks – before the arrests were made.'

'What?' Woodend asked.

'I was just saying there must have been quite a considerable time between the burning and the arrests, don't you think?'

'Aye, probably,' Woodend agreed.

'Is something the matter, sir?'

'I'm thinkin',' Woodend said, perhaps a little more harshly than he'd intended.

And he was. Fragments of the puzzle had been drifting idly around his brain ever since he had first become involved in the case.

But that was all they'd been.

Fragments!

Slivers of a whole picture, each of which meant nothing on its own.

But now, at this Witch Burning which represented for the villagers the truth as they saw it, the fragments were coming together – and he was beginning to see a truth of his own.

The village was a kingdom, ruled over by

the Witch Maker. He'd always known that. But until now he'd never seen the true extent of it – had never fully understood the depth of the obligations which were imposed on the monarch's subjects!

'*She didn't have the mental strength of the other women,*' Alf Raby had said of his dead wife.

'*What other women? The ones who killed themselves?*'

'*No, the ones who didn't. She couldn't take it any more, you see. She just couldn't convince herself that she was doin' the right thing. I tried to tell her it was the same for everybody in the village – that we all did what we had to do – but ... but ... she just wouldn't see it.*'

And she wasn't the only one.

'*She hanged herself, did my Beth,*' the postman had said mournfully to Monika Paniatowski. '*I found her myself. It was so hard, so very, very hard. I really did love her, you know.*'

'*I'm sure you did,*' Paniatowski had agreed. '*Did you ever wonder why she did it?*'

'*I know why she did it. She did it because she didn't believe. But I believe. I have to believe. It's the only thing that stops me from goin' completely mad.*'

But did the man who'd driven those two women to their deaths care? Of course not! He was above such petty considerations. He had been put above the law by others, and had become a law unto himself.

'*The Witch Maker never marries,*' Constable Thwaites had said.

'*Never?*'

'*Never.*'

'*Not in the entire history of the Witch Burnin'?*'

'*No, sir.*'

But that wasn't to say he was always celibate – as Woodend had pointed out at the time.

Sacrifice was what they all talked about in this village, the Chief Inspector reminded himself – and to understand what that sacrifice entailed was to understand this case.

'*Have you actually made a sacrifice yourself, Mr Dimdyke?*' he'd asked Tom caustically.

'*Oh aye. Twenty year ago now. It was hard – but it was necessary.*'

'*An' what form, exactly, did your sacrifice take?*'

'*That's none of your business!*'

But it *was* his business. It was *central* to his business.

There was more.

There were fragments he didn't even need to think about now – because once he'd seen the general shape of things, they slotted *themselves* into place.

There were details which were still not clear, but didn't matter – because he had no need to appreciate individual brush strokes once he had the whole canvas spread out before him.

'Sir?' Monika Paniatowski said worriedly. 'Are you all right, sir?'

'No! I'm far from all right. But at least I've finally got my sense of direction back.'

'I don't understand.'

'It's time we had a talk with them Dim-dykes, Monika,' Woodend said. 'An' I mean a *real* talk this time.'

Forty

The blackboard outside the Black Bull had the words 'CLOSED FOR A PRIVATE PARTY' crudely chalked on it.

'Some party, eh, Monika?' Woodend said, hammering on the door. 'More like a wake for the death of Free Will, if you ask me.'

The landlord opened the door a couple of inches. 'Can't you read?' he demanded, pointing at the blackboard.

'Can't *you* read?' Woodend countered, holding up his warrant card.

The landlord reluctantly opened the door wider, and Woodend and Paniatowski stepped inside. The villagers were all still in their traditional dress, but now they had shed some of their earlier seriousness and austerity.

They're drunk, Woodend thought.

He didn't blame them. He'd be drunk himself if he was caught in the same trap as they were – if he, too, could feel the jaws of history clamped tightly around his soul.

Tom Dimdyke and his son were sitting in the centre of the room, as befitted the guests of honour.

'Glad to see the sheriff's men were all for show, an' that you've not *really* been arrested,' Woodend said jovially to them. 'Or should I say, not really been arrested *yet*.'

Tom Dimdyke stretched across the table for his drink, and Woodend saw the rope burn on his wrist.

The visitors probably thought that when Tom was dragged away by the soldier's horse, he had used some clever trick to prevent himself from being hurt. But no such trick existed. And even if one had, Tom and Wilf would never have employed it – because there had been no tricks the first time this had all happened, so there could be no tricks now.

Woodend shook his head, amazed at how easy it had become for him to tune his brain into the villagers' way of seeing things. He had learned a great deal during his time in Hallerton, he thought, but perhaps the biggest step was to finally accept that the villagers didn't *mind* making sacrifices and undergoing discomfort.

Didn't *mind?* he repeated mentally.

No, it was worse that that – and far more frightening. They *welcomed* the opportunity to suffer!

'What is you want?' Tom Dimdyke demanded.

'To talk,' Woodend said.

'Now?'

'Now!' Woodend turned to the landlord. 'Have you got a room where we can have a bit of privacy?'

The landlord glanced in Tom Dimdyke's direction for guidance, but it was Wilf who nodded his assent.

'There's a little parlour at the back,' the landlord said. 'You'll be private enough there.'

'I'm sure we will,' Woodend agreed. 'Well then, let's get it over with, shall we?'

And though he could have been addressing anybody at all in the bar, it was only Tom and Wilf who rose to their feet.

'There's some good comes out of the way you lot take the law into your own hands in this village, an' I won't deny it,' Woodend said, once they had adjourned to the back parlour. 'Take that old feller I was talkin' to yesterday, as an example.'

'What about him?' Tom Dimdyke asked suspiciously.

'The Great War was a terrible thing,' Woodend said. 'Whole villages just stood by, while their young men were led away to be slaughtered like cattle on the battlefields of Flanders. But that didn't happen here, did it? Your young men deserted before they got to France, an' the village hid them. In fact, fifty years later, the village is *still* hidin' them.'

'I don't know what you're talkin' about,' Tom Dimdyke protested.

'Of course you do,' Woodend said dismissively. 'The old feller I had a drink with said his name was Oswald Warburton. But that was a lie. The real Oswald Warburton died in 1912. I know, because I've seen his grave. This Oswald Warburton borrowed his name – because he didn't dare use his own.'

Tom Dimdyke suddenly looked frightened. But he was not frightened for himself, Woodend thought. He was frightened that he had failed in his responsibility to others.

'You'll ... you'll not tell the Army, will you?' he asked.

'No,' Woodend replied. 'I assured old Oswald – or whatever his real name is – that he had nothin' to fear from me. An' I meant it. As a policeman, I can't condone what the village did in 1914, but I like to think that if I'd been here at the time, I'd have done the same myself. So I'll overlook it. But there are other things I can't overlook – other things which *nobody* should overlook. Do you know what I'm talkin' about, Mr Dimdyke?'

Tom Dimdyke shook his head forcefully.

'All right, if you won't come clean, I'll just have to spell it all out,' Woodend said. 'An' that could be a long process, because we have to go a fair way back in history to start makin' any sense of this whole bloody mess, don't we?'

Dimdyke said nothing.

'How far back, I'm not sure,' Woodend continued. 'Maybe you can help me there, Tom. When *was* it that the Witch Maker was given licence to have his pick of the women in this village?'

Tom Dimdyke glanced briefly at his son, and then turned his attention back to Woodend.

'Does Wilf have to be here?' he asked, in a tone which was as close to a plea as the Chief Inspector had ever heard him come.

'Why *shouldn't* Wilf be here?' Woodend countered. 'He *is* the Witch Maker, when all's said an' done. What we're goin' to talk about surely can't come as any news to him.'

'The new Witch Maker isn't told of his ... of his rights ... until after the Witch Burnin' is over,' Tom Dimdyke said. 'I would have had a word with him about it tonight.'

But he already knew, Woodend thought, looking at Wilf's face. Somebody had *already* told him.

'So it wasn't to be until tonight that you revealed the fact that he could get his end away whenever he felt like it?' he said to Tom Dimdyke.

Dimdyke shook his head in disgust. 'It isn't like that. You don't understand,' he said.

'Then explain it so I will.'

'The Witch Maker has needs like any other

man. But he *isn't* like the rest of us. He must dedicate his life to the Witch. He must abandon all thoughts, from the very beginnin', of a normal childhood and a normal young manhood. He must give up any hope of havin' a family of his own – for that can only deflect him from his true purpose.'

'I'm not sure you're bein' strictly honest with me there, Tom,' Woodend told him.

'I don't know what you're—'

'Still, I suppose we can leave the subtleties for later discussion. As far as the point I was about to make goes, the simple truth of the matter is that every woman in the village – except, of course, for the Dimdyke women, who are excluded on the grounds of bein' immediate family – is expected to offer herself as fodder for the Witch Maker's bed whenever he feels the urge. Isn't that right?'

'No.'

Woodend sighed. 'You're playin' games with me, Mr Dimdyke. You know as well as I do that what I meant when I said *every* woman was every *married* woman. Because that's the way it is, isn't it? The Witch Maker gets all of the fun out of it – an' none of the responsibility.'

'The women are expected to give him relief, yes,' Tom Dimdyke said. 'It is a service they perform for him, just as others perform the service of workin' to keep him clothed an' fed.'

323

'It can't be as simple as that. Human relationships never are.'

'It *is* that simple,' Tom Dimdyke insisted. 'It is duty, not lust, which drives them. They are not being unfaithful to their husbands – because the husbands both know and approve.'

Woodend nodded. 'Yes, I can almost see that workin' out,' he said. 'At least, I can see it workin' out *some* of the time. But what happens when the man who becomes Witch Maker is an evil bastard – like your brother was?'

'For a man to be either good or evil, he must have choices,' Tom Dimdyke said. 'And the Witch Maker has *no* choice. His path is set for him, an' all he can do is to follow it.'

He believed in the words he was speaking, Woodend thought, but they were not his own. He was quoting – reciting an article of faith which had been passed down from generation to generation.

The minds of the people in this village were chained to a rock of belief almost from birth – and if a chief inspector from the outside was going to produce a solution to this case which would stand up in court, he would first have to break that chain.

Woodend turned his head towards Wilf Dimdyke. 'The path is set,' he said. 'Is that what you think, an' all?'

'You heard what my father told you,' Wilf

replied.

'Aye, but I was askin' you, not him,' Woodend said. 'An' you're the one who should really know what you're talkin' about – because you're the Witch Maker now.'

'The path is set,' Wilf said firmly.

'You're sure about that, are you?'

'There was a time when I thought it might not be – but I was mistaken.'

'Now that *is* interestin',' Woodend said. 'So you're willin' to admit that you've had your doubts.'

'Leave the boy alone!' Tom Dimdyke said angrily.

'He's *not* a boy,' Woodend replied harshly. 'He's the Witch Maker. If he can't defend himself, how the bloody hell can he be expected to defend the rest of you?'

Tom Dimdyke bowed his head, but said nothing.

'However, I *am* prepared to leave Wilf out of it for the moment,' Woodend conceded.

'Thank you,' Tom Dimdyke said humbly.

'So shall we get back to talkin' about choices, Tom?'

'If that is what you wish,' Dimdyke answered, his expression saying more clearly than words ever could that he was very willing to put himself in the firing line if, by doing so, he could take the pressure off his son.

'You're wrong when you say the Witch Maker doesn't have choices,' Woodend said.

'The path may be set, but there are many different ways a man can walk along it. For instance, when he takes another man's wife to his bed he can treat her like a human bein'. Or he can be so brutal with her – treat her so much like an object – that she ends up killin' herself. Am I ringin' any bells for you here, Tom? Would it help if I came out with a few names of women who've been brutalized in that way?'

'If the women truly believe in the nobility of their purpose, then there is no shame nor humiliation in whatever they have to endure,' Tom Dimdyke replied.

'The problem is, some of them didn't,' Woodend reminded him. 'An' neither did Zelda Todd. Why *should* she have? She wasn't from the village. She wasn't devoted to any sacred mission.'

'You're mocking us now,' Tom Dimdyke said accusingly.

Woodend shook his head gravely. 'No, I'm not. I'd have to think somethin' was ridiculous before I mocked it, an' I've learned to take very seriously what's been goin' on in this village for the last three hundred an' fifty years. But what about Zelda Todd, Tom? She was an innocent young girl. A virgin. An' then she met your brother, who had just burnt his Witch, just been told he could have any woman he fancied, an' thought he was God Almighty. An' he raped her. How's that for stickin' to the path?'

'He did wrong,' Tom admitted. 'Very great wrong.'

'Shut up, Dad!' Wilf said. 'Don't admit anythin'.'

'Why not?' his father asked, with a shrug. 'What's the point in denyin' somethin' to him that he clearly already knows.'

'Your brother Harry wasn't worthy to be the Witch Maker, was he?' Woodend demanded.

'No,' Tom Dimdyke said reluctantly. 'He wasn't.'

'It should have been you there in his place, shouldn't it?'

'That we will never know. Perhaps I would have been as unworthy as my brother.'

'You might say that, but you don't really believe it. Not deep down inside yourself,' Woodend told him. 'Anyway, we're gettin' side-tracked again. After Harry had raped the girl, even *he* saw that he'd gone too far. He came back to the village in a complete panic, didn't he?'

Tom Dimdyke nodded.

'He needed somebody to get him out of the mess, an' that somebody was you. You gave him a ten bob note, an' told him to go back to the funfair to try to buy the girl off. But at the same time, you prepared yourself for any trouble there might be as a result of what he'd done. An' there was trouble – in the form of a young lad called Stan Dawkins.'

'Please shut up, Dad!' Wilf begged.

'Why should you *want* him to shut up?' Woodend asked, sounding puzzled. 'What's he got to hide? Isn't the whole life of this village built on doin' what you see as the right thing?'

'Yes.'

'An' isn't part of that bein' prepared to stand up afterwards an' *admit* what you've done?'

'Yes, but...'

'Ah, I see your problem,' Woodend told the young Witch Maker. 'You think your dad killed Stan Dawkins for an *unworthy* reason – that he only did it to protect his no-good brother. But that wasn't the case at all, was it, Tom?'

'No,' Tom Dimdyke said.

'Dad...!'

'When he killed Dawkins, it wasn't his brother he was protectin' – it was the office of the Witch Maker. He did it for the village. An' for you!'

'For me?' Wilf Dimdyke asked.

'Of course.'

'I was a baby!'

'But you were destined to grow up to be the Witch Maker. An' who could teach you the necessary skills if your uncle was servin' a long prison sentence for rape?'

'Is this true, Dad?' Wilf Dimdyke demanded.

'Even if the girl had been willin' to keep quiet about what had happened, Dawkins would never have let it rest,' Tom Dimdyke said regretfully. 'He'd have gone to the police, whatever I said.'

'So it *was* you!' Wilf gasped. 'You really did kill him!'

'I only wanted the best for you.'

'But I never asked ... I never wanted...'

'There was so little else I could do for you. The Witch Maker was all, and I was nothing. This one thing, at least, was within my power.'

'Let me get this straight, Mr Dimdyke,' Woodend said. 'You're confessin' to the murder of Stan Dawkins now, are you?'

'Yes, I'm confessin'. I did it. I knew he didn't deserve to die, but I couldn't see any other way out.'

'I've no real evidence against you, you know. Even now, if you retracted your confession, I'd probably be hard put to get a conviction.'

'I know.'

'So why confess at all? Is it that it doesn't really matter whether or not you confess to this murder, since you're just about to confess to another one?'

'That's right,' Tom Dimdyke agreed. 'I not only killed Stan Dawkins, I also killed my own brother.'

'Why? Because you resented the fact that he'd become Witch Maker instead of you? Because, over the years, your resentment grew into hatred?'

'Yes.'

'It'd be a very neat an' tidy endin' to the case if that was the truth,' Woodend said. 'The only problem is, it's a load of bollocks.'

'I swear—'

'Oh, I don't doubt for a second that you killed Stan Dawkins – that you beat him to death. But your brother Harry wasn't beaten, was he? He was garrotted.'

'What does it matter how I killed him?'

'Which is a funny method for any killer to choose,' Woodend continued, ignoring the interruption. 'There's somethin' of the ritual about it, isn't there? Its stated aim is to cause death, but there's also an element of punishment in it. An' it's a tricky thing to do properly, is garrottin'. At least, it would be for anybody who'd not been practicin' doin' it on a dummy for the last few weeks.' Woodend switched his attention from Tom Dimdyke to his son, who had slowly been turning paler and paler and was now the colour of chalk. 'Do you want to tell me about it, lad?' he asked gently.

Forty-One

Wilf, working alone in the barn, looks up and sees his beloved sister standing there. He can tell from the way her cheeks are puffed up that she has been crying.

'What's the matter?' he asks.

'What do you th ... think's the matter?' she replies angrily. 'In th ... three days they're goin' to cut off all my b ... beautiful hair.'

'It'll grow back,' Wilf tells her, knowing the response is inadequate – wishing he could say more.

'You're the Assistant Witch M ... Maker, Our Wilf,' she says. 'Can't you st ... stop it?'

'I might as well try to stop an express train,' he says.

And even as he speaks, he realizes how odd it is to hear the phrase coming out of his mouth. What meaning does 'an express train' have for him? He's hardly even seen an express train, let alone gone anywhere on one. Trains are for other people – people who lead lives which are not centred on this village.

'We're nothin' but sl ... slaves,' Mary says, as fresh tears run down her cheeks. 'Sl ... slaves to

331

somethin' we had no part in st ... startin' – which was all over an' d ... done with three hundred an' fifty years ago.'

'It can never be over an' done with,' Wilf tells her. 'Evil is with us always. We must fight with our hands when we can, and with our minds and spirits when we cannot. We must burn the Witch, or she has won. We must burn the Witch to show others that we, at least, are pure of heart.'

He has known these words since he was a child. Yet only now does he start to realize that they are not his words – that though his greatest wish is to console his dear sister, these words will not do it.

He struggles to gain some understanding of this new insight. The words are a barrier, he tells himself. They fill his mind, they clog his soul – they leave no space for the thought he really wishes to express.

'I'll have a talk to Uncle Harry,' he says, as he feels himself drowning in a sea of inadequacy. 'I'll see if he can do somethin' to save your hair.'

'It's n ... not about my h ... hair. It's about everythin'!' Mary almost screams at him.

'I don't understand,' he says.

But he is starting to.

'God, I h ... hate you!' Mary says. 'I h ... hate you all!'

And then she turns and flees.

'Do you want to know why I killed my uncle?' Wilf demanded. 'I did it to save

Mary! An' to save the children – the ones who haven't even been born yet, but are already marked down to go through all this, just like we did.' He waved his hands helplessly in the air. 'I'm ... I'm tryin' to make you understand, honestly I am, but I can't ... I can't...'

'What you want to say is that you were tryin' to derail the express train,' Woodend suggested.

'Yes, that's it,' Wilf said gratefully.

'But when the train didn't come off the lines with your uncle's death, why did you slip straight into the driver's seat?'

'Because I felt the spirit of a score of dead Witch Makers urgin' me on – and I didn't have the courage to resist them.'

'You've got what you wanted,' Tom Dimdyke said, his voice a mixture of anger and misery. 'Why can't you leave the lad alone now?'

'Because my job's not just to catch murderers, it's to see that justice is done,' Woodend explained. 'Wilf has to be punished for his crime – there's no way round that – but I want it to be a *fair* punishment. An' if he says no more at his trial than he has now, the punishment *won't* be fair. The judge an' jury will have no sympathy for him, an' he'll be given the maximum sentence. That's why he has to be completely honest. That's why I have to have the whole truth.'

'I've told you the whole truth!' Wilf protested.

Woodend shook his head. 'No, you have not. If you'd killed Harry for no other reason than to derail the Witch Burnin', you'd have left him in the barn. But you didn't. You tied to him to the stake and garrotted him. An' why? Because you thought he was evil. But what had he done or said to make you think that?'

'Nothin'!' Wilf said defiantly.

'You're lyin',' Woodend told him.

'Why would I?'

'If I'm right,' Woodend said softly, 'then the reason you're lyin' is to spare your dad's feelings.'

'My feelings!' Tom Dimdyke exploded. 'What have *my* feelings got to do with it?'

'Nothin' at all!' Woodend admitted. 'That's perhaps the saddest part of this whole sorry business. Because what we're talkin' about here isn't your *real* feelin's – it's the feelin's that Wilf *thought* you'd have when you learned what he'd just learned in that barn.'

'What do you mean?' Tom Dimdyke demanded.

'The first time we met, you told me that you'd done your part twenty years ago. An' it was plain to me then that you considered it a very important part. It had been hard, but it had been necessary, you said. For quite a while, I couldn't work out what it could possibly have been. Then, when I was thinkin' about your brother's concubines, it came to me that there was only one thing it *could* have been. An' it wasn't somethin' you really *did* at all, was it? It was somethin' you *allowed* to happen!'

This is perhaps the wrong time to have the talk, because Harry is obviously drunk, but Wilf is not sure there will ever be a right time, and so he decides to speak anyway.

He wants to ask his uncle about the things which have been troubling him since Mary fled from the barn.

He needs to know whether it is all worth it.

He wonders if, after three hundred and fifty years, there is any point in the Burning any more.

He has been agonizing about the question of whether there might be something else the village could do – some other way in which its energies might be channelled.

But he is new to using words of his own, and the question, when it comes, is not exactly what he intended it to be.

'Why are we Witch Makers, Uncle Harry?' he asks.

Harry plops down on to the orange crate, where Mary has so often sat and watched her brother work.

He grins. 'Why are we the Witch Makers? Because we're lucky bastards, that's why.'

335

'Lucky?' Wilf repeats – not knowing quite what his uncle means, but understanding the conversation is already going in the wrong direction.

'Bloody lucky,' Harry says. 'You might think that what we do is hard work, but it's a doddle compared to what the rest of those stupid sods have to put up with. We don't get up at dawn to milk the cows. We're not out there in all weathers, mendin' fences an' deliverin' letters. We make the Witch, an' that's it.'

'Yes, but—'

'An' just think of the compensations.' The grin on Harry's face turns into a leer. 'We can have any woman we want. Did you know that?'

'No, I—'

'Well, we can. Take it from me. An' we do what we like to them.' Harry chuckles. 'Some of the things I've done to the women of this village, I tell you, even the lowest whore wouldn't have let me do.'

'You ... you never talked to me like this before,' Wilf stutters.

'You were a boy before,' Harry answers. 'Now you're a man.' He climbs shakily to his feet, and drapes his arm over Wilf's shoulder. 'You're my lad, an' you're about to start reapin' the reward.'

He is happy. He is proud. And though he doesn't know it yet, he has just signed his own death warrant.

'What was it your uncle told you that made

you decide you needed to execute him?' Woodend asked Wilf Dimdyke.

'That bein' the Witch Maker didn't mean anythin' more to him than havin' the power to do whatever he wanted.'

'An' that was the *only* thing?'

'Yes!'

'You're still holdin' out on me, lad!' Woodend said, the tone in his voice almost pleading. 'For God's sake – for your *own* sake – tell me the rest!'

'There is no rest!'

Woodend lit up a cigarette, took a deep drag, and grimaced as if he were inhaling cyanide. 'You're makin' it more difficult – more painful – than it needs to be,' he said.

'I can't help that,' Wilf told him.

Woodend sighed. 'All right, if that's the way you want it.' He turned to Paniatowski. 'When a king dies, who usually succeeds him, Monika?'

'His natural heir?' Paniatowski replied, making it sound as if she were guessing.

'That's right,' Woodend agreed. 'Irrespective of talent or ability, his natural heir – his son or his daughter – takes his place. It's all in the magic of the name, you see. An' it's not only kings that the name works for. Look at what's happenin' in India, as an example. It won't be long before Mrs Gandhi's voted in as Prime Minister, an' her main claim to the job – as far as I can see – is that her dad held the same post for donkey's years.' He paused to take another poisoned drag on his Capstan. 'But what happens if there isn't what you call a "natural heir"?'

Paniatowski feigned a puzzled frown. 'Then I suppose it's a close blood relative who takes up the slack,' she said. 'Like in the United States.'

'Spot on,' Woodend agreed. 'Jack Kennedy – the shinin' white hope of all America – is assassinated in Dallas, an' people immediately start to wonder who can fill his shoes. He does *have* a son, but that son's too young – so it's his brother Bobby who starts to look like a serious contender for the presidency. Now for all I know, Bobby Kennedy might turn out to be a great leader, but that's not the point. He's where he is because of *the name.*'

'True,' Paniatowski agreed.

'Of course, if Bobby had been John's *cousin* rather than his *brother*, the magic wouldn't have been quite so strong,' Woodend continued. 'It's a risky business movin' away from the direct line – an' the further away you move, the riskier it is.'

'How do you mean?' Paniatowski asked, still playing Woodend's straight man.

'You've only to look at history to find countless examples of the king's cousin succeedin' to the throne – an' of civil war breakin' out almost immediately. Now why do you think that might be?'

'Because there were always *other* cousins – from other branches of the family – who thought they had just as much right to the throne as the man who was claiming it?'

'Exactly!' Woodend agreed. 'The magic gets so watered down that it isn't even magic any more.'

'What's any of this got to do with us here in Hallerton?' Tom Dimdyke demanded.

And though he was doing his best to sound impatient, it was his unease which came across most strongly.

'Every king who's ever ruled has done his best to ensure that it's one of his *direct* descendants who succeeds him,' Woodend said. 'It's the only way to maintain stability, you see. It's the only way the king can be certain that things go on as he thinks they were meant to.'

'But we have nothin' to *do* with kings!' Tom Dimdyke said.

'Don't you?' Woodend asked. 'One of the first things that struck me when I arrived in this village was how like a king the Witch Maker was.'

'That's rubbish!'

'Is it? Tell me, who was the first Witch Maker, Mr Dimdyke?'

'A cousin of Tom an' Harry's.'

'An' the second?'

'Does that matter?'

'Of course it bloody matters! It's bloody crucial! It was Harry's son, wasn't it? The fruit of his second marriage – the one who was born after his father had been hanged.'

'Who ... who told you all this?' Tom Dimdyke asked.

'A local historian called Tyndale told me a son had been born. I'm only guessin' he was actually the second Witch Maker. But I'm right, aren't I?'

'Yes, you're right,' Dimdyke admitted.

'An' what about the *third* Witch Maker? Was he the son of the *second*?'

'Yes.'

'So the Witch Maker *did* get married in those days?'

'I never said that.'

'No, you didn't, did you? Well, now we've got that settled, let's skip a few hundred years. Tell me, Mr Dimdyke, who'll be the next Witch Maker – after your lad?'

'I don't know,' Dimdyke said.

'You're lyin',' Woodend told him, though not harshly. 'You *do* know. It's just that he hasn't been born yet. That's the real truth, isn't it?'

'Yes.'

'But *why* hasn't he been born? Wilf was a baby at the time of the last Witch Burnin', wasn't he? An' I'd be willin' to bet that Harry was a baby at the Witch Burnin' before that. So what went wrong?'

'Nothin' went wrong. I just thought it'd be better to wait a bit longer this time.'

'*You* thought? Or your *brother* thought?'

'*I* thought!' Tom Dimdyke said fiercely. 'He's my lad. I didn't want it to happen until he was ready – until he was strong enough.'

Woodend nodded sympathetically. 'Because he's not a callous bastard like your brother was,' he said. 'Because you knew it'd be hard for him to give up to somebody else's care a thing he'd probably already have begun to love.'

'Yes,' Tom Dimdyke said.

'What the bloody hell's goin' on?' Wilf demanded. 'Why won't somebody tell me what the bloody hell's goin' on?'

'I'll tell you,' Woodend promised him. 'But before that, I'm goin' to ask you one question. Did your dad bring a girl to see you recently – a girl who was just about to get wed? An' was it a Dimdyke she was goin' to marry?'

'Yes, but what's that to do with—?' Wilf stopped suddenly, as if he'd been hit by a truck. His face turned even paler, and his hands started shaking. 'Why *did* you bring the girl to see me, Dad?'

Tom Dimdyke looked at the floor, and said nothing.

'I think he brought her to you for the same reason that your grandfather took your mother to see your Uncle Harry – except that in Harry's case, it was over a year before he became the Witch Maker,' Woodend told Wilf.

'You ... you don't mean ... You can't mean...'

'The Witch Maker never marries, but his successor, in order to have legitimacy, has to carry his blood – which is the same blood as that of the first Harry Dimdyke, the local hero who tied Meg Ramsden to the post an' then garrotted her. Now do you think you can work out how that's *managed*?'

'I ... I don't know.'

'Yes, you do. The only way a king can ensure a child is his is to impregnate a virgin. Why should it be any different for Witch Makers?'

A look of almost indescribable agony came to Wilf's face. Slowly, he turned towards Tom.

'When Uncle Harry told me he was my real dad, I thought he was lyin',' he said, almost sobbing now. 'But he seemed so sure of himself that, in the end, I was forced to believe him. An' do you know what I thought then? I thought Mum an' him had betrayed you, Dad. I thought they'd slept with each other behind your back. An' *that's* why I killed him. That's why I took him all the way to the Witchin' Post and garrotted him like the evil slime he was – to get revenge for you! But you *knew* about it! You knew all

342

the time.'

'Yes,' Tom Dimdyke agreed. 'The Witch Maker had to have an heir, an' that heir had to be brought up in the right kind of home. An' what better kind of home could there have been than the one we gave you?'

'So you an' my grandfather forced my mother to sleep with your brother before you'd marry her!'

'Nobody forced her. She went willingly. She saw it as her duty to the village. We both did. But for two people who were as much in love as we were, it wasn't easy. God knows, it wasn't easy.'

'But you did it anyway,' Wilf said bitterly. 'An' when it was all over, you took in your brother's bastard – an' called him your own.'

'You *are* my own,' Tom said firmly. 'You might not be the seed of my loins, like Mary is, but you're still mine. When I held you in my arms as a baby, do you think it mattered to me that the monster who was my half-brother had actually *fathered* you? I didn't love you any the less for that.' He paused for a moment, as tears streamed down his face. '*I'm* your real dad, Wilf,' he continued. 'I always was.'

Epilogue

The weather forecast had predicted this would be the last day of the real summer, and if that were true, then the summer had chosen to go out in a blaze of glory. Those who could, flocked to the beach or lay in their gardens. Those who couldn't, looked longingly out of their office or factory windows, and promised themselves they would get in at least a short walk before darkness drew the curtain on this final golden day.

The three women, separated from each other by distance, but united in their connection to a dead Witch Maker, belonged to the group who could not take advantage of the day. They were all working. At least, that was what they told themselves. And, in fact, they were all, more or less, right.

Hettie Todd was helping her mother on the coconut shy. They were doing good business, and they needed to – because a long workless winter lay ahead. She knew now who her father was, and considered that she had come to terms with it. What did it matter who had planted the seed, she asked herself, when it was Zelda – wonderful, warm, kind Zelda – who had harvested it?

As she took the money and handed out the balls, she let her mind wander freely. She wondered where their winter quarters would be this year, and if Pat Calhoun would come with them, instead of going back to Ireland. She hoped he would, for though she had not yet fallen in love with him, she thought she very well might.

Monika Paniatowski was behind the wheel of her MGA. The bonnet had been re-sprayed, but the scars were far from healed. Her boss was on his first foreign holiday – he had taken his wife to Spain – and with Woodend away, the sergeant was finding she had more time on her hands than she was comfortable with.

When she had to drive across the town, as she often did, she had taken to going down the road where the Rutters lived. She'd convinced herself it was a short cut, and sometimes it was. She occasionally saw Maria and the baby out on the street during these journeys – the baby gurgling happily in her pushchair, Maria holding the pushchair handle with one hand and her white stick with the other. Paniatowski never made the other woman aware she was there, but sometimes she'd park and watch – just to make sure that Maria and the fruit of her womb reached the corner of the road safely.

She secretly suspected that she hoped that seeing Maria in all her need – and with all her courage – would lead to a dampening of the fires of passion she felt for the other woman's husband.

It hadn't worked yet!

Mary Dimdyke, lying on her back, on a moor scented with gorse and wild primrose, looked up at a single swallow which was riding on the air currents above her. What joy it seemed to have, she thought. How much it seemed to relish its freedom. And what a fool it was not to have noticed the kestrel hawk which was hovering close by, and just waiting for its opportunity to strike!

Mary shifted her position slightly. The bracken against her back was a little irritating, but nowhere near as uncomfortable as the weight of the sweating, grunting youth who was pressing down on her front.

'Have you nearly finished, Teddy?' she asked.

She didn't stutter. She had quite lost her stutter now.

'I ... uh...' the boy gasped.

'Oh, do get on with it,' Mary said irritably.

His name was Edward Thwaites. He was the constable's nephew and, because he was

346

from the village, he was probably also some distant relation of hers, too. He had been drooling over her ever since he had first started paying attention to girls, but she had kept him at a distance until now.

She had chosen him for two reasons. The first was that he was not very bright. The second was that what he lacked in brain power, he more than made up for in brawn. Though he was only eighteen, he was already bigger than his own dad – and that made him bigger than any other man in the village.

He hadn't been able to believe his luck when she'd suggested this walk together. He didn't care that her beautiful hair was gone for ever – that the new hair which was growing to replace it lacked its sheen and softness, and even contained the odd strand of white.

And why should he care, when she had breasts she would allow him to clumsily massage, and legs she would open when he asked her to?

That was all he wanted. That was all that any man – whatever he might claim – *truly* wanted.

Teddy gave a last strangled cry, and rolled off her.

'That was lovely,' he said.

He was lying, of course. She knew that. It had been – at best – mildly satisfactory. But that wouldn't stop him coming back for more. Now he had had a taste, he was as dependent on her as any alcoholic is on his bottle.

'Have you heard anythin' about your dad an' brother?' Teddy asked.

'They come up for trial next month.'

'You must miss them.'

He was not really interested, she thought. It was all pretence, so she wouldn't think him shallow – so she wouldn't come to believe that all he cared about was what she had between her legs. But pretence or not, it gave her the opportunity to say what she had been planning to say all along.

'Yes, I miss them,' she told him. 'It's hard for me to get by now they're in prison.'

'It must be,' Teddy said awkwardly, already beginning his retreat from the subject.

'Maybe you could help me out,' she said, as if the thought had only just occurred to her.

'Me?' Teddy said, moving further away from her.

'You,' she repeated.

'But I'm just a farm labourer. I don't earn much.'

'I never said you did. But you don't have to *earn* money to get your hands on it.'

'How do you mean?'

'Oh, there are lots of ways to do it. You could take it out of that cash box that you told me your dad keeps hidden in the barn.'

'But that'd be stealin'!'

'Or when you're workin' behind the bar at the Bull, like you sometimes do, you could slip a few bottles of whisky into your pocket. I'd sell them for you, and you'd get half of the money I made.'

Or a quarter, she thought. Or perhaps even less than that.

'It's wrong,' Teddy said.

'An' once we had a bit of what you might call "capital", we could put it to work for us,' Mary continued. 'I could lend it out, you see, like banks do. An' charge interest. An' if people fell behind with their payments, you could go an' see them an' persuade them to cough up.'

'I'm not sure...' Teddy said.

'You want us to keep on doin' this, don't you?'

'Yes, but...'

'Then you'll do what's necessary to keep me happy. Besides...'

'Besides what?' Teddy asked tremulously.

'You know what my Uncle Harry did to that girl from the fairground, don't you?'

'He ... he raped her.'

'An' if it had ever come out, he'd have gone to prison for a long, long time.'

'I know that.'

'An' if *I* said *you'd* raped me, the same would happen to you.'

'You wouldn't—'

'I was a virgin until half an hour ago. Did you know that?'

'But you can't have been, or you'd never have...'

'Given in so easily?'

'I didn't say that.'

'If you don't believe I was a virgin, just look down at your willie.'

'Oh God!' Teddy groaned. 'It's covered in blood.'

'Yes,' Mary agreed. 'But don't panic, because it's mine, not yours. That's what happens when you deflower an innocent girl.'

'I never ... I didn't even...'

'So you will think about what I've said, won't you?'

'Yes, I'll...'

He'd do more than think about it, she told herself. He'd do *exactly* what she told him to.

Her father and her brother had been fools, she thought. The choice in this world was not between good and evil, as they had always believed – and *still* believed. It was both starker and simpler than that – it was whether you chose to become a victim or a predator. They didn't see it. They would *never* see it. Which was why they were now languishing in Lancaster Gaol.

Meg Ramsden – though she had lived and died nearly four hundred years earlier –

would have been more at home in the modern world than they could ever have been. She had understood it for what it was. Yes, she had ended her life at the stake. But that was not because she had been playing the wrong game – it was because she played the *right* game *badly.*

Mary looked up at the sky again, just in time to see the hawk swoop down and dig its cruel talons into the soft flesh of the swallow.

'Well, have you thought about it?' she demanded.

'If I took a couple of pounds out of the box, I don't think my dad would miss it,' Teddy mumbled. 'Will that do?'

'For a start.'

But *only* for a start. A smile of triumph spread across Mary's face. She was on her way. She was no longer the girl who would sit there meekly while her beautiful hair was shorn from her head. She was a woman now. But not a new woman, exactly. More a new version of an older woman.

She could feel the blood of Meg Ramsden suddenly beginning to gush powerfully through her veins.